Five minutes later, Captain Tengut sat at his desk. On the way from the medical room, he had decided not to call the harbor officials first. For one thing, they wouldn't care what kind of story he told; they simply would not let him dock if he had an undocumented man on his ship. For another thing, they wouldn't believe him.

He didn't believe it himself. Forty-six years of total isolation? Not only unlikely, but plain unbelievable.

Probably.

So he called the Operations Desk. After being put on hold twice, he reached a petty officer in the JAG office. He introduced himself and said, "We inbound, a few day out from San Diego, and yesterday we find a stowaway on ship."

"Uh-oh," the bored petty officer said.

"Better than uh-oh," Tengut plied. "This guy say he POW from Vietnam."

Other Books by Nishi Giefer

Brennan's Odyssey
Redemption on the High Plains: A Collection of
       Short Stories
Convergent Trails
Doctor of Veterinary Murder
Keep Your Enemies Closer
The Jim Russet Trilogy

Acknowledgements

The idea for this story germinated in my mind thirty-some years ago. I never expected to write it, for I lacked the experience and worldliness. Only with the generous assistance of some extraordinarily knowledgeable people was I able to pull it off. Responsibility for any error is strictly mine.

Ben Jetton, one of my dad's best friends since childhood, served as an officer in the United States Naval Reserve, including a tour in Vietnam in 1967-1968.

Don Shepperd was one of the elite Misty pilots during the Vietnam War. Graduate of the United States Air Force Academy, he retired as head of the Air National Guard and has written numerous books on aviation, pilots, and the Vietnam War.

Jeffrey L. Ward, Navy Intelligence Specialist First Class Petty Officer (Retired), is currently deployed in Afghanistan. Like many, he is apparently not very good at being retired.

When he was a child, Loung Quach and his family abruptly left Vietnam in the middle of the night. Two years later, they immigrated to the United States and, fortunately for my family, settled in our community.

Also thanks to Pat O'Dell, Myrna Schlegel, Marty Peters, Kendall Ottley, Jan and Sandy Burkhard, and Diane Giefer. Special thank you to Jerry Peters who penned the limerick found on page 97, except his first line was "Nishi Linn O'Dell went down to the well. . ."

not Quite Forgotten
©2018 Nishi Giefer

ISBN-13: 978-1986011181
ISBN-10: 1986011186

High Plains Fiction
www.GieferRanch.com
WaKeeney, Kansas
United States of America

not

QUITE

FORGOTTEN

NISHI GIEFER

HIGH PLAINS FICTION

In Memory of

Those Who Did Not Return

Dedicated to

Those Who Still Wait

For Them

Wednesday, January 31, 2018

The woman who was a second cousin to the man's late wife had appointed herself to check in on him daily. He had been increasingly frail over the past few months. His two children both lived too far away to look in on him. And they both worked. And she didn't mind.

It was a Wednesday afternoon when she found him slumped in his favorite chair.

The first call she made on her cell phone was to alert the local authorities. The second was to the son, the elder child. She had planned to let him notify his sister, but he was so overwrought that she didn't think he could talk intelligibly on the telephone. So she asked if she should call the girl, too.

The answer was not clear, so she said she would call.

Two hours later, both teary-eyed adult children were sitting in the old man's house. Their dead mother's second cousin was fixing tea when she overheard the sister in a choking sob trying to whisper to her brother.

"What are we going to do with his pet?"

The woman fixing tea thought to herself, "Pet! I should think!" The old man had all kinds of pets, mostly in rusty old cages or bamboo crates. Others, like the dogs and pigs destined for his table, ran loose in the huge wild area behind the house.

What the old woman did not know, because plurals and singular forms do not exist in the Vietnamese language, was that the younger woman referred to a specific pet.

A very specific pet.

Thursday, February 8, 2018

The sailor was growing increasingly edgy as the giant cargo ship steamed closer to its final port. His elderly aunt, who had approximately four remaining teeth and who had seen at least ninety birthdays, had warned him he would encounter trouble on this journey. He had been across the Pacific twice so far. Both trips had been uneventful. He had no reason to think this one would be otherwise.

Except for the old aunt.

By western standards, she was actually his grandmother's aunt. But in his culture, she was an aunt. Just plain aunt.

And she was known to have visions. And some of them were very accurate.

Now, six days from San Diego where they would pull into the harbor and unload the supplies for the US Navy, he was getting jumpier every minute.

Damn her. He wished she had just kept her omens to herself. This ship was perfectly safe. There was nothing wrong with it. There were no major storms in the forecast. The captain was a fine man—even if they didn't share a common language. And if anyone fell ill, there was a medical officer on board who was as good as a doctor.

Seeking a snack, hoping it would ease his mind, he pulled open the big steel door of the pantry. Nothing on the top three shelves interested him, so he dropped onto his knees to check out the lowest level. He pulled back a couple unopened jars of pickled vegetables and a case of noodles and peered into the depths of the cupboard.

Then he screamed.

Positioned far back on the deep shelf was a skeleton lying on its side with its back toward him. Not just a skeleton, but a mummified skeleton over which was stretched grimy skin covered with wicked red sores. In the instant before he leapt to his feet and hastily backed from the pantry, he saw ribs and backbone, stringy hair, and pelvic bones that had no meat on them at all.

He darted from the pantry and ran through the galley where the captain happened to be smoking a cigar. The tiny grizzled officer, who had far more salt than pepper on his head, put out a hand and stopped the terrified sailor.

After a moment of the younger man's hysterical gibberish, they went together to the pantry. The captain led the way while the sailor reluctantly followed several paces behind.

Unbelievably to the young sailor, the old captain reached toward the cadaver and touched it. Then he became animated and shouted an order to the teenager. Despite the language barrier, the kid recognized the name of the medical officer. As much to fulfill the order as to get away from the dead body, he raced off.

Minutes later, the medical officer trotted into the room. Having been born and raised on the same small island as the captain, there was no communication difficulty between them. They carefully pulled the man from the back of the shelf and gently laid him on the floor.

"I can't believe he's alive," the medical officer breathed.

"My god," the captain whispered. "My god."

The man was naked except for what appeared to be years of grime. His beard was thick and tangled, his hair was slightly longer than shoulder length, thin, brittle, graying and matted. But the underlying color of the hair was not black, as was the case with the captain and his entire Asian crew. This man's hair was brown mixed with gray.

The medical officer lifted an eyelid to expose a very dilated blue eye.

"Drugs?" the captain asked in their shared native tongue. "Could a person on drugs live so long as to become this skinny?"

Wrinkling his nose, the medic asked, "How come nobody smelled him before now?"

With a shrug, the captain replied, "Because the ventilation system pulls air from the galley and expels it through this room. This guy only been stinking to the fish outside."

They moved the man to the infirmary and covered him with a blanket. While the medic made a cursory evaluation, the captain found a wash cloth and began bathing the patient, starting with the right hand.

In his notes, the medic wrote, "Pulse 42. Pressure not determinable—too low to register. Temperature 35.4C. Emaciated. No response to light on eyes. Obtained blood sample for doctors at USA." It took several minutes longer than usual for him to obtain the blood sample from the limp vein in the fleshless arm. But finally, he filled a pair of tubes and stuck them in the tiny refrigerator.

When he finished, he looked at the right hand the captain had been scrubbing.

"He's pale," he commented.

The old captain nodded and scowled. "Where do you suppose he's been? And how in the hell did he get on this ship?"

"He must have been on board when we left Da Nang," the medic said unnecessarily.

"Is he in a coma? How could he survive so long without eating or drinking? We been at sea eight days," the captain implored.

"His metabolism is very slow from his illness," came the explanation. "He looks like he might have cancer. Or some type of autoimmune disorder."

"Or starvation."

When he finished with the right hand, the captain dumped the water basin and refilled it with clean water. After rinsing out the washcloth, he continued working his way up the arm. At the same time, the medical officer added more notes to his record. "Multiple skin lesions—appear to be infected insect bites. Perhaps rodent bites, as well. Mucus in eyes; eyelids red." He tried to recall the medical term for reddened eyelids, but he couldn't. Twelve years ago—after three interminable years of pre-medical training—he had given up the struggle of studying for hours a day memorizing long words and physiological processes. That's when he had gone to sea.

Now it was sometimes hard to recall those terms.

Finished with his notes, he inserted an IV catheter and began pouring intravenous fluids into the living cadaver. Captain Tengut relieved him of his other ship duties, allowing the medical officer to devote his full attention to the patient.

Friday, February 9, 2018

The following morning, the living skeleton turned his head slightly on the pillow. A few hours later, his eyelids fluttered and his left hand twitched.

Finally, seventeen hours after being discovered, the man opened his eyes—flat, dull, and unseeing eyes for the first several minutes. Then the eyes blinked. And blinked again. Then they began to water.

He swallowed, which rendered a rasping noise in his dry throat.

Then he focused on the smiling medical officer who gave a small bow.

The man on the bunk stared and blinked and stared. He startled when the medic asked him a question. He made no reply. Either he didn't understand the language, or he couldn't respond. But then the medic held up a cup and raised his eyebrows to ask the question: "Would you like something to drink?"

The patient only stared for the first minute. Then he slowly raised his left hand and tried to grasp the cup. But he was too weak and uncoordinated, and he had to keep blinking to clear tears and mucus from the red-rimmed eyes set deeply into his fleshless face.

When the medical officer reached a hand to help him lift his head to the cup, the man flinched.

Raising both hands to show that he was friendly, the medic said something foreign but soothing. Then he again reached out and helped raise the head that seemed incongruously large for the skeletal body.

Three sips were all the skinny man could take at first. But a few minutes later, he drank more. In the first hour, he drank a full cup.

The captain stepped in through the doorway and said something. The medic nodded. They talked for a few minutes before the old man left again. Then the medic procured a cup of beef stock.

Within an hour, the patient was partially sitting, propped on pillows. He had gradually consumed a full cup of broth and then another. The dullness in his eyes was slowly being replaced with wariness. As he became better hydrated, his eyes began to water profusely.

After the broth, there was fruit flavored gelatin. An hour later, there was soup with rice and tiny bits of vegetables.

Throughout the feeding session, a parade of crew members filtered through, one at a time. Each addressed the patient in any language he knew. The man responded to none of them.

But the medic thought his patient's expression flickered once. He quickly asked the crewman what language he had used.

French.

Nodding, he said, "Tell him no one wants to hurt him. We are sad that he is so thin. We want to help make him better."

The crewman relayed the message in his best broken French.

The patient's expression did not change. But his eyes shifted from the speaker to the medic and back again.

The second day, the medic helped the man sit on the edge of the bunk. There he sat for over an hour. He had another bowl of broth with rice. Then he drank a cup of tea.

As he was finishing the tea, he began to look around the tiny cabin. Behind him and to the left was a tiny lavatory. He stared at it for a long time until the medic said something.

Then the medic rose from his chair and moved to the lavatory door, making gestures that indicated it was okay for the man to use the facilities. He gently took the bony arm and helped the patient to his feet. To the surprise of the medic, the man walked nimbly.

The skeletal man did not close the door upon entering. He turned to his right and looked into a mirror over the tiny stainless steel sink. The medical officer saw the expression on his face.

Shock.

The patient seemed so shocked, in fact, that he touched the mirror. Then he touched his hair. Then he ran a finger down the crease from the edge of his nose to the corner of his thick moustache.

After a few minutes, the medic pointed to the shower nozzle in the back corner of the room. From a small door below the mirror, he pulled a bar of soap which he offered.

The skinny man swallowed and stared at the soap. Then he gingerly took it and moved to the shower. The medic had to demonstrate how to make the water run and adjust the temperature. Then he tapped his watch and held up five fingers indicating five minutes.

The patient reverently reached his hands toward the warm spray. Then, very slowly, he moved forward until his face was in the stream. When the recommended five minutes was up, the man still stood, merely letting the water run over his head and down his scabby and raw body. Then he began in earnest the process of removing the filth and stench.

Ten minutes later, the medic produced a bottle of shampoo. The bony man blinked hard to clear his eyes as he squinted at the label that was written in Chinese. The medic demonstrated pouring an imaginary dab in his own hand and rubbing his hair. Taking the bottle, the skeletal man proceeded to scrub and scour. The first application yielded no lather. But by the fourth time, the stringy, brittle hair began to resemble normal human locks.

The medic left the bathroom and the infirmary for several minutes. When he returned, the skinny man was drying himself with a thick towel. Despite taking great care, he deposited blotchy stains of blood on the towel. The medic held up a pair of shorts and a t-shirt, which he then laid on the bunk. Due to his own fondness for sweets, his shorts would have been too large to stay around the foreigner's bony pelvis. So he had procured the pants from the kid who had found the man in the pantry.

The scrawny kid was nearly five-foot-one. The skeleton man was several inches taller than anyone on the crew. The medic watched with wonder as the skinny man carefully pulled on the shorts and slipped the shirt over his protruding collar bones and ribs. Then he lowered himself onto the bunk and began gingerly running his fingers over the cloth.

While the stranger sat fondling his new-found clothes, the medic dished up a bowl with chicken, cucumber, and rice. Then as the bony man slowly sipped the broth and then licked the remaining contents from the container, the medic flipped open a laptop computer. When it had booted up, he found a world map and turned it toward the stowaway.

He asked a question, not expecting a reply. Next he pointed to himself, and then to an island of Malaysia. He then pointed to the patient and gestured toward the map. A shrug added a question mark to his mimed sentence.

"I'm American," came the vocal reply as he pointed to the United States.

The medic smiled and bowed.

The American stared at the laptop, studying the keyboard, the screen, the hinges. When the medic tapped the bright screen and brought up a new picture, the American's brow lowered in quandary.

Setting the computer aside, the medic stood and motioned toward an electronic scale. He invited the stick man to step upon it. But there was no response. So the medic stepped on the scale and waited until the device beeped and displayed a number.

After he dismounted, he again invited the foreigner to stand on the scale. Finally, he did.

The medic noted the weight. Thirty-seven kilograms.

The American did a quick calculation in his head and converted the number to eighty-two pounds.

Blake Moffat awoke with a start. Such a start, in fact, that he found himself sitting bolt upright. He looked over at his wife to see if he had disturbed her. She grabbed the covers and yanked them toward her. Then her breathing returned to a deep and regular pattern. He doubted she would remember it later.

Softly, he padded from the room and donned the sweatshirt and sweat pants he always left folded just outside the bedroom door. After a trip to the bathroom, he went to the dark living room, sat on the couch, and stared out the big picture window toward the empty street.

It was the same dream. Well, mostly the same. He wished he had kept track of how many times he'd had the dream since he began working this project. Dozens of times. Maybe hundreds. Maybe even a thousand times he had dreamed of finding the skeletons. Bones in long trenches.

Sometimes the bones lay in the same relative positions as they had been in life. Sometimes they were scattered. Sometimes they were whole. Sometimes only fragments.

10

But on this night, the bones had become a skeletal man and the man in the trench had reached toward him, pleading. It was only the one man, not the many he usually dreamed. And this man was very insistent. He reached toward Moffat as though he would grab him and pull himself into Moffat's world of the living.

Or pull Moffat into his world of the dead.

Sometimes in the dream, Moffat was shoved into the trench or into a cell, sitting with his ankles secured, his head tipped to one side because the ceiling of the bamboo holding cell was so low.

Staring out into the suburban street, failing to register the streetlight glinting on the patches of snow, he still felt the intensity of the dream. He tried to remember if he had ever awakened sitting up like that.

Four hours later, having returned to bed and a restless sleep, he arose for the day. After a half hour on the exercise bike, he showered and shaved the heavy black whiskers from his chin. Then he put on his dress greens and his shiny black shoes and went to the kitchen.

For breakfast, he warmed a couple of burritos from the night before. When his wife appeared in the kitchen, he set a plate and a cup of coffee on the bar for her. She stood on her toes and gave him a sleepy kiss before she sank onto her chair and wordlessly began eating.

By the time he left for the office, he was still haunted by the insistent prisoner reaching, clawing toward him.

At the first stoplight on the way to the office, he perused today's list on his phone. All of the names were familiar to him. Some families he knew better than others, of course. Some were old friends. Some were sworn enemies. But he called every one of them as they came up on his schedule. He called to tell them some clue had been unearthed. Or he called to tell them there was nothing new.

11

After he reviewed the list, he pulled up the itinerary for next month's trip to Vietnam. The light turned green. He drove for forty-five seconds and found himself at the next red light. This one was always long. He looked again at his phone.

The Vietnamese officials had allowed him to add an extra name this time. He had evidence of eleven men's final resting places. Three Navy, one Marine, two Army, and five Air Force. Seven of them had last been seen at the site of a crash-rescue-crash site. The other four had also died within a relatively small area. On each semi-annual trip, Moffat was allowed to search for the remains of only ten service members. The only way he could add anyone to the list after he was in-country was if the joint American and Vietnamese team received credible evidence of the location of remains near the planned search area.

He hoped the late-March departure date would coincide with good weather in the north where they would be searching this time. Traveling the rural areas during the rainy season was infinitely more difficult. And slow.

But that was the common link in all his trips, two of them a year for the past fourteen years—the first three years as an underling and the last eleven as the team leader.

Slow.

Difficult.

Frustrating.

It had led him to develop patience he would never have guessed possible.

The ship's captain ducked through the hatch and returned a quick bow from the medical officer. Then he turned and bowed to the foreigner who had just stepped off the scale.

"You speak Engrish?" the captain inquired slowly.

The skinny man swallowed and looked warily from one man to the other. Then he came to attention and said deliberately, "Lance Corporal D. E. Weller." He recited what sounded like a US Social Security number, then added, "March 4, 1956."

The captain said, "Okay. My name Captain Tengut. This my ship. You American Army?"

The man who called himself Weller repeated the Big Four sequence. Name. Rank. Service number. Date of birth.

The captain scowled. "You know where you at?"

Again, Weller repeated his mantra.

The captain sighed and pulled around a chair. When he was seated, he motioned for Weller to sit on the bunk. "Okay. I got it. You not going to answer. So, why you on my ship?"

Now, for the first time, the American's face revealed something.

Confusion.

"You a stowaway," Tengut replied. "We find you day before yesterday. You look sick. You got cancer or something?"

No reply.

Tengut said something to the medical officer, who then scurried out of the room. When he was gone, the captain said, "I tell him get you food. You look like you no eat for long time. Why you so skinny—and don't tell me name and date of birth again. I got that memorize already."

Weller swallowed.

Tengut sighed again. "So do you mind tell me where you been? You drug addick?"

"I'm a prisoner of war."

Tengut's face folded into a thousand lines. "You a what? What war you think you prisoner of?"

Weller did not reply.

Tengut tried again. "When you become prisoner of war?"

Weller hesitated for a moment, debating whether his answer would compromise any military secrets. Deciding it wouldn't, he replied, "April 9, 1972."

The medical officer returned and set down a steaming bowl containing a concoction of pork, rice, and chunks of brightly colored vegetables. Tengut waved toward it. "You eat."

Weller stared at the food but made no move toward it, though all of them distinctly heard his stomach growl.

Feigning exasperation—feigning because Tengut was a very patient man with a well-developed sense of humor capable of transcending language barriers—the captain reached out and plucked up a piece of the meat. Simultaneously chewing and talking, he said, "There. Now you see I no die from poison. Food okay for you to eat." He picked up a sliver of eggplant. "You eat; I talk. I tell you, you on a military civilian cargo ship, under Indonesian flag. We taking supply to San Diego for US Navy. I not Indonesian; I am Malaysian. Same with your doctor, here. He not really a doctor. But he go to medical school for three year before he go to sea. He still know some big word from medical training. Only in Chinese, though. Not Engrish. But we call him medical officer. He usually sailor, but if someone sick or hurt, he become our doctor. He take good care of you?"

Weller slipped a piece of pork into his mouth and very slowly began to chew it. He closed his runny, red-rimmed eyes. Before he swallowed the tiny morsel, tears began to course down his cheeks. Tengut wasn't sure if

14

the tears were from the infection in his eyes or if it was simply from the pleasure of eating.

"You want chopstick?" Tengut asked, holding out a pair of disposable wooden chopsticks.

Weller opened his eyes and shook his head.

The medical officer picked up another set of chopsticks and with many bows, kindly demonstrated how to hold them. After a long moment of scrutiny, Weller reached with his left hand and took the offered utensils. After two botched attempts, he used one of the sticks as a spear and picked up a piece of cabbage. This, too, he savored for a long time.

Tengut said, "I have to find out why you on my ship, or they no let me dock in port and unload my cargo. If I have to turn around and go back to Da Nang, my boss not be happy with me. And I not be happy with you."

"Da Nang?" Weller repeated.

Tengut nodded. "Yes. We load in Da Nang and leave there ten day ago. Find you in pantry on eighth day. Yesterday, you in la-la land. So how you get on ship?"

Again, Weller hesitated, but for different reasons. "I don't know."

Tengut ate another chunk of the pork. Then he asked, "You like milkshake?" Without awaiting reply, he spoke to the medical officer. This time, the officer did not need to leave the room; he opened the tiny refrigerator tucked under a built-in desk, picked out a can, and set it in front of Weller.

But Weller was peering past him into the refrigerator. "Coke?" His voice was laced with near reverence.

With a bow and another big smile, the officer quickly returned the canned milkshake and pulled out a plastic bottle of Coca Cola.

Weller stared at the bottle for half a minute before Tengut picked it up and twisted off the lid. "They don't put it in glass now. Somebody cut lip or something. Sued the Coke people. Now they put it in plastic. Better, really. Now you can put lid back on. No spill." He held the bottle out to Weller.

But Weller just eyed it suspiciously.

With another sigh, Tengut took a swig and handed it back. Then he watched as Weller took a long drink and let the liquid prickle in his mouth before he swallowed.

Then Weller smiled for the first time. "Thank you."

Tengut chuckled. Then he asked, "What date you think it is now?"

Weller shrugged. "I lost track."

"The year is two-thousand eighteen."

Weller snorted.

Tengut scowled. "You no believe me. But I tell you truth. Now you tell me. What prison you been in?"

Weller took another drink of Coke. Then a bite of meat. It was a full two minutes before he answered. "Dong Phu Prison Camp."

Tengut asked, "Where that? Vietnam?"

Weller nodded. "Is the war over? I haven't heard any shelling for a while. I didn't know if it was over or if it just moved farther away."

"American Vietnam War? Over for long time. How long you in that prison camp?"

"I'm not sure," Weller answered. He took another bite, relishing it as much as he had the first. "I think five or six days."

"Then where after that?" Tengut inquired.

"In a box."

"What do you mean when you say box?"

"Steel. Concrete. Thatch roof. Leaky roof."

Tengut stood. "You eat. I go make phone call."

Five minutes later, Tengut sat at his desk. On the way from the medical room, he had decided not to call the

16

harbor officials first. For one thing, they wouldn't care what kind of story he told; they simply would not let him dock with an undocumented man on his ship. For another thing, they wouldn't believe him.

He didn't believe it himself. A POW for forty-six years? Not only unlikely, but just plain unbelievable.

Probably.

So he called the Operations Desk and reached a man with a strong Hispanic accent.

Tengut explained his situation, and then asked, "So can you transfer me to Intel or somebody?"

"Not if the dude is a US Person, sir. That would be more in line with SJA. Hang on."

Before the line switched, Tengut said, "Hey, wait! I don't understand you. Talk slower. You and me don't talk same kind of Engrish. You transfer me to what?"

"Staff Judge Advocate, sir," the operator said slowly.

There was a pause. "You mean JAG?"

"Yeah. Judge Advocate General's office. Same thing. Hang on, sir."

The next person on the line was a Petty Officer Wong in the JAG office.

After introducing himself again, Tengut said, "We inbound, a few day out from San Diego, and yesterday we find stowaway on ship."

"Uh-oh," the bored petty officer said.

"Better than uh-oh," Tengut plied. "This guy say he POW from Vietnam."

The petty officer scoffed. "Yeah, right! Did he tell you about his pet unicorn, too, sir?"

"He tell me name, rank, serial number, and birth date. In fack, he tell me about ten time. I have it memorize by the time he finally answer a real question. So, I tell you his name, rank, and birthdate, and you tell me he crazy, or you tell me he might be that guy. Okay?"

"Sure. Go ahead, sir. But that's, like, thirty-five years ago or something."

"Forty-six," Tengut said dryly. "And since you so good with math, you prob'ly notice that if he born March 1956 and capture April 1972, he sixteen year old. Last I check, America not put school boys in uniforms."

The petty officer chuckled. "You got that right, sir. You ready to give me the information?"

Tengut relayed Weller's name, rank, Social Security number, and date of birth.

The petty officer took down the information. Then he said, "Okay. Let me do some checking and get back to you, Captain."

"Okay. But you don't wait too long to get back to me. Because I got to unload cargo. They not gonna let me into port if I got a guy with no passport, no visa, no clothes, no nothing. Okay? And I don't want to have to throw him overboard just so I can unload. He so skinny, he not even enough to feed two small fish."

"Okay, sir. I'll let you know as soon as I find out anything."

Before he could do anything with the information, the petty officer was called to a meeting. Then he went home and completely forgot about the foreign ship captain and his stowaway. In fact, it was three days before Petty Officer Wong cleared his desk and rediscovered his note. With an oath under his breath, he hopped up and strode to see his commanding officer.

Tuesday, February 13, 2018

At Wong's knock, a voice called out, "Enter."

In less than a minute, Wong outlined the issue.

The admiral, whose desk was covered with a slew of paperwork he was trying desperately to clear before he left that afternoon for a three-day conference at Pearl Harbor, scowled as he listened. Dismissively, he said, "There's a guy who handles all POW-MIA issues from the Vietnam era. Hell, maybe every era. I don't know. Can't remember his name. I heard him talk at a conference a few years ago. Colonel Burton. Barton. Something like that. Find him, and see what he wants you to do. I'm sure he has some kind of protocol. Dismissed."

The petty officer went back to his cubicle. A quick internet search revealed that Burton had been replaced by a Lieutenant Colonel Moffat, US Army. A minute later, he had Moffat on the line. He briefly explained the situation.

With Moffat's first words, it became clear that he was concise and efficient. With absolutely no hesitation, he said, "Petty Officer, first let me tell you that if you breathe a word of this to anyone except me, I'll have you court-martialed and sent to the brig for a thousand years. And let me tell you why. There are over sixteen hundred families who sent a son, brother, husband, or father to Vietnam and never knew what happened to him. Every year, we find remains of a few of them. But most of the families will never know what happened to their men. So I don't want to turn on the television in a half hour and watch some dingbat who couldn't find Vietnam on a map of Southeast Asia blabbing about a POW who has returned home. Because all those families will get yanked around again. Hopes dashed. The whole nine yards. Do you understand?"

"You could have stopped at the thousand years of brig time, sir," the petty officer said mildly.

"Who else knows about this?" Moffat asked.

"My CO, Admiral Seitzman."

"Give me the information you have on the alleged POW and the contact number for the ship captain. Then patch me through to your CO, so I can give him the same spiel I just gave you."

The petty officer chuckled. "You gonna threaten a two-star with brig time, sir?"

"Yes," came the terse reply. "I have the backing of the Joint Chiefs and the White House on this."

After relaying the same threat to the admiral, albeit with somewhat more civility, Moffat added, "I will be in San Diego in four hours, sir. No one is to question this man until I get there."

"Understood," the admiral drawled. "I'll make arrangements for a driver and car for you. You'll have full run of my base."

"Thank you, sir. I appreciate it."

"Uh, Colonel," Seitzman posed, "just when will you release information about this guy?"

"As soon as I expose him as a charlatan, Admiral."

"And how long will that take?" the admiral asked.

"Not long, sir."

During the phone conversation, Lieutenant Colonel Blake Moffat had already walked out of his tiny office, slung his go-bag over his shoulder, and made arrangements for a flight from Chicago to San Diego. The plane would lift off as soon as he could get to the air base.

As he drove to the airport, he called the captain of the Indonesian cargo ship. After introducing himself, he assured Captain Tengut that the ship would be able to dock in San Diego. But no one would be able to disembark until the stowaway had been taken off.

"Okay. Thanks, Colonel," Captain Tengut replied.

Then Moffat said, "I'd like you to do me a favor. I'd like you to hand something to this guy and see which hand he uses to reach for it."

"He left-handed, if that's what you want to know. He try to use chop-stick. Picked them up with left hand. But he don't know how to use them. If a guy not know how to use chop-stick and he right-handed, he wouldn't try to learn with left hand."

"Okay," Moffat answered.

"I got picture of him with my phone. You want me to send it? By the way, I on the way now to infirmary so you can talk to him."

"Don't send any pictures on an unsecured line," Moffat stated. "What is your impression of the stowaway, Captain?"

Tengut was slightly out of breath, walking as he spoke. "He sound genuine. But who knows? He probably crazy and need to be in hospital. But if he telling the truth, he need to be reunited with his family. If any of them left, that is."

"Right. Who has spoken with him, other than you?"

"Nobody. There is sixteen guy on my crew. The Indonesian kid who found him don't speak Engrish and medical officer also don't speak Engrish. Other crew members all try whatever languages they know, but Weller don't respond to any until I talk to him in Engrish. Of course, I think he maybe was still too loopy from drugs when they all talk to him."

"Drugs?" Moffat pressed.

21

"Yeah. He in a coma or something when we find him eight day after we leave Da Nang. Take him a couple day to wake up."

"Captain, you know I don't have any legal right to ask you this, but I'm going to ask as a favor. I would like you to keep this incident to yourself until I can verify who this man really is. The families of those men who never returned from Vietnam have mostly given up ever seeing their men again. But they still have a little tiny spark of hope down deep. If they find out there is a guy claiming to be a returning POW, it will cause that hope to mushroom. And when he turns out not to be their loved one, they will be crushed. Do you understand?"

"Sure. I already think about that. My uncle disappear in Borneo in World War II. My mother never stop wondering what happen to him. I not talk to anybody else. And nobody else on ship know what Weller tell to me. My medical officer only guy in the room when I talk to Weller, and like I say, he don't speak Engrish. He think Weller got cancer or something because he so skinny."

"Good. I'm glad you understand. Trust me, after I find out if he's really Weller, you can have all the press you want. But don't get your hopes up. We haven't had a live returned POW for decades."

Tengut chuckled. "I be ready for my interview on Sixty Minute. Here we are. I standing in front of Weller now. You want to talk to him?"

"Yes, please."

Tengut held out his cell phone. "American man want to talk to you."

Weller stared at the device. "What do you mean?"

Tengut waved the phone in front of Weller's face. "This a phone. Here. You listen here. You talk here. Put to your head like this."

22

Skeptically, Weller took the device. He sounded hesitant when he asked, "Hello?"

"Hello, Sergeant Weller. My name is Lieutenant Colonel Blake Moffat, US Army POW-MIA coordinator. I need to ask you some questions."

"Okay. But I'm a corporal, not a sergeant, sir."

"If you're Weller, you were declared Killed in Action in 1981. Between capture and death, you were promoted to the rank of Gunnery Sergeant. What did you call the friendly steer?"

"You said 1981?" Weller's face furrowed for a moment until he focused on the question that had rounded out Moffat's speech. "Friendly steer? Oh, you mean back home? We had a black calf we called C-3. He would lick you to death if you stood still long enough."

"Do you have siblings?"

"Three older brothers."

Moffat continued, rapid-fire. "What are their names?"

"Hiram is the oldest. Then Sam. Then Kiel. Then me."

Moffat noticed that he pronounced the third brother's name *Kee-ay*. So far, so good. "How is your first name pronounced?"

"Deeth. It is spelled D-y-d-d. But it's Welsh. Pronounced like D-e-e-t-h."

"What did you and Sam and Kiel find in the neighbor's barn?"

Again, Dydd hesitated. "You mean the booze? I wasn't with them. That was just Sam and Kiel. They were nine and eleven. I was six. I stayed home because I was supposed to take a nap. Nobody lived at that farmstead anymore. There was no house, just an old abandoned barn. And the boys were playing there— without permission from the owners or from Mom and

Dad—when a couple guys pulled up outside. The boys hid in the mow while the guys buried two cases of whiskey and some cash under the old hay. After they left, the boys ran home and told Dad, and he called the sheriff. Turns out those guys had robbed the liquor store in Lander."

"Tell me about the Charolais steer."

Dydd chuckled. "The one whose hide we tanned? We chased that bastard around the feedlot for a half hour before we got him loaded to go to the locker, so he didn't bleed out right. Dad said we should've tanned the meat and eaten the hide. It would have been more tender. Mom cooked the steaks like usual, and we couldn't eat them. So she stuck them in the CrockPot for a couple days. Still couldn't chew them. The dog wouldn't even eat them. Just carried them around for a while and then buried them or something."

"Tell me about the horse team Becky and Bessy."

Dydd hesitated. "Colonel, I don't know where you got your information, but that's all wrong. Becky was a nanny goat. She was crippled; her back leg was messed up."

"Where did she spend most of her time?" Moffat pelted.

Chuckling, Dydd replied, "On the chicken house roof. She'd scramble right up there. Darnedest thing. And Bessy was a milk cow. Big old brindle crossbred. Dad figured she was part Jersey, part Shorthorn, and part dog. She followed us around like a puppy. Loved to be scratched on her withers."

"When is your birthday?"

"Well, the Marine Corps thinks it's May 7, 1953. But that's Kiel's birthday. I was born March 4, 1956. I lied about my age so I could sign up. Kiel told me he was going to report me and get me sent home. That was a couple days before he was killed. When my CO told me he was dead, I admitted what I had done. He told me to stand down. Then that night, my platoon leader came to get me for patrol. I asked him if I was supposed to go. I guess the CO hadn't talked to him yet. So I went. We got ambushed. I ended up in a prison camp."

"Which camp?" Moffat pelted.

"Dong Phu."

"How long were you there?"

"I'm not sure. I think five or six days. Then I woke up in a room made of concrete and steel with a thatch roof. That's where I was until I woke up on this boat."

"Why aren't you sure how long you were in the camp?"

"Because I was unconscious part of the time."

"Did you talk to anyone there?"

"Just for a few seconds. There were two officers in a, well, a cage, I guess you'd call it. I was being led past them, and they said it's very important for us to learn each other's names. One of them was Lieutenant Commander James Blevins. The other was Captain Lew Whipple. They asked me who I was, but someone clobbered me on the back of the head. I don't know if I told them my name or not before I went unconscious."

"Have you seen any other Americans?" Moffat pressed.

"I haven't seen anyone until I woke up here."

"What about guards? Would you recognize any of your guards?"

"I never saw any."

"Since when?" Moffat sounded exasperated.

"Since a week or so after I was captured."

Moffat was silent a moment. Unconvinced, he asked, "You've been in isolation the whole time?"

"Yes, sir. Someone slid a bowl of food through a slot at the bottom of the door. That was as close as I came to contact with anyone. But if I was too close to the door or made a sound, no food."

Moffat said, "Let me talk to the captain."

Tengut took the phone and spoke into it. "Hang on, I go out of the room." He ducked out of the cabin hatch and trotted down the hallway before he said anything. "So, what you think? He pass the test?"

"Our policy is *believe but verify*. I won't know until I get fingerprints and DNA," Moffat said noncommittally. "Captain, if a couple of guys share a cell for a while, they talk. They learn details about the other's life. He could be a total fraud. Tell me the color of his hair and eyes. How tall is he?"

"How tall? I don't know. He taller than anybody on my crew. But we all Asians. Little guys. I five-four. He maybe five, six inch taller than me. He got blue eye and brown hair. Lot of beard. I would offer him razor, but his skin covered with so many sores that I afraid he cut off his face if he try to shave. We got him some shorts, a shirt. But we got no shoe for him. His feet bigger than anybody here. He real white, too. Like he not be out in sun for a long time. And he smell better today after long, long shower. When we first find him, he smell like dead dog on hot day."

"Okay. Listen, you will tie up at the harbor, as usual. No one will disembark until I take custody of your stowaway. Understood?"

"Yeah, sure. We not move until you say move."

"When do you expect to arrive in San Diego?"

"We get there about midnight, but we wait for tide at three in the morning. I'm glad somebody finally call me back. I was getting nervous."

"I'll see you in port."

Moffat checked a couple of text messages and stepped from his car. Three minutes later, he snapped his lap belt and settled in for the four hour flight to San Diego. When they were airborne, he placed another call.

"Good morning, Colonel Whipple. This is Blake Moffat."

"Hi, Major. Long time, no hear. What time zone are you in these days?"

"Headed for GMT plus eight. And I got a promotion a while back. It's Lieutenant Colonel now."

"Congratulations. You didn't call just to tell me about your promotion, did you?"

"You told me once about a skinny kid you saw at Dong Phu Camp. Tell me that story again."

"You're right. I've already told you that story. At least four times. Why do you want to hear it again? Weren't you paying attention the first four times?"

"Humor me, sir. It might be important."

"Why? Did you find the guy's remains? Or are you looking for them?"

Moffat didn't answer. He simply waited.

Whipple let out a long sigh. "Jim and me saw a kid being led by two guards. And when I say *kid,* I mean *kid.* We'd seen him there for four days. He hadn't had a chance to shave, but he didn't need to. Peach fuzz. He was still skinny like a kid, you know. Hadn't filled out yet; his ribcage was still real small. Anyway, they were dragging him past us, and we had just a few seconds to talk to him, knowing that we would get the hell beat out of us for talking. We told him how important it was that we know each other's names in case some of us got out alive, so we could report who else had been there, you know? And we told him our names. I still remember— forty-however-many years later—the terror in that kid's eyes. He looked at us with such. . . I don't know.

27

Pleading, I guess. And he started to call out his name and this one bastard guard—if I had that son-of-a-bitch in front of me right now, I'd strangle him to death—he took a club and knocked that kid in the back of the head. Dropped him like a bag of rocks."

"So he didn't tell you his name?"

"Nope."

"What did the kid look like?"

"Brown hair. Marine cut. You know, eighth on top, sixteenth on the sides. Like I said, peach fuzz on his face. Blue eyes."

"You sure about that?"

"Sure. I looked right into his eyes. I still look right into those eyes once in a while in my dreams. He still haunts me. Poor bastard."

"How tall was he?"

"Hell, I don't know. They were kinda dragging him. Probably five-seven or –eight. Skinny, too. Maybe a hundred ten or so. Not more than a buck-twenty."

Moffat was thinking.

Whipple asked, "So why are you asking me about this again? You got a line on the kid?"

"I might. It's a long shot."

"Are you on your way to Vietnam again to hunt down bones?"

"Not yet. Late March. Next month. Is there anything else you can tell me about that encounter?"

"Just that I got the shit beat out of me later in the day."

"Did you ever see the kid again?"

Whipple thought for a moment. Took a deep breath. "Yeah. I mean, they dragged him by a couple more times. But then he disappeared the ninth day after he was brought in."

"Disappeared?"

"Yep. We figured they killed him. Probably tossed him in a shallow grave someplace. How many graves have you uncovered around Dong Phu?"

Moffat's thoughts blocked the question from his consciousness. "Lew, if I sent you some photographs, do you think you could identify the kid?"

"Well, it's been nearly fifty years, but yes. I think so."

"All right. Look for an email in a few minutes." Moffat disconnected the call and flipped open his laptop. It took more time for the computer to boot up than it did for him to assemble ten photographs. He was stacking the deck against Whipple. He picked nine photos of guys who looked enough like Dydd Weller to be his brother. They were all skinny and young with brown hair and blue eyes, all the photos taken in uniform and during the same era.

With the ten photos assembled and numbered, he hit Send.

His phone rang almost immediately.

Lew Whipple said, "It's the fourth guy."

Moffat's heart began to pound. "How can you be sure?"

"Like I said, Moffat, the kid haunts me in my dreams."

The driver who met Lieutenant Colonel Blake Moffat at the airport was an Asian-looking petty officer. The hard plastic nametag pinned above the shirt pocket on his peanut butter uniform identified him as Wong.

Moffat returned the salute. "You the guy I talked to this morning?"

"Yes, sir. The admiral figured if this thing was so top-secret, we better keep the personnel to a minimum."

"Good. I'm starving. You got a McDonalds around here?"

Moffat kept busy with paperwork through the afternoon and evening and imposed on Wong to find them a good restaurant for dinner. After that, they worked out at the gym to kill time. Then they drove to the harbor where Moffat made arrangements at the harbor office to take custody of the stowaway on Tengut's ship.

Wednesday, February 14, 2018

Lieutenant Colonel Blake Moffat's first impression of the docks was amazement. As he stood leaning against the front of the car, he asked, "Petty Officer, does anyone actually know how many ships are tied up here? I've never seen so many water-going vessels in my life."

With a shrug, Wong replied, "Beats me, sir. But I suppose somebody has to go out and count them once in a while."

"Is there anybody in the Navy who can count that high?" Moffat muttered. "Every pier is lined with them. Big ones. Little ones. Giant ones. Tiny ones. Everything from aircraft carriers to rowboats. Jesus."

Wong snickered.

For almost an hour, they re-hashed the recent Super Bowl victory of the Eagles over the Patriots, dubbed by many as the most patriotic of all Super Bowls. After that, they discussed the medal count in the on-going Winter Olympics in South Korea. Then they ruminated over the upcoming college basketball championships. Eventually, they talked of various armed forces installations, though because they were in separate branches, there were very few they had visited in common. They agreed that being assigned to Fort DeRussy in Honolulu would be the cherry of all assignments.

Finally, they could make out the lights of an approaching ship on the horizon. But then the lights seemed to stop.

After a time, Moffat inquired, "What's taking so long?"

Wong pointed. "See those other lights moving toward them, sir? That's the pilot ship. It will drop off a captain to steer the ship through the dredged deep draft channel.

He knows the channel, the local winds, currents, that sort of thing."

Moffat scowled. "How does he get into Tengut's ship?"

"Jacob's ladder," Wong answered simply.

When it became apparent that Wong had nothing further to add, Moffat turned and stared at him. "Hey. Look closely at my uniform."

Wong responded, "Sir?"

"Do you see an anchor anywhere on this thing? I know a lot about guns, bombs, and tanks, but only three things about the ocean. One. Never turn your back on it. Two. Never go in deeper than your ankles. And three, it hurts like hell when a wave knocks you ass-over-teakettle and drags you across sand and rocks. But I know nothing about ships or boats. I know there's a difference. But I don't know which is which. And I sure as hell don't know what a Jacob's ladder is."

"Well then, sir, let me educate you," Wong grinned. "If a vessel leans outward when it turns, it's a ship. If it leans inward, it's a boat. And if it's a sub, it's always called a boat. A Jacob's ladder is a rope ladder with wood rungs. Fortunately for the pilot, the swells are pretty tame tonight. It can be a real bear to make that transfer in, say, ten foot swells."

"So," Moffat exhaled. "We hurry up and wait. That's the military for you, Wong. Hurry up and wait."

Even after the ship approached, it seemed to take forever to tie up at the dock. A full hour later, Moffat strode onto the ship, introduced Petty Officer Wong, and shook hands with Tengut.

Tengut handed the petty officer a small hard plastic cooler just the size to hold a six-pack. "My medical officer say give this to doctors at hospital. He take blood sample from Weller when we first find him. Maybe lab

32

NISHI GIEFER

can find out what drug someone use to knock him out. Must have been a lot of drug. He not wake up for nine day. Also in the box is notes medical officer take from physical exam. He write in Chinese, so I translate for you. My Engrish writing not too good. If you have question later, you call me. I try to explain."

"Thank you, Captain," Moffat said.

"My officer bringing Weller up now. They got to go up some flight of stair. Weller not too good at stairs. He do okay walking straight, but officer call me a couple minute ago, say they got to go real slow, stop on every landing to breathe."

When Moffat saw the man claiming to be Dydd Weller, he sucked in his breath. He had seen photos of concentration camp victims. He had seen photos of returning POWs from Japan and the Philippines and Korea and Vietnam.

He had never seen a human being as emaciated as this one. The sight of the mucus and tears exuding from Weller's eyes made his own water. The oozing, open sores on all visible skin appeared infected and inflamed and left the stringy hair and beard matted in places.

Moffat was instantly reminded of the dream and the skeletal man reaching for him. Shaking off the feeling and showing no reaction to the physical condition of the man before him, he asked, "Are you Weller?"

"Yes, sir. Colonel Moffat?"

"That's right. Place your index finger here." Moffat held out his cell phone, screen side up.

Weller studied the apparatus. "Why?"

Tengut reached out his finger and placed it on the screen. "He read your fingerprint. Not electrocute you. Do it like this."

33

Moffat scowled at the captain for disrupting the test. He reset the fingerprint reader and again held it out toward Weller.

Dydd Weller pressed his finger onto the screen. At Moffat's request, he then touched the phone with his next finger, and so on until he had done all ten digits.

Moffat studied his phone for a few seconds. Then he looked up at the emaciated stowaway. "Welcome home, Sergeant Weller. You have a hell of a lot of questions to answer."

Dydd shook hands with the medical officer and then with Captain Tengut. To the latter, he said, "Thank you, sir. Would you please tell him thank you for me, too?"

Tengut bowed and said, "You bow. He understand."

Dydd returned Tengut's bow and repeated the procedure with the smiling medical officer. Then he followed Moffat and Wong to the parking lot. Just before he slid into the official car, he waved again at the two men still standing at the rail of the ship.

Wong took the wheel while Moffat climbed into the backseat beside Dydd Weller.

Dydd glanced at the front of the car and admired the seat belt as he buckled it. "The dash looks like a spaceship. And since when are there shoulder belts in the back?"

"For a long time now," Moffat said coolly. "Have you seen other Americans during your captivity?"

"No, sir. You asked me that on the phone. I never saw anyone."

Moffat's face clouded. "I'm going to be frank with you, Weller. I don't believe you. I don't believe that any human being could be in total isolation for forty-six years and not be nuts."

Dydd had been looking around the interior of the car, trying to blink the mucus from his eyes so he could see.

34

Now he snapped around to face Moffat. "What did you just say?"

Moffat proceeded carefully, concerned that what he had said was truer than he wanted to find out in the close confines of an automobile. "I said I think someone couldn't stay sane in those conditions."

"*Forty-six years?* Tengut said this is 2018. But he was snowing me, right? That's not really the date, right?"

Realizing that it wasn't the insinuation of insanity that had so affected Weller, Moffat exhaled and nodded. "Forty-six years. You tell me you were in Dong Phu Prison Camp for less than a week. If you went directly from there to the cell you tell me you've occupied ever since, that's almost forty-six years."

Weller looked sick as he mentally ticked through the ages his parents must now be. His aunts and uncles. Grandparents.

No. No grandparents. All of them would be well over a hundred years old.

Dydd Weller swallowed and gazed out the window past Moffat. His eyes caught on something, and he perked up. "McDonalds is still around?"

Raising his eyes from the screen of his cell phone, Moffat glanced over his shoulder. "Yeah. McDonalds is still around. You want something?"

Dydd laughed, sounding like a kid. "Oh, you have no idea how many Big Macs I've dreamed about!"

Catching Wong's eye in the rearview mirror, Moffat nodded.

As Wong switched lanes to pull into the McDonalds drive-through, Weller's smile dropped. "This is silly. It's the middle of the night. McDonalds isn't open at this time of the night."

35

"The drive-in is open," Moffat replied as he tapped out a text message. "But they're serving breakfast. No Big Macs until ten-thirty. You want an Egg McMuffin?"

The blank expression returned to Dydd's face.

Wong ordered for all three of them, pulled through, and used his cell phone to pay.

Scowling, Dydd watched the exchange as well as he could through infected eyes. He muttered something.

Moffat stowed his cell phone, took the bag of food handed over the seat by Wong, and asked, "What did you say?"

Dydd turned toward him and smiled slightly. "I feel like Rip van Winkle. I fell asleep for forty-six years, waited for Colonel Hogan to come rescue me from the Twilight Zone, and then woke up in the Jetsons."

For the first time since they met, Moffat cracked a lopsided smile. "Wong, there, won't even know what you're talking about. He's too young to remember the Jetsons."

"I watch the Cartoon Network," Wong replied defensively, stopping at the end of the restaurant's exit lane. "And my old man's favorite show is the Twilight Zone. He has, like, every episode on DVD. Here, check this out."

Wong extracted his cell phone and within seconds had an episode of The Jetsons on the tiny screen. He handed it over the seat to Dydd.

Squinting at the tiny device, Dydd laughed. "My god! I guess if you can get color on a TV this small, the big ones must all have color now, too."

"You can't even buy a black and white television now," Wong vowed as he pulled back onto the street. "Shoot, you won't recognize televisions now. I barely remember our old tube TV. We got a flat screen when I was, like, five or something."

Wong and Moffat downed their food quickly. Dydd was still savoring the last half of his sandwich when they parked in front of the medical clinic.

"Bring it along," Moffat indicated the sandwich. "They're ready for you inside. You'll get a preliminary physical exam today. There will be more testing later."

"Colonel, I'd like to make a phone call." Dydd climbed out of the car behind Moffat. Blinking and squinting, he staggered.

Moffat caught his skinny arm. "Okay?"

"Yes. Thank you. Sir, if I could just use a phone, I'd like to—"

Moffat said, "While you're getting checked out, I'll call your brother Sam. He runs a restaurant in your hometown. Lives in the back of the place with Cal and Kevin."

Dydd gingerly negotiated the entry to the hospital, slowing as they passed through the sliding doors and encountered the bright indoor lighting. Within a few steps, he stopped and mumbled, "I can't see. It's too bright. I can't keep my eyes open."

Someone helped him into a wheelchair.

"I can walk," he protested. "Just can't see."

Moffat assured him as he was pushed away, "I'll find you in a little while."

Moffat entered the conference room the admiral had arranged for him. A glance at his watch told him it was just past zero-five-hundred hours in Wyoming. So he first called his commanding officer in Washington, DC. He gave his preliminary report and promised to provide more details as they became available.

Then he again consulted his watch and placed a call to Sam Weller's restaurant in Whispering Pines, Wyoming.

As Moffat expected, the phone was answered on the first ring. The boys were early risers.

"Hey, Moffat, how's it going?"

"Good morning. Is this Cal?" Moffat asked.

"Yessir. You're on speaker phone. Sam's at the counter chopping veggies for today's lunch special. Beef and vegetable stew, I think. I hope so, anyway. It's colder than a witch's broomstick here, and a big bowl of soup will hit the spot come noon time. I didn't figure we'd hear from you until about July. You have something new?"

"Actually, I do. Sam, put down the knife and have a seat."

Cal laughed. "Sam's giving me the hairy eyeball. His hands are busy, so he can't sign to me, but his eyes are saying, 'What the hell is so important that I have to stop chopping?'"

Blake Moffat let out a long breath. "Sam, please. Have a seat."

Sam Weller, who had been mute since a scrap of shrapnel had torn through his head during the siege at Khe Sanh in Vietnam, left the knife on the countertop and took a seat across from Cal.

"Are you both sitting?" Moffat asked. Then he quickly caught himself. "Jesus, Cal. I'm sorry. That was in incredibly poor taste."

Cal laughed. "I love sitting, Blake. I love sitting so much that after I scrapped Uncle Sam's pretty F-4 Phantom all over the runway at Nakhon Phanom, I've done nothing but sit. So, what's up?"

"Fellas, I don't know how else to say this but to just come out and say it. Dydd walked off a ship this morning in San Diego. I just dropped him off at the clinic to get checked out."

38

Moffat happened to be staring blankly at his watch as he finished speaking. He continued staring until a full minute had passed in silence. Finally, he asked, "You guys still there?"

He heard Cal swallow. Then sniff. Clearing his throat, he mumbled, "Holy shit, Blake. You're kidding."

"His fingerprints match. And Sam, he answered all your security questions. Even the trick questions. He told me he was taking a nap when you and Kiel saw those guys hide the liquor store loot. And he identified the goat and the milk cow."

Moffat let that soak in for a moment. Then he went on. "He says he was in Dong Phu for about a week after he was captured. And I have pretty reliable verification of that. Then he says he woke up in a cell. Says he's been in that same cell ever since. When I get off the phone with you guys, I will be in touch with investigators in Da Nang. We'll try to find out where Dydd's been."

Cal sniffled again. "Christ. Have you ever found one alive before?"

"No. Never."

"Blake, Sams's asking," Cal relayed the sign language from his cousin, "is he okay?"

"Guys, I have honest-to-god never seen a human being so skinny. He has some kind of eye infection, so there's tears and goop running down his face. His skin is covered with open sores and infected bites. Frankly, he looks like hell.

"But he actually seems okay mentally. He's getting checked over right now by all kinds of docs. But I'll tell you straight: not a single doctor in the world has ever encountered a guy who's been through what he says he's been through."

Sam did not miss the innuendo. Through Cal's translation, he asked, "What he *says* he's been through? Do you mean to say that you don't believe he's telling you the truth about where he's been?"

"Honestly? How the hell should I know? I mean, we'll find answers eventually. But how could a person survive in total isolation that long? You know the guys who came home from Hoa Lo had emotional problems—drinking problems, marital problems—and they were there for a lot shorter time than this." Moffat hesitated, then he added, "But at least he says he wasn't beaten or tortured once he was placed in that cell. You know what those fellas went through. It was hell. They were dragged out of their cells and—"

Moffat stopped himself and rubbed a hand over the stubble on his chin. "God, I'm sorry for rambling, guys. I'm punchy. I need some sleep. Listen, I gotta call my counterparts on the other side of the Pacific and get the ball rolling on just where the hell your brother has been."

"Blake, we'll be there in a few hours," Cal asserted.

After the call, Moffat glanced again at his watch and did a quick mental calculation. Seven-thirty in the evening across the Pacific. He found a number for the People's Public Security Forces in Da Nang. After two telephone transfers, and some confusion, as Moffat's Vietnamese was barely passable, he reached a Constable Tran.

Moffat introduced himself slowly. Then he said, "Constable, this morning a man arrived in San Diego by ship. The ship's captain claims to have found the man, apparently drugged, in his ship when he was between Da Nang and San Diego."

"I am ready to write, Colonel. Could you please give me the man's name and nationality?"

Moffat relayed and spelled the name and gave the date of birth. Then he said, "He is an American, and I have verified his identity by fingerprints. He claims to have been taken captive in 1972 during the war."

"And he says he's been held against his will since then?" the constable asked with disbelief. "And you are intimating that he has been held by the government of Vietnam?"

The final sentence was delivered as something of a challenge.

Knowing he must proceed cautiously—and expecting the next exchange to be a request for money—Moffat responded evenly, "Frankly, no. But I would like to know where he's been for the last forty-five years."

There was a momentary hesitation. "Colonel, you realize this man was sixteen years old in 1972?"

"Yes. He said he lied about his age in order to enlist in the United States Marine Corps. Look, Constable Tran, I know there are conspiracy theorists who believe Vietnam is still holding prisoners. Let me assure you that I am not among them."

No demand for money.

Yet.

In Moffat's experience, that was a refreshing surprise.

Tran said coolly, "Do not look for contact from me tomorrow, as I will be detained in meetings, but rest assured I will look into this matter."

Moffat thanked him and disconnected. He doubted he would ever again hear from Constable Tran—or anyone in the People's Public Security Forces—regarding a former US Marine who claimed to have been detained for forty-six years.

In fact, Moffat figured Tran and his cronies were doubled over at the office water cooler laughing about the whole ludicrous matter right now.

Moffat was dozing in his chair when Dydd Weller entered the conference room three hours later. Carrying a box of tissues in one hand and a crumpled tissue in the other, he was dressed in a set of sweats with *US Navy* emblazoned down the leg and across the chest. On his feet were brand new running shoes. "Colonel? You wanted to talk to me some more?"

Moffat blinked a few times and looked at the fresh haircut and trimmed beard, both of which accentuated the emaciation. "Nice duds."

Breaking into a big smile, Dydd answered, "Yeah. Like I said. I woke up in the Jetsons. These shoes look like something George would've worn to the office. And the nurse said the sweatpants add thirty pounds to my appearance. She said nobody wants an extra thirty pounds anymore and offered to give me some of hers."

Dydd slid onto a chair opposite Moffat. "Sir? Has the Navy really let down their standards? I mean, well, a lot of the people working here in the hospital are pretty fat."

Moffat nodded slowly. "America is fat."

"Why?" Dydd inquired.

With a dismissive shrug, Moffat replied, "Because we eat too well and exercise too little." Holding up his phone, he added, "And we waste too much time with these things. How did the exams go?"

Dydd scoffed. "Well, it's almost a darned shame I feel so good because I have parasites on me and parasites in me and my bones are out of whack and my teeth need some work and my heart isn't ticking right. They asked me to sign my name on a bunch of forms. I couldn't see where I was writing. And it was hard to hold the pen." Suddenly he laughed. "Shoot, I'm nearly sixty-two years old! That's unbelievable! My grandpa wasn't even that old when I left home. I'm older than you are, Colonel."

"That's a fact. I see you got a haircut, too."

Dydd nodded. "They wouldn't let me shave the beard all the way. This is what my dad would call a mow-it-or-grow-it beard. We had a hired man once who looked like this. Dad said he thought the guy shaved once a month with a pair of scissors."

"It's fashionable these days," Moffat offered.

Dydd laughed. "Man, the haircut sure feels good. After I went into the box and my hair started growing, I thought about yanking it out one hair at a time. I mean, what else did I have to do, right? But I wondered if it would ever grow back. I didn't want to be totally bald. So I broke it off when it got long enough to pinch between my fingers and thumbs. I thought about letting it grow long enough to braid. But it was so filthy, I just wanted to get rid of it."

"Is that how you trimmed your beard?" Moffat inquired. "By breaking off the whiskers?"

"Too tough to break. I had to bite them. I hated to, because I tried to never touch my mouth. I knew I'd get worms." He laughed. "I looked like a mountain man when I first saw myself in the mirror on the ship."

Moffat still wore the same expression he'd had since first meeting Weller. Skepticism. "Tell me about the holding cell."

Without hesitation, Dydd began. "The south wall was steel with a steel door set into it. I never saw that door open. I figured it was rusted shut." He looked contemplative a moment. "Maybe they took me out through the roof. It was getting pretty leaky. I could almost see daylight through it at the north end. Anyway, the other three sides were concrete and—"

"Hold on." Moffat held up a hand to apologize for interrupting. "Do you want something to eat or drink?"

"No wonder America is fat. Everybody I've met since I got back has asked me that. Even on the ship, they kept putting food in front of me. Yeah. I'd take a slab of cheesecake if one's handy. And a Coke."

Moffat tapped on his phone for a few seconds and set it back on the table. "By the way, I'm recording this conversation."

"You are?" Dydd asked as he looked around the room for recording equipment.

Moffat pointed to his phone. "On that."

Dydd nodded slightly. "What can't those things do? They are phones, they read fingerprints, and they are tape recorders. How in the world do you put a cassette in that little thing? It's no bigger than an envelope."

"It's digital," Moffat answered. "No cassettes."

Studying the phone more closely, Dydd continued as though by rote. "The north wall was the lowest and about an inch taller than I could reach when I jumped for all I was worth, so I couldn't quite hook my fingers over it. The south wall was higher than that by about ten inches. Thatch roof. Sloped downward south to north. Are my parents still living?"

Moffat shook his head. "No. I'm sorry."

Weller nodded slowly. "I thought so. First it was Great Aunt Felicia. I dreamed about her so clearly one night, it was like she was there with me." He looked into Moffat's eyes, and then blinked to clear the drainage. "I think she came to say goodbye. Then Grandma Lois. Then Dad. He went first, didn't he, I mean before Mom? She stayed longest. I felt like she was there with me for four days. In my dreams. When I was awake, too."

Sliding his finger down his phone and tapping a few times, Moffat verified. "Your dad passed away in June of '98. Your mom had a heart attack in 2008."

Dydd was silent for a while. Then he asked, "Why are you petting that thing? Does it purr?"

Moffat turned the phone and slid it toward Dydd. "I'm looking into your records."

Squinting, Dydd studied the face of the device. "How do you read it? It's so tiny."

"Have you seen the ophthalmologist yet?"

Looking up at Moffat, Dydd answered, "They gave me some eye drops for the infections and said I would probably need glasses, but they can't measure me for them until the swelling in my eyes goes down."

"Infections?" Moffat asked. "More than one?"

"Yeah. I can't pronounce all of them. Infection in the eyelid, infection in the uvea—whatever that is— infection in the something else. Can't remember. I feel like I just took every class in medical school in the last two hours. Oh, gingivitis. I think that was the name of the eyelid infection."

"Infection of the gums," Moffat amended. "Let's get back to the description of your cell."

"Not *my* cell," Dydd stated. "I never claimed possession of it. My name wasn't on the deed. You can call it *the* cell or *the* box. But please don't call it *my* cell or *my* box."

"Okay," Moffat responded blandly.

Dydd went on. "The floor sloped very slightly to the northwest, so that was the bathroom corner. There was a two inch gap at the bottom of the three concrete walls with two four-inch-wide supports equidistant in the long walls and supports in the corners, all contiguous concrete. There was a six-inch gap between the roof and the tops of the concrete walls. For ventilation, I guess. No gap at the south end."

"What happened with any solids you deposited in the northwest corner?" Moffat asked. He had heard horror stories from former prisoners about giant piles of human waste they were forced to climb atop in order to defecate.

"I kicked it out under the wall. There were pigs outside. And chickens. They were my sewage treatment plant," Dydd answered. "The southeast corner was the bedroom. It was the driest during the rainy season. And the northeast corner is where I sat when I waited for chow at midday. If I made a peep, no food. Sat too close to the slot under the door, no food."

"What did you do during the course of a day?" Moffat probed.

A sheepish look came over Dydd. "You already think I'm crazy, so I'll tell you. I had a rigid schedule. I woke. I waited for it to get light. Then I went through the motions of changing into my clothes. Folded my pajamas and put them away in the imaginary dresser. Made the bed I didn't have. Maybe did some ironing. Washed the dishes. Then I walked. Two hours. At first I counted, but then I got to know how long I'd been walking, so I did it on autopilot. Twenty-five laps to the right, twenty-five laps to the left, twenty-five laps to the right, and so on for two hours." He laughed. "You'd be surprised how dizzy you get walking the perimeter of a five-by-eight rectangle if you don't switch directions. You know when we walked up the sidewalk to this building from the parking lot this morning? That was pure bliss. A straight line!

"Then after I walked, I waited for chow. It came in a bowl two inches high and eight inches wide, just the size of the slot in the bottom center of the door. I never got water by itself, just the broth that came in the bowl. On about the fourth day, I grabbed his arm and yanked it through the slot as far as I could. I held on for a long time. He never made a peep. Finally, he jerked, and I lost my grip. No food for three days. So after that, I sat in the corner farthest from the door. The food wasn't anything fancy. Broth, rice, little chunks of fish or some other kind of meat—I never knew what kind it was, just that it wasn't beef—and a few chunks of some kind of chopped up vegetables."

Moffat prodded, "What happened next?"

"After I prayed, I drank the broth first. Then ate the food. I would've liked to savor it and keep some for later, but I didn't want to get sick if the food went bad. So I ate it while it was still hot. Then I pushed the bowl back through the slot."

Someone knocked on the door. At Moffat's bidding, the door opened and Wong stepped inside with a paper sack. Wordlessly leaving the parcel on the table, he ducked back out.

Moffat slid the bag across the table. "Cheesecake and Coke."

Dydd scowled. "How did you do that? This room is bugged?"

Moffat pointed again to the phone. "I sent him a text."

"Show me," Dydd said skeptically.

"*Show me.*" With a scoff, Moffat said, "I thought you were from Wyoming, not Missouri." He tapped on the screen to awaken it. Then, typing with his thumbs, he sent another message to Wong that said, "Demonstrating txt. Knock three times to show you got this."

Within seconds, there were three taps on the door.

Dydd laughed. "Now I'm not so sure if I'm in the Jetsons or a James Bond movie."

47

"A lot of 007's gadgets have come true," Moffat said benignly. "What do you want to eat after the cheesecake?"

"Anything you bring in," Dydd said honestly. He picked up the plastic spoon with his left hand and resumed relaying his typical day in captivity. "After I ate, I started reciting. Songs. Poems. Stories. Books. Movies. Speeches. Television shows. Scriptures. Anything I could remember. I bought and sold ranches, tractors, cows, implements. I had rental houses and tenants. I bought and sold stocks and followed the markets on my imaginary New York Stock Exchange. I hired and fired and calculated payroll taxes and workmen's comp. I dated lots of girls. Nurses. Teachers. Secretaries. Once I even went out with a hairdresser. But I had to dump her. Even in my wildest imagination, I couldn't imagine what a hairdresser would say on a date. Say, when did women start doing all these other jobs? I mean, half the doctors I've met in the last couple hours were gals. That's cool."

Moffat said, "Women have been doing almost every job for a long time now. Go on."

Not ready to leave the topic just yet, Dydd inquired, "Are they serving in combat?"

"Not totally," Moffat replied. "But the lines between combat and support are sometimes blurred now. We are fighting a war against a nebulous enemy that doesn't ally to a single country and doesn't limit itself to fighting in any particular geographical region. Please continue with your story."

"What do you mean?" Dydd plied.

"Please continue," Moffat said, his voice carrying an edge that may have belied irritation or simply exhaustion.

Dydd sighed and relayed, "I dressed up and went to weddings and cocktail parties and graduations. I gave lectures. I taught chemistry labs. I had a very full fake life. See, I didn't want to forget how to think. How to talk. How to do the mundane things you do in a day. So I thought. And I talked. And I pretended to get dressed and wash dishes and set the table. I cleaned and oiled my rifle, polished my boots and brass, swept the floor with an imaginary broom.

"I had a four-day week, sort of. I spoke English one day. German the next. Then French. Then Welsh. There was a kid at my school who moved to Wyoming from Italy when he was in fifth grade. When he got there, he didn't know a word of English. By seventh grade, he couldn't remember how to speak Italian. I didn't want to forget how to speak. So I practiced."

"Remind me," Moffat broke in, "how you happen to know four languages."

"My great-grandpa and his brother came from Europe and spoke German and French. They both learned English, but they never used it with their kids or grandkids. I was seven when my great-grandpa Stondt died. He never spoke English to me. Only German. My dad's dad came from Wales and he kind of picked up that trick. Only spoke Welsh to his kids. So Dad only used Welsh with us boys. Except sometimes when he was mad. You can get the point across better cussing in German."

Moffat scowled. "You didn't cover French."

Dydd shrugged. "My great-grandpa's brother spoke French to all the kids. His wife was Arapaho. I guess she taught their kids that language. They must've learned English at school. But everybody I grew up with could speak German, French, and English. We're all kind of proud of it, I guess. When we played another team in sports, we'd chant in German just to piss them off."

Dydd smiled at the memory and waited for another question. When none came, he said, "During recitation time, I cooked. I made all the recipes I could remember—I mean I went through all the motions, you know? I turned on the oven to preheat it while I mixed together all the ingredients. My favorite one to make is cinnamon rolls. The kind with the gooey caramel. And chocolate chip cookies. With walnuts. And lasagna. Man, I love lasagna! I made stew and biscuits and apple pie, with the apples sliced real thin. Mom didn't peel them, so I didn't either. Not that I had anything better to do than peel imaginary apples. Oh, and sausage. I made tons of sausage. With extra seasoning." He broke into a huge grin. "It smelled so good! I mean, it smelled as good as it could in a sewer. You have to really work hard to imagine anything smelling good in a sewer."

Dydd took a long draw on the Coke and another bite of cheesecake. Then he went on. "I invented things. I designed a better sickle bar for mowing hay. I improved the mounts for saddle tanks on a tractor. I made a safer step for getting in and out of the tractor cab. I invented a set of screwdrivers to get into tight spaces. I added power to several hand tools. I even made some of them run on a battery, so you don't need a power cord. You know, there are times you want to fix something out in the field, and you don't have electricity or a generator handy.

"I built concrete forms and framed buildings and designed machine sheds and came up with a far better method of pulling a motor. I came up with a way to put three gearboxes on one system so I could tie three rotary mower blades together. I designed a set of working corrals, alleys, and a chute—with a scale because how else can you measure how well a cow performs for you unless you know her calving interval and the calves' weaning weights? I improved the swells on a bronk saddle."

Dydd stopped in case Moffat wanted to ask him anything. No questions were forthcoming, so Dydd took another long drink, smiled as the Coke stung his tastebuds, and continued. "On English days, I also practiced the little bits of other languages I knew. A little Latin, Spanish, a few words of Russian. Then after recitations, I practiced piano. You know, when I played on a concrete floor, I never hit a bad note.

"Then I did a few calisthenics and stretches. And when it started to get dark, I prayed. I recited every rote prayer I ever learned. I thanked God for my life and health and sustenance. Then I asked God to let the war end. And to bless my family. And to not let them forget me. And I asked God to bless my country. And to not let it forget me."

Moffat took a ragged breath and cleared his throat. Then he muttered, "Jesus."

"Colonel? What's the matter?" Dydd asked.

Swiping a tear from his eye, Moffat cleared his throat again and said, "Nothing. Go ahead."

"That's it. Next day started just the same. Different language in the afternoon. Same pattern. Every day. I didn't know what day it was when I got there. And I never knew what day it was after that. Once in a while, I got two bowls of food instead of one. I figured that was the Tet."

Suddenly, there was a flurry at the door. Wong poked his head in, but then his whole body abruptly entered as he was shoved from behind. "Sorry, Colonel Moffat," he bleated. "Colonel Walsh is here."

51

Moffat scowled and looked up. Then he stood. "Sir, if you could please give us a few moments, we're—"

Colonel Sheldon Walsh of the United States Marine Corps stepped past Wong and saluted Dydd Weller. "Welcome home, Gunny."

Dydd stood and looked uncertainly from Walsh to Moffat and back. "Sir, am I allowed to salute when I'm out of uniform and indoors and not wearing cover?"

Walsh's eyes went to Dydd's feet and back as he dropped his hand. "Good god, Colonel Moffat. This is unacceptable. What the hell is this man wearing?"

Moffat began, "Sir, we couldn't get him a uniform. Nothing would fit him in the—"

Face dismayed, the Marine officer broke in. "Jesus, even a ground pounder ought to have better sense than to dress a Marine in a goddamned squid costume."

Moffat cracked a smile.

Walsh added, "And yes, Gunny, you can by god salute. It doesn't matter if you're in your Class A's or your skivvies. They changed the rule since you went underground."

Dydd snapped a salute and held it until Walsh responded.

Walsh looked at Moffat and said, "I appreciate you keeping this homecoming under the radar, Colonel, but good news travels almost as fast as bad. I didn't want you to whisk this man off someplace before I got a chance to welcome him home and thank him for his service."

To Dydd, the colonel said, "My oldest brother was in the third wave of POWs returned from Hanoi in '73." He hesitated before he added softly, "He had some trouble adjusting. First he took solace in a bottle. Then he took his life in '94." Returning to his full volume, he added, "But you won't have that problem, Gunny."

"Which branch was your brother in, sir?" Dydd asked.

Nodding toward Moffat, Walsh said reluctantly, "Ground pounder, like him. Army."

Dydd snorted. "Then don't worry, sir. With all due respect to Colonel Moffat, here, we all know Marines are tougher than army grunts. I'll be fine, sir."

"Very true," Walsh agreed. "Very true. Thank you for your service and your sacrifice, Weller."

"Thank you, sir."

As he grabbed the door to leave, Walsh grunted, "And I'll see to it you get some goddamned decent clothes."

When the Marine Colonel had gone, Moffat returned to his chair and said, "Colonel Walsh said something you need to pay attention to, Weller. I know you are in euphoria right now because you're home. But real people aren't going to act like the fake people you've been dealing with."

Nodding, Dydd admitted, "I know, sir. I know that. But everybody else in the world figures out how to work with other people. I'll figure it out, too. I know I'm behind. But I'll figure it out."

"Tell me about your capture," Moffat prompted.

"Where do you want me to start?" Dydd asked.

Moffat flipped his hand in the air. "What the hell. We have all day, and I haven't slept for thirty hours. Start wherever you want to."

"Speaking of other people not saying things I expect," Dydd said dryly. He dabbed at both eyes with a new tissue. Then he said, "I saw Kiel in Saigon on April second. He was madder than a wet hen. Said he was going to report me for being underage. And for lying about already having a brother in combat—you know,

53

because they don't put two brothers in harm's way at the same time.

"Sam had already got hurt by then and was still in a stateside hospital when I shipped out." Dydd looked up and said, "You know, Hiram is the only one of us who didn't get injured, killed, or captured. But he lost his wife. Anyway, Kiel was hopping mad. He told me if I didn't 'fess up in a week, he would report me. He sorta gave me a chance to do the right thing on my own.

"So I went back to my unit, and I thought hard about how to tell my commanding officer what I'd done. And I was still working on it when Major Ellis hunted me up. I figured Kiel had ratted me out. But the Major came to tell me Kiel was dead. Then he chewed me out for being in a combat zone when my brother was there, too."

"So did you tell him your real birthday?" Moffat asked blandly.

Dydd nodded. "Yeah. He was pretty pissed off. Told me to go pack my gear and get on the next flight out."

Moffat held up a hand for Dydd to stop while he tapped a note to himself in his phone. "Okay. Then what?"

"I packed my gear and waited for a flight. When it was close to dark, my platoon leader came to get me and asked why I wasn't ready to go on patrol. I asked if I was supposed to go. He said he didn't know of any reason I wasn't. I figured he hadn't talked to Major Ellis yet. So I went. We got ambushed in a narrow coulee that night. The NVA was all around us. Shots coming from everywhere. I saw some of our guys go down. Then I woke up tied to a spit."

"A spit?" Moffat probed.

Dydd nodded. "Yeah. Remember how they hauled Bing and Bob in *Road to Zanzibar*? They tied their hands to one end of the pole and their feet to the other end, then two guys propped the pole on their shoulders and carried them. That's where I was when I woke up. Slung under a pole that way."

"Then what?"

"Then they threw me into a bamboo cage that wasn't tall enough to stand up in. Or sit up, really. I felt like shit. I mean headache, gut ache. Everything ached. And I was thirsty. God, was I thirsty. After a while, a couple guards came to get me. They dragged me through the camp and tied my hands to a post. There was a Vietnamese guy in civilian clothes who started asking me questions. He spoke pretty decent English. When I didn't answer the way he wanted, he smacked me. He whupped on me until I was unconscious. Then I woke up in the hut again. I think it was the third or fourth day when I saw Lieutenant Commander Blevins and Captain Whipple. I don't know if they got my name or not."

"They didn't," Moffat verified. "But Lew Whipple identified you from a set of photographs yesterday."

"He's here?" Dydd asked with surprise.

"Arizona."

"How did you show him the pictures?" Dydd asked.

"Email," Moffat explained. "Look, you can learn all about that later. What happened next?"

"They beat me up a few more times. Then I woke up in the box."

Moffat's phone vibrated, making a buzzing noise on the table. "Excuse me a minute." He read a message and tapped a reply.

When he looked back up at Dydd, he reported, "I've been in contact with authorities in Da Nang. If you were held by the government, that'll be the last contact I have with them. They'll shuffle my request under a rug for ten years, and then burn the rug."

Dydd nodded slowly. "Why would the government hold a prisoner of war when the war is over? It doesn't make sense."

Moffat shrugged. "Communist governments don't have to make sense."

Dydd's eyes widened. "Communist? What are you saying? We lost the war?"

"Well," Moffat said carefully. "We attempted to make a graceful exit. Some would argue that it wasn't all that graceful."

"We lost the war?" Dydd snapped, leaning toward Moffat across the table.

Moffat swallowed. "Essentially, yes."

Dydd probed him with his runny eyes until Moffat started to become uncomfortable.

Voice rising, Dydd pressed, "Do you have any idea what my family paid for that war? Sam can't talk because of shrapnel in his head—or at least he couldn't last I knew. Hiram got called home because his wife died in childbirth—and I know that wasn't because of the war, but he wasn't home with his family when she died. Kiel got killed. I got captured. My cousin Kevin broke his neck punching out of his jet over the Gulf of Tonkin. Then Cal crash landed his plane in Thailand because he didn't want to eject and break his neck, too. Turned out Kevin recovered okay. But Cal was paralyzed. We paid, man. We paid heavily."

"I know," Moffat said softly. "I know you did. That's probably why I've been drawn toward your family, Dydd. Your family exemplifies sacrifice for country. You collectively took your licks and kept coming and coming. You're the kind of family recruiters love to talk about."

Dydd let out a sigh of frustration. "I don't know why they would talk about us. If you told me about a family that was dumb enough to keep sending their boys into that mess—and still lose the war—I'd say they were nuts."

Shaking his head, Dydd went on. "My great-grandmother's ancestors fought in the Revolution and the War of 1812. We won those wars. Her dad fought in the Civil War. For the Union. My grandpa and his older brothers fought in World War I. We won that one, too. My dad and my uncles were in World War II. We won."

Seemingly at the end of his ire, Dydd's voice softened. "My uncle was a POW in Korea where a priest named Father Kapaun saved his life. But the priest died before they got out. I guess we didn't really win that one, either."

Sensing it was time to change the subject, Moffat pulled his phone toward him. After a few taps, he turned it toward Dydd. "Here's a photo I took of Sam, Cal, Kevin, and Devon a couple years ago when they dropped in to see me in Chicago."

"Your phone is a photo album, too?" Dydd leaned over the screen and squinted at it. He swiped a tissue at his leaking eyes. "Sorry about the sniffling. Mom would smack me. But my eyes water, then my nose runs."

"I have a kid," Moffat said wryly. "I know all about snot."

Dydd alternately blinked, dabbed at his eyes, and studied the photo. Smiling, he said, "Jeez! Sam looks just like Grandpa. Grandpa Stondt, not Grandpa Weller. I only know Grandpa Weller from pictures. He died when I was a baby."

Frowning, Dydd continued. "And Calvin's still stuck in that chair. Man, he's spent more of his life in that thing than on his feet. And Kevin hasn't changed a bit. Neither has Devon, for that matter. I mean, I can still pick them out almost fifty years since I last saw them. They're all so old!"

Moffat said, "Devon is an international celebrity."

Dydd laughed aloud. "Well, he can't carry a tune in a bucket, so he didn't get famous in a band. And he never was one to watch a movie, so I can't imagine he is a movie star."

"He's a financier," Moffat explained.

"That makes sense," Dydd mused. "He always knew a lot about money. He invested his extra scholarship money from college and had a mint by the time he went in the Navy. He helped me set up an investment account to put all my pay into." Dydd looked at Moffat. "He knew I was underage in the Corps. But he didn't care. He just wanted to make sure I took good care of my money. So he's a millionaire, huh? I'm not surprised."

"Billionaire," Moffat amended. "At any given time, he's among the top five wealthiest people in the country. Top twenty in the world."

Dydd's eyes opened as far as they could in their infected condition. "*Billionaire?*"

"Many times over."

Dydd sighed. He sounded contemplative when he asked, "How am I going to find out about everything I've missed?"

"The internet," Moffat answered easily. In reply to Dydd's questioning expression, he said, "I'll let your kin explain that to you when they tell you about email. How long did it take to get from your cell to the shipyard?"

"No idea," Dydd replied. "I slept right through it. And you already asked me about it. And I already told you about it."

Moffat made no reply. He started to consult his phone, but it vibrated again. He flicked into a message. Then he stood. "Let's go."

58

Before they made it to the door, Wong knocked and stuck his head inside. "Sir, Colonel Walsh dropped these off."

With a grin, Dydd reached for the sweats with *USMC* printed on them. "You mind if I change, sir?"

"Won't bother me," Moffat replied. "As long as you aren't shy."

Dydd yanked the Navy sweatshirt over his head and dropped it on the table. "Shy? I grew up with three brothers. And I haven't had a stitch of clothes for a long time. Years, I guess."

Swimming in the oversized clothing, Dydd followed Moffat and Wong out of the room. At the door, they turned right and went down a hallway. Then they turned left and went down a longer hallway.

Moffat turned to Dydd. "You doing okay?"

"Sure. Fine, sir. It's nice to walk in a straight line."

The hallway opened into a large room. As they crossed it, Dydd suddenly stopped and stared toward the far left side of the room. Moffat glanced in the same direction and saw an American flag on a pole. Beside it was a piano. He looked at Dydd and tried to deduce which item had so enraptured him.

Moffat gestured toward the piano. "Go ahead if you want."

Breaking into a broad smile, Dydd strode across the room. He dropped the box of tissues on top of the upright, pulled out the bench, and slid onto it.

Practicing on a concrete floor hadn't been a perfect substitute. But for a man who hadn't touched a real piano in over forty-six years, he didn't do too badly either.

Reaching for the box of tissues, Moffat felt his eyes welling up for the second time that day as he listened to the enthusiastic, if flawed, "Maple Leaf Rag". Moffat recalled Sam laughing while relaying through Calvin that Dydd had driven the whole family nuts playing the Scott Joplin song over and over. Sometimes fast, sometimes slow. Sometimes jazzy. Sometimes soulful.

Always loud.

Midway through the second repetition, Moffat caught movement at the opposite side of the room. He touched Dydd's shoulder and turned toward the five men approaching them.

The piano went suddenly silent.

The tallest and leanest of the quintet wore jeans and a long-sleeved t-shirt. His hair was mostly silver with a few remnants of light brown. Except that they were clear, his eyes looked much like Dydd's. Bright blue and inquisitive.

From the two-year-old photo Moffat had shown him, there was no doubt in Dydd's mind that this was his brother Sam.

Three of the others, including the one in the wheelchair, wore dress shirts and khaki slacks. Devon Stondt's hair was still darker than that of his brothers, the twins Calvin and Kevin. But all three had the unmistakable pale blue eyes of their Grandpa Stondt.

Dydd broke into a huge smile as he walked into an embrace with Sam, the brother he hadn't seen in nearly fifty years.

On one side of the cavalcade, Wong was recording the event on his phone. He had trouble holding the camera steady when his breath caught and his eyes welled up.

Moffat plucked a tissue from the box still resting on the piano. Then he passed the box around.

After a full minute embracing his brother, both of them laughing and sobbing, Dydd leaned down to hug Calvin in the wheelchair. Then he draped an arm over the shoulders of each of his first cousins, Kevin and Devon. Then he hugged Sam again.

When Dydd pulled away from Sam, he saw for the first time the fifth man hanging a few steps behind Sam. Clad in jeans and a heavy sweatshirt, he was broad in the shoulders, thick in the chest, and three inches taller than Dydd. His hands were thick and calloused. His thick moustache was dark, almost black, with a few silver hairs sprinkled throughout.

Dydd's jaw dropped. "*Kiel?*"

Offering a handshake, the man replied softly, "I'm Neil. Hiram's son."

"Holy cow!" Dydd exclaimed. "I held you in my arms when you were a tiny baby. *Golly!* You look like your Uncle Kiel! I thought maybe he hadn't been killed after all. Wow! Hey, where is Hiram? And your big brother Nolan?"

Moffat interjected, "Sergeant, I'm sorry. I didn't get a chance to tell you about Hiram. He passed away a few years ago."

Dydd turned again to Neil. "I'm so sorry."

"Thanks," Neil mumbled. "Welcome home."

Beaming, Dydd said, "Thank you. Jeepers, it's so good to see you guys! Even if you are a bunch of old geezers!" He put a hand on Neil's shoulder. "I guess you must be about forty-seven, huh?"

Neil nodded. "Forty-eight next month." His voice cut off quickly as he reached for one of Moffat's tissues.

Even Devon, known for his steady nerves and cool demeanor, swished at a tear in his eye. He said, "Leave it to a bunch of old soldiers to stand around bawling. Start waving a flag or playing Taps, and we all turn into a bunch of little girls."

The comment broke the tension and everyone began talking at once. After a few minutes, Moffat's phone buzzed. He answered it and quickly held up a hand for silence.

"Yes, Mr. President. It is true. . . Yes, sir. . . He's just been reunited with his brother Sam and nephew Neil, and his cousins Calvin, Kevin, and Devon Stondt. . . Yes, sir, just a moment." He held the phone toward Devon. "He'd like to speak with you, sir."

Dydd laughed and looked at Devon. "You know the President of the United States personally?"

Ignoring the question, Devon took the phone. "Hi, Todd. . . Yep. This is the one I've told you about. And yes, we are ecstatic to have him home. . . Today? Not a chance. He looks like hell. Looking at him makes your eyes water. He has some kind of eye infection. His skin is in awful shape. He's pale as hell, and he's so damned skinny you can shine a flashlight through him. Dydd, how long until your eyes clear up?"

Dydd said, "They told me I would have to use eye drops for five days."

Devon spoke into Moffat's phone. "Todd, we'll be there next week. . . No, we're staying here on base tonight in BOQ. . . What do you mean, *what's that?* Bachelor Officer's Quarters, for Christ's sake. What kind of Commander-in-Chief doesn't know what BOQ stands for?" Straight faced, Devon winked at Colonel Moffat. "Sure. I'll keep you posted. See you next week. Here's Moffat." Devon held out the phone.

Moffat shook his head doubtfully at the verbal exchange.

Devon said, "Don't you talk to your boss like that once in while, just to shake him up?"

With a wry chuckle and shake of the head, Moffat whispered as he took his phone, "I like living in a house, not a cell." He moved to the edge of the room to resume his conversation.

Kevin snorted at Devon. "The Prez probably knows the term TOQ or TEQ because that's what we in the military call temporary base housing."

Scowling, Devon asked, "What do you mean 'we in the military'?"

Grinning, Cal explained, "Military is Army and Air Force. You squids and jarheads are considered naval forces. Armed forces, yes, but not military."

Devon snorted. "Horse shit."

Eventually, several enlisted personnel came in to set up a large round table in the room. They brought in take-out in paper sacks. Devon reached into a bag and his face screwed up. "Jesus. Who would bring us rice? This is going in the can."

He started carrying two containers toward the trash can in the corner. But he didn't make three steps before Dydd grabbed his arm.

Face plaintive, Dydd bleated, "Don't waste that!"

Devon looked into the weepy, infected eyes for a long moment. Softly, he said, "Okay. Out of deference for you, I won't pitch it. But you don't have to eat this crap. Eat something else for a change."

Dydd stared into his cousin's eyes until his own blurred. He blinked several times to clear them. "Okay. But don't throw it away. Please."

Before anyone started eating, they said grace.

Then Moffat said, "Gentlemen, I'll be taking off immediately after we dine. Press conference in the White House first thing in the morning. But regulations require that I ask you one question before I go. Do you think this is really him?"

Calvin was the first to crack up laughing.

"Okay," Moffat grinned. "I will have the DNA tested just for the sake of regulation. But I will tell the lab there's no hurry. Congratulations to all of you."

"And to you," Devon said, holding up his plastic drinking cup as though offering a toast. "This is a first for you, I believe."

Nodding, Moffat agreed. "That it is."

Everyone but Dydd ate quickly and automatically. But he savored every bite, only managing to eat a fraction as much food the others consumed. When most of them were finished, a nurse wearing surgical scrubs came in and administered his eye drops.

An hour later, after Dydd had begun yawning almost constantly, Sam nudged Calvin and signed something.

Cal looked over and asked, "Dydd, you ready for some shut-eye?"

Lifting his head, Dydd countered, "Not me. I don't want to sleep for twenty years. I have a lot of lost time to make up for."

"Tomorrow," Sam signed. "We'll start making up lost time tomorrow. After some sleep. Then we'll go home." As Cal relayed his signs into words, Sam glanced at Moffat as if for verification.

Colonel Moffat gave a half smile and nodded. "He's free to go when the docs clear him. But you better find him some warmer clothes. I checked your weather back home. Eight degrees with blowing snow."

Dydd looked around suddenly. "What is the date?"

"Valentine's Day," Kevin answered. "February fourteen."

"Where's the chocolate?" Dydd asked seriously.

Again, Calvin burst out laughing.

Devon did not laugh. He strode from the room and returned fifteen minutes later with a giant chocolate heart. Tossing the big red box in the center of the table, he said, "There you are. Happy Valentine's Day."

As they broke off pieces of the confection, Dydd looked around and asked, "When is Easter this year?"

Sam signed something. Calvin relayed, "April first."

Dydd scowled as he did some quick calculation. "Hey! What day of the week is it? It's Wednesday. This is Ash Wednesday, isn't it?"

Tipping his head with feigned disdain, Devon sneered, "I suppose you want a priest to smear ashes on your forehead. That won't be as easy as a chocolate heart." He dropped both hands on the table and pushed himself to his feet. Twenty minutes later, he returned with a priest in a Navy uniform. The man of the cloth explained that he preferred to provide a whole Mass with the ashes, but given the circumstances and the late hour, he was honored to apply blessed ashes to all of them.

For Dydd's sake, they stood in line and allowed the priest to smudge a black cross on their foreheads, though none of the men had attended church regularly for years. Afterward, the priest asked Dydd, "Would you like me to administer the Sacrament of the Sick to you?"

Looking confused, Dydd asked, "What is that? They invented a new sacrament since I was captured?"

With a casual shrug, the priest responded, "We used to call it Last Rites, but we encourage people to ask for the sacrament now if they are ill or preparing for a medical procedure."

With a warm smile, Dydd shook the priest's hand and said, "Save your oils for someone who needs 'em, Father. I'm in great shape."

Kevin chuckled aloud. "You always were a scrappy little bugger."

"Hey, who you calling little?" Dydd joked. "I grew an inch and a half in the box."

Calvin commented, "This Easter we'll be celebrating two resurrections."

Dydd smiled at him. "You think I've come back from the dead?"

"I know you have," his cousin replied softly.

As Dydd had formerly been the only enlisted man among them, they teased him all the way to BOQ, saying perhaps he'd be more comfortable in the enlisted quarters.

Sam draped a protective arm over Dydd's shoulders and signed one-handed to Calvin, who relayed, "Don't worry about our teasing. Sam's not letting you out of his sight."

Sam and Dydd shared a queen-sized bed for the night. At least five times during the night, Dydd woke and realized where he was. Or, more importantly, where he was not. Each time, he reached over and gently touched Sam, resting a hand on his arm or shoulder.

And each time, Sam broke into a smile as his eyes filled with tears.

Thursday, February 15, 2018

Despite his claim that he would not sleep for twenty years, Dydd slept for nearly sixteen hours. While they waited for him to arise, the others sat in the living room of their quarters, all of them staring at their phone screens.

Devon was alternately monitoring the stock markets around the world, conducting negotiations with a business cohort in Germany, directing an employee who was lining up accommodations in Brazil for a business trip next month, and checking with a nephew/employee who was translating a series of letters from a consortium in Lyons, France. Though Devon, like all of his cousins, could speak French fluently, he could barely read it. And none of the other committee members working on the project knew any French at all.

On Calvin's phone was a video demonstrating the steps to installing an apparatus on a mainframe. To keep the instructions to himself, he listened to the narrative through ear buds.

Neil was investigating options for purchasing the potentilla shrubs he needed for landscaping around a client's new office building.

Sam was scanning the restaurant's sales from the previous night—one of the busiest of the year—and making notes for his assistant chef regarding the upcoming evening's menu.

Without looking up from his phone, Kevin, who was playing a video game, suddenly piped up, "We could hook him up with Molly Addison."

As was common, his cousin and brothers ignored the comment. But Neil, though he knew from years of experience that it was pointless, engaged him. "Molly Addison?" he asked dryly. "Molly with the tattoos on

67

her neck? Molly with the brassy purple hair? With the breast enhancements? With the ear gauges and six piercings up each ear? With the cheek stud, the tongue stud, the lip stud, the belly button ring, and I-don't-even-want-to-know what other piercings? Molly who has lived with six men in the past three years and currently lives with two? Molly who brags about her abortions and her orgies and her drugs? Really?"

"Yeah. She's not married. And she's Sam's assistant, so she'll be around a lot," Kevin reasoned.

Rolling his eyes, Neil said, "And you think she's a good match for a guy who walked out of four decades of solitary confinement and the first thing he wants is a haircut, a shave, and Ash Wednesday ashes?"

Although four of the six men at the breakfast table, out of concerns for their midlines, would ordinarily not consider eating pancakes slathered with butter and syrup, they polished off a large platter of cakes along with a vat of butter, a quart of syrup, and a couple pounds of ham, all the while laughing and telling stories.

Between his first and second cake, Dydd looked around the table and asked, "Where's Colonel Moffat?"

"Washington, DC. Remember?" Kevin answered.

Devon relayed, "He's giving a press conference at the White House, telling the world about you. You're about to be inundated with your fifteen minutes of fame."

Eleven miles southwest of Tyler City, Kansas, in rural Tyler County, twelve-year-old Willa emptied the last of twelve buckets of grain into the long row of steel feed bunks. Then she climbed into the passenger seat of the big diesel pickup, slipped off her insulated leather mittens, and held her blanched fingers to the heater blower. Her stepdad Zeb slid out of the driver's seat and walked slowly along the bunks, counting the cows as they lined up for their breakfast.

When he climbed back into the pickup, whose motor he had left running in deference to the girl's frozen fingers, he heard the last scrap of a newscast on the radio.

". . . was declared Missing In Action in 1972. His status was later changed to Killed In Action in 1981. In other news, the Dow Stock Exchange dipped. . ."

"What was she talking about?" Zeb inquired, pointing to the radio.

Eagerly gesturing toward the pasture gate, Willa said, "Something about a guy coming home from Vietnam. We have to go. I still have to eat breakfast and get ready for school."

Zeb shifted the big pickup into gear and turned toward the gate. "They found his remains, you mean?"

"No. They said he was alive."

Shaking his head, Zeb said, "You must've misunderstood it. Every now and then, they bring home a handful of remains from those guys."

As the pickup was rolling to a stop, she opened her door and said, "Do you mean they find a handful of remains, or they find remains from a handful of guys? Hang on a second."

She closed the door, trotted to swing open the gate, and waited for him to pull through. After securing the gate again, she hopped back into the passenger seat.

Zeb answered, "It works both ways, I guess. I know a family whose son was finally found. There was part of a collar bone and some teeth. That was it. Everything left of him would fit in a tea cup."

She scowled. "How do they know it was him? DNA testing?"

He nodded. "Yep. Sam gave a sample in case they ever found his brother."

"You mean the one who was killed? I thought he was buried in Whispering Pines. He's the one whose name has an *L* in it, but it's pronounced the French way. Is his body really there in the cemetery? Or is there just an empty coffin?"

"He's there," Zeb avowed. "But the youngest brother was killed in Vietnam, too. They never found his body."

She nodded slowly as she absorbed the news. "Isn't he the one with the Welsh first name?"

"Yes. Dydd. It means—"

"Day," she filled in. "*Dydd da.* Good morning. Well, good day, technically. Or day good."

With a nod, he recited the first line of a poem in Welsh. Willa filled in the second line, her American accent barely noticeable.

Zeb chuckled. "*Swydd da!*"

She turned and grinned at him. "Good job. Right?"

"Aye. *Swydd da!*"

At the house, Willa darted inside. Taking his time, Zeb sauntered in and found his mother—who was due to conclude her weeklong visit from Wyoming tomorrow—watching his wife roll out a pie crust. Bypassing the chatting women, he refilled his coffee cup and went into the living room. Opening the computer on his lap, he pulled up NewsNet online.

A moment later, he gasped, choking on the coffee. "*Mom!*"

Leaving his cup in a puddle of spilled coffee on the end table beside his recliner, he trotted into the kitchen and held the laptop in front of his mother. "Is this possible?" he begged.

Her eyes widened as she read the headline. Already she was reaching for her phone with shaking hands. A

70

second later, she spoke into her cell, her native Welsh accent becoming nearly staccato. "Devon? Zeb just showed me a headline about Dydd."

She was quiet for a moment as she listened. Then she murmured, "Thanks be to God!" Overcome with emotion and unable to speak, she handed the phone to Zeb.

"Hello?" he snapped into the device.

On the other end of the line was Devon Stondt's cool, even voice. "I will assume Colonel Moffat has concluded his press conference. You want to talk to Dydd?"

Zeb's mouth fell open.

There was a scuffling sound as the phone was handed over. Then a different voice asked, "Zeb?"

Instantly recognizing the voice, though it was a little deeper than the last time he'd heard it, Zeb sputtered in Welsh, "*Dydd?* Is that really you?"

"Hi, Zeb!" Responding in Welsh, Dydd blurted, "It's sure good to hear your voice! We're flying to Whispering Pines in a little bit. I'll see you when we get there."

Swallowing hard, Zeb cleared his throat. "My word. My word."

"I can't wait to see you, Cousin!" Switching to English, Dydd blurted, "I'm so glad you're alive. I mean, with sugar diabetes and all, I didn't figure you would still be around."

Laughing and swiping at his eyes, Zeb asked, "Where are you? I'm on my way!"

"We're leaving San Diego soon in Devon's plane. We're heading home." His voice softened. "Home to Wyoming. It's been a long time."

Zeb yelped, "Hell! I don't live in Wyoming anymore. But I'll be there as soon as I can get there. I can leave inside the hour."

"Hang on, Zeb." Dydd seemed to be talking to someone else when he asked, "What did you say?"

Dydd came back on. "Zeb, Devon said we can stop by. He said your mom is there. He wants to know if she wants a ride home today."

"Absolutely! Not because I want to get rid of her, but because I will bring her to the airport, so I can give you a hell of a bear hug!"

Two hours later, the Stondt Industries Gulfstream jet was en route to Wyoming via Kansas.

When they were clear of San Diego airspace, Devon left the controls to Kevin and made his way to the main cabin. From the galley, he retrieved a Coke, which he handed to Dydd. Taking a seat opposite him, he said, "Unless you are opposed to the notion, I'll be dictating your schedule until things blow over and you can start living your life."

"You always were a good dictator," Dydd said, straight-faced.

From across the aisle, Calvin chuckled.

Dydd broke into a smile. "Hey, I figure you're qualified. Anybody who calls the Prez by first name and chews him out for not knowing the meaning of BOQ is tops in my book. Say, whatever happened to all that pay you invested for me?"

Devon pulled out his cell phone and consulted the screen. After a moment, he said, "Your current balance is somewhere north of one-point-seven million. That doesn't include your back pay and pension from Uncle Sam since 1981. I've already begun negotiations on that front."

Dydd was unconvinced. "There's no way I have over a million bucks. I was a lance corporal."

"Your parents asked me to invest your pay for you in case you came home. After you were declared KIA, they asked me to set up a memorial scholarship fund at our school with the life insurance money. Which I did. To date, you have helped over three hundred Whispering Pines graduates go to college."

"So that money is all used up," Dydd prompted.

Devon shot him a patronizing look. "Give me a little credit. And don't forget your Stondt Family Ranch dividends. You're set for life. Don't worry about money. I've got you covered."

"Enough to buy a ranch?" Dydd probed skeptically.

"You can't think of an easier way to go broke?" Devon scoffed. Then he switched the subject. "We'll have dinner at the White House next week. Then we'll go on Caleb Chamberlain's radio program the following day. He's a political commentator. His show airs in the whole country. Hell, the whole world if you stream it online. Then we'll fly up to New York and appear on Brian Wirth's televised news program."

"Which channel is that on?" Dydd asked.

"NewsNet," Devon answered. Seeing that it meant nothing to his cousin, he explained, "Since you went into your time capsule, Uncle Sam deregulated telecommunications. There are hundreds of television channels now. Most of them have to be paid for by subscription—and usually a person pays for a package that includes a set number of channels."

Without looking up from a magazine he was perusing, Cal added, "There are news channels, drama channels, garden channels, home improvement channels, history channels, old rerun channels, cop channels, fashion channels. You name it."

"Cartoon channels," Dydd posed, recalling the scrap of a Jetsons episode he had seen on a tiny screen the previous day. Then he added, "The first paid channel was HBO. It was being debuted when I was in Vietnam. I mean when I was still fighting—before I was captured. I read about it in *Popular Science*."

Devon nodded impatiently. "Now, listen. The press will be all over you for a couple weeks. Then they will drop you like a hot rock and collectively forget all about you. Honestly, that's how it works."

"Fine by me," Dydd replied. "I don't need to be a fish in a fishbowl. Say, Devon, what got Hiram? How did he die?"

Devon shifted his gaze out the window. Below was a tributary of the Colorado River, a side branch of the Grand Canyon. He let out a long breath and finally said softly, "He didn't adjust well."

"To what?" Dydd asked. "The war or Judy's death?"

Again, Devon was slow to answer. Still peering through the window, he said, "All of it."

"What happened?" Dydd pressed.

"He drank himself to death," came the slow reply.

Two hours later, they began their descent for a landing at the Tyler City, Kansas, airport which, according to Kevin, was ridiculously oversized for a county with a population of fewer than two thousand.

"What do you mean?" Dydd asked from the right seat in the cockpit.

"I mean they must have big plans. They have enough runway to land a 747 on, but not enough people to fill one."

Dydd laughed before he gave up his seat to Devon and returned to the main cabin. Before he was buckled, Cal handed him a tangerine.

"You still like these?" he grinned.

74

With a boyish grin, Dydd replied, "I probably forgot a lot of things, but I never forgot these. I bet they're still tops. You remember how Grandpa used to get a big box of these at Christmas every year? He would count them and make us do the math so everybody got the same number."

"I remember. If there was a remainder, it was Grandpa's share." Calvin grinned. "Hell, now we get these in the store all winter. They're better these days. They must be different hybrids or something. They're sweeter, easier to peel. And cheap."

Twelve minutes later, they taxied toward the three small metal hangars next to the wind sock. Parked beside the fuel pumps was what appeared to Dydd to be a huge pickup with a flatbed instead of a standard bed and with a back seat. Leaning his back against the grille was a tall, whipcord thin man with a salt and pepper walrus moustache that seemed to engulf the lower half of his face. If he had weighed fifty pounds more and stood five inches taller, he could have been Dydd's uncle David Weller.

But a quick calculation informed Dydd that David would now be over eighty. This man was younger than that.

Standing beside the tall thin man was a slender woman perhaps ten years his junior. She had a long brown braid hanging off her shoulder. Both of them wore Wrangler jeans, long-sleeved shirts, vests, and silky neckerchiefs.

And there was Marion! She had put on some weight since 1971 when he had last seen her, but she still looked like Marion.

The hatch was barely open before Zeb, nearing sixty and the veteran of a broken back and a myriad of other ranching catastrophes, bounded into the cabin and grabbed Dydd in an embrace.

Neither of them could talk.

The first words spoken came from Devon. "Hey, the doctors said he's fragile. Don't squeeze him too hard or you might break his ribs or his spine."

When his words appeared unheeded, Devon slapped the back of Zeb's head and barked, "I said be gentle!"

Zeb pulled back and held Dydd at arm's length. "God! I can't believe it! You've come back from the dead. Didn't they feed you in Hell? Criminy, people say I'm skinny."

Laughing, Dydd replied, "You look like a tub of butter! Marion, how are you?"

Keeping one hand on Dydd's back, Zeb stepped aside to let his mother have a hug.

Then, after another squeeze from Zeb, Dydd asked, "Are you going to introduce me to the woman crazy enough to marry you?"

Straight-faced, Zeb announced, "This is Shiloh. Be nice to her. She removes unnecessary testicles for a living."

Marion scoffed and shook her head with disdain. "She's a doctor of veterinary medicine, he means."

Shiloh hugged Dydd and said, "Welcome home. It's so good to meet you."

"How long will you be in Wyoming?" Zeb asked.

With a shrug, Dydd answered, "For the rest of my life, I hope."

"If you change your mind, come to Kansas," Zeb offered. "There's plenty of room for you. We'd love to have you. Go home and say hi to everybody, then come back. The weather here is a hell of a lot better."

Devon smirked. "If you like living in a furnace for six months of the year. Shoot, it's fifty degrees warmer here than at home right now."

While Zeb pulled Dydd in for another hug, Dydd asked, "Where's David?"

Letting his smile droop, Zeb said, "He died a few years ago. Heart attack."

Nodding thoughtfully, Dydd said, "He's in a good place."

Four states to the east, Reggie Ellis was in his man-cave polishing one of his twin forty-five caliber handguns. They were beauties, having belonged to his dad in a war before Reggie's.

As he lovingly caressed the weapon, Reggie gazed at the shadow box displaying his Purple Heart and commendation for bravery—two items of his personal history that he never, *ever* let his two children or three grandchildren forget.

Reggie Ellis was a war hero. He knew it. Everyone knew it.

In fact, everyone in his life was tired of hearing about it. After coming home from Vietnam, Reggie had done little with his life other than domineer the woman he had once loved and who was too old-fashioned and obedient to ask for a divorce, crush the ambition out of his kids, and threaten the workers in the plant where he had retired as a supervisor.

He always wondered why he had never moved up the ladder after forty years working at the same plant.

The radio was droning in the background as he replaced the first pistol in its case and took up the second. There was a speck of rust on the barrel near the muzzle. That wouldn't do. He reached into his kit for the old penny he kept for this purpose just as the news broke at the top of the hour. The penny, oddly, was minted in 1972. Those made after 1982 contained too much zinc to be effective at buffing off a spot of rust.

The radio's lead story caused Ellis's heart to pound. He broke out in a sweat. His big hands shaking, he let the penny fall to the carpeted floor.

In the twenty paces between the business jet and the heated van waiting for them at the airport in Whispering Pines, Wyoming, Dydd began shivering. In fact, he would not feel warm again for several hours.

But before he stepped into the van, he stared westward at the silhouette of the Wind River Mountains against the setting sun. Chattering teeth did not prevent a huge smile crossing his face.

When they reached Sam's place, Calvin translated Sam's sign language and asked if Dydd would sleep in Sam's room.

"No," Dydd replied. "I'll like your couch just fine if there aren't any spare beds."

Sam's brow furrowed. "But I can't put you on the couch. That's no way to welcome you home after all you've been through."

Dydd laughed. "That couch beats a concrete slab any day. It's twenty-four carat luxury."

"When Kevin is out of town, you can have his bed," Calvin suggested.

"No thanks," Dydd answered. "There's probably a naked girl under his covers."

Kevin made a guttural noise that might have been intended as a laugh. "You should be so lucky."

When Blake Moffat pulled up to his driveway, he saw three familiar vehicles parked at the curb in front of the house. A grin crossed his exhausted face. Linda must have thrown together an impromptu celebration in honor of his newly returned POW.

Quickly, he tried to remember if he had showered or shaved in the past forty-eight hours. Yes, on the shave. That happened this morning an hour before the press conference in the White House at 0800 hours, Eastern Time. And he had changed into a fresh uniform on the flight to Washington.

But there had been no shower. And the little bit of sleep he'd caught on the flights between California and Washington, then Washington to Chicago, had been sporadic and interrupted.

Still, it was nice that she had invited their friends.

She met him at the door that led from the garage into the kitchen. As she gave him a quick kiss, she leaned toward his ear and said, "I'm sorry. I didn't know you'd be so tired. You look like you've had a long day."

"Long two days," he amended. "But don't sweat it. I could use a tall, cold one. Might as well have a good chat with friends while I'm drinking."

She led him into the living room where one of his oldest friends, Carroll Beale, greeted him with an enthusiastic handshake. "Hey, Buddy! Congratulations. How long has it been since a living POW came home from Vietnam?"

Taking the beer handed him by his wife, Blake answered, "Since about the time you and I were born. Thanks, everybody, for coming over. It's quite an occasion."

"I'll say. So, Blake, do you believe him about where's he's been?" Carroll posed.

With a wry face, Moffat replied, "Our policy is believe but verify. I haven't verified anything yet. That will take time. But the captain of the ship that brought him home described him as genuine. Until I know differently, I'll accept that."

By the end of the first beer, they moved to the dining room table. As they were taking their seats, Linda Moffat said apologetically, "I should've gotten some take-out, but I had already put this casserole in the oven this morning before I went to work. Threw together a salad. Dumped some pickles and olives on a platter. It's not much, but it'll fill the belly."

"It looks beautiful," Blake said before any of the others could speak. "I love your cheeseburger casserole." To the others assembled, he said, "She makes these on weekends and puts them in the freezer. Then in the morning, all she has to do is set it in the oven and program the timer. When we come home, voila! Hot, tasty dinner."

Linda beamed at him. "I didn't know you liked plain old cheeseburger casserole that much. Heck, I make it a couple times a week. I figured you were bored with it."

Blake placed his napkin on his thigh and looked around the table. Forks were already beginning to lift when he said, "Let's say grace."

His request was met with total silence for an awkward moment. Then Blake said, "Carroll, you asked me about the man I just met. I haven't yet verified, but if I can believe what he says, he has lived in a state of deprivation beyond imagination. No freedom. No clothing. No possessions. No human contact. No hygiene. Barely any food. But before he ate his one paltry bowl of food a day, he prayed. And before he went to sleep buck naked every night on a slab of filthy concrete, he prayed. He *thanked* God for what he had. And he had nothing. He asked God to bless his family and not let them—"

Blake Moffat tried to swallow the lump that suddenly developed in his throat. He thought to himself, *He prayed that his family would not forget him. That his country would not forget him.*

But we did!

Clenching his jaw, he stared at the huge bowl of leafy green salad. The colorful relish tray. The lace tablecloth his wife had bought on their trip to Venice a couple years earlier.

Resolved, he looked up again and said, "If a guy who has absolutely nothing can express that much faith, a guy like me who has everything," he caught Linda's eye and smiled slightly, "should at least express a little gratitude."

Linda Moffat's face softened. Looking around the table, she recognized that none of their friends attended church. She and Blake didn't. She wondered if any one of them even knew how to pray. But she suddenly remembered a scrap from a long past conversation. "Carroll, didn't you tell me your grandfather was a Baptist minister? Would you give thanks for us, please?"

"I'd be happy to. Please bow your heads." Carroll paused for a moment. Then he began, "Heavenly Father, we just ask that you bless those gathered around this table. We thank you for the fellowship and for the food and ask that you bless it to our bodies that we may serve you more fully. Bless the hands that prepared this meal. Be with our friends and family scattered around the world. Bless those who have gone on before us. And bless our troops deployed around the globe to secure our liberty.

"We ask this in your name and in the name of your son, our lord and savior Jesus Christ. Amen."

Friday, February 16, 2018

On his first morning home, Dydd strode into the big kitchen that separated restaurant from living quarters. Sam, dressed in jeans, a sweatshirt, and running shoes, was busy at the sink, but when he saw Dydd, he waved him toward a chair, pulled a plate from the oven, and set it down on the table.

"Thanks. I can't even begin to tell you how good it smells in here!" As Dydd passed the sink, he reached into a plastic bucket and plucked out a piece of lettuce.

Returning from setting down Dydd's plate, Sam burst, "Stop!"

Dydd looked up, surprised. "Did you just say that?"

Grabbing the lettuce from Dydd's hand, Sam dropped it back into the bucket and gently pushed his brother toward the plate he had placed on the table.

Picking up his phone, he typed, "COMPOST. DON'T EAT THAT!"

Dydd blinked several times and squinted at the words.

Sam enlarged the print and held it toward Dydd again.

"Oh. Okay," Dydd said. "Guess the chickens need some breakfast, too. I didn't know you could talk at all."

Unable to explain that sometimes a knee-jerk word popped free, Sam resumed chopping vegetables.

Dydd grinned as he picked up the fork. "I kept practicing so I wouldn't forget how to eat like a human. But this fork sure seems heavier than the imaginary version."

Sam grinned.

Midway through the scrambled eggs, Dydd asked, "What happened to Hiram?"

Letting out a long breath, Sam dried his hands and picked up his phone. He tapped on it for a few seconds. Then the phone-generated voice relayed his words. "It's a long story. Cal will have to tell you. Be back soon to take you to the doctor."

"Okay. You said the doc is Ben Stondt. Would that be Charley's middle boy?"

Sam nodded.

"They were little tiny babies when I left," Dydd mused. "What do the other two do?"

Sam tapped on his phone. Then it spoke. "Oldest runs the home ranch. Youngest is veterinarian here in town."

Smiling, Dydd said, "I'm glad to hear somebody is still ranching."

At first, Sam took the comment as a barb. But then he realized Dydd hadn't meant it that way.

A rush of cold air came into the kitchen from the house end of the building. Then Neil appeared. Before he could say anything, Sam pointed toward a drawer and signed something fast.

"Okay. Uncle Dydd, are you game to crush garlic?"

"Good morning," Dydd bade. "Sure."

Neil opened the indicated drawer and extracted a hand-held garlic press which he dropped on the counter before Dydd. Then from the pantry, he procured a repurposed ice cream tub full of garlic bulbs. He placed the garlic and an empty soup bowl next to Dydd. Then, after washing his hands, he demonstrated the press.

"Where do you get so much garlic?" Dydd asked as he crushed the first clove into the bowl. "And what do I do with the crud that's left over?"

"Here," Neil set another ice cream bucket—the one that had been in the sink—next to his uncle. "Sam raises it in the back yard. He's got an acre of it."

Sam chuckled.

"Okay," Neil amended. "Half an acre. He's a regular old woman. Good cook. Good garden. Bunch of chickens."

Sam signed something.

Neil replied, "I know. If you weren't a gardener, I'd be in some other business. I wouldn't have grown up loving dirt and seeds and plants." To Dydd, he explained, "I run a landscaping company. And if it weren't for Devon and his two hundred imported New York employees, I'd have to supplement my income by being a roughneck. Or starve."

Neil snapped his head up and said, "Oh. I'm sorry, Dydd. I shouldn't have said that."

"What? About starving? Don't sweat it."

Again, Sam signed something quickly to Neil.

Neil shot Sam an odd look. Then to Dydd, he relayed, "Sam says don't eat the stuff in the compost bucket. And he says sometimes he can say a word or two. It's like a reflex thing. Yes. No. Shit. Those words come pretty freely."

Sam lowered one eyebrow in reprimand.

Neil laughed. "Well, it's true. Those are the three most common words I hear out of you. Of course, they aren't always the right word for the moment. Sometimes *no* means *yes* and *yes* means the stove is on fire."

Dydd asked, "So you live here in town, Neil?"

Neil nodded and broke a bulb of garlic into individual cloves. As he brushed the chaff off the counter and into his hand, he said, "Dad talked about you a lot in his last weeks."

"I'm surprised he didn't come see me when he died," Dydd mused.

Neil shot a sideways glance at Sam. Sam stopped stirring.

With a dismissive grin at their reactions, Dydd explained, "I think I knew when Grandma Lois died. And the folks. They came to say goodbye. I felt like they were there, anyway. But Hiram didn't visit."

"Oh." Neil shook his head and let out a sigh. "Maybe you only get visiting privileges on your way to heaven."

"You don't think that's where he went?" Dydd inquired.

With a shrug, Neil answered, "When he came back—couple months before he died—it was hard for me to reconcile the dad who used to come home drunk and beat the hell out of us every night with the pathetic old man on my doorstep."

"Where is your brother Nolan?" Dydd asked.

Shooting him a wry stare, Neil replied, "He took after one of his uncles. Ran away from home when he was sixteen. He called me once. About ten years ago. Wouldn't tell me where he was, and that was before I had Caller ID."

"What's Caller ID?"

Crossing the kitchen, Neil picked up Sam's phone and placed it before Dydd. Then he pulled out his own phone and said, "Watch the screen when I call Sam."

A moment later, the screen lit up and Neil's name and photo appeared.

Breaking into a broad grin, Dydd said, "Wow! The Jetsons."

From across the kitchen, Sam chuckled. Neil had no clue who the Jetsons were.

"What did your wife think when Hiram came back to stay with you?" asked Dydd.

"My live-in. She was the one who said we should take him in. Otherwise, he would have probably gone to a nursing home or something. And she's the one who had to do all the extra cooking and cleaning. She's a trooper."

"What do you mean 'live-in'?"

"We aren't married," Neil replied casually.

Dydd's hands went silent. Brow lowering, he asked, "What do you mean?"

"We never got married," Neil answered. "Most people don't anymore."

Shooting a look at Sam, Dydd got verification in the form of a nod.

"That's not right," Dydd muttered as he resumed crushing garlic. "Since when is matrimony out of style?"

"I don't know." Neil shrugged. "I've known people all my life who were living together and not married."

Neil relayed Sam's sign language. "Sam says someone coined the term 'palimony' in the late Seventies. I never heard that one before. Oh, and he says that's enough garlic, Dydd. Could you get a couple quarts of ricotta cheese from the fridge and stir them in there with the garlic?"

It was no problem finding the tubs of gritty white cheese. But when he pulled off the first lid, Dydd asked, "What's with the Saran Wrap on the top?"

"Tamper resistant," Neil answered. Then, realizing that Dydd had been incarcerated during the Tylenol murders, he began to explain the event and the subsequent advent of tamper-resistant closures on most items. Looking up, he asked Sam, "When did those murders happen?"

Sam shrugged.

Neil pulled out his phone and looked it up. "Chicago, 1982."

Scowling, Dydd lamented, "How am I going to catch up on everything?"

Preceded by another rush of cold air, Calvin rolled into the room. "Internet," he said as tossed a plastic grocery bag on the counter. "Sam, they had a boatload of poblano peppers in the store. If you like these, we'll pick up some more on our way back from the clinic."

Crossing the kitchen, Sam peered into the bag to examine the anchos. He nodded and signed something to Cal.

Pointing to the remains of Dydd's breakfast, Cal asked, "You about ready to go? You're gonna need to dress in more layers. It's ten degrees."

After brushing his teeth gently but very thoroughly, Dydd sifted through the clothing Devon had sent by messenger before their arrival last night. He settled on sweats over fleece long underwear over silk long underwear. The running shoes supplied to him on the base would not lace over the thick woolen socks. That problem was solved by a larger pair of running shoes from Sam's closet.

Tossing his pickup keys to Dydd, Cal pointed through the window at his pickup and said, "Start it up."

Dydd started to cross the living room floor, but Cal said, "No, start it from here. See the button with the little curved arrow on it? Point the key fob out the window and push that button."

Dydd squinted at the key fob. A moment later, he looked out the window in amazement. "Wow! That's neat-o!"

Cal chuckled. "Nobody says *neat-o* anymore. Everything is awesome or radical or bomb or dope."

Following Cal out the door onto the porch, Dydd asked, "Mind if I drive?"

"Three problems," Cal answered. "First problem, my pickup is modified for a driver in a wheelchair. Second problem, you can't see with your eyes running like that.

Especially out here in the sun. You turned into a faucet when we stepped out the door. And third, you don't have a driver's license. And the sheriff hereabouts is your cousin, so you don't want to piss him off."

Dydd laughed. "Really? What happened to old Biehn?"

"He retired and moved someplace warm. Cheyenne, I think."

Dydd laughed even more loudly as he moved toward the passenger door. Last night, Sam had shown him his phone's weather radar. The forecasted high in Cheyenne for the day was a whopping fifteen degrees Fahrenheit. "Cal, what happened to Hiram? I know he was a drunk. But what killed him?"

"Aw, hell," Cal said as he rolled toward his door. He didn't answer until he had maneuvered himself into the pickup cab. As he began backing through the parking area, he said, "Shit, I guess you're gonna hear it eventually. Might as well be now.

Dydd supplied, "I know he was drinking a lot when I left home. And he dropped off the boys with Mom a lot. I just figured he would get things straightened out once he got over Judy."

Cal pulled onto the street. "He worked with your dad for about a year. But they couldn't get along. Your dad was grieving, too, and they were at each other's throats day in and day out. Then Hiram quit and went to work for a fella south of town. That didn't last too long, so he worked for the county for a couple years, mostly driving a road grader. But he was drinking too much, and he got fired. I think your dad was paying his rent there at the end. Just so the boys would have a roof over their head, you know?"

Turning left at the four-way stop, Cal continued. "Then one day Nolan came to school all black and blue.

88

The teacher asked him where Neil was. He said Neil wouldn't wake up to get on the bus. So the teacher called the law. Biehn went out and found Hiram passed out on the couch. The place was so filthy that it took him a bit to find Neil. Eight years old, for Christ sake. He was unconscious, all balled up in the corner, a bunch of newspapers or something on top of him."

Cal let out a deep breath as he slowed to turn. "When he got to drinking, Hiram would start ranting about how Neil killed his mama. He whipped both of the boys, but it was always worse for Neil."

They pulled into the clinic parking lot, but Cal didn't shut off the engine. He turned his head to face Dydd. "The boys came to live with us, and Hiram did eight years in the slammer. He was out for a few months, then got rung up selling dope. When he got out of jail that time, he left. Nobody heard of him for years. Then, a few months before he died, he showed up on Neil's doorstep looking for forgiveness. Neil took him in, took care of him until he died. It was cancer that got him. Liver cancer."

Though he said nothing, Dydd was intently watching his cousin's face.

Cal added, "I know what you're thinking: Hiram was always so strong. He was an ox, physically. Six-two and one-ninety. And strong between his ears, too. It just goes to show that you never know. I mean, it could've been me. Could've been any of us. He stumbled, and he just never could get it back together."

Cal shut off the key. "You had it the worst of any of us, and you seem pretty sane."

Dydd pushed open his door and said aloud what his cousin was thinking. "So far."

When the nurse called Dydd's name, Cal rolled as far as the exam room and asked, "Are you guys gonna keep

89

him for long? Because I can run over to the office and get some work done, and you can give me a call when he's ready to go."

"Just a minute," the nurse answered. She pulled a cell phone from the shirt pocket on her scrubs and touched the screen. A second later, she asked, "How long do you need to visit with Dydd?"

The voice that came through the speaker reminded Dydd a lot of his grandpa's. "Just long enough to get a baseline."

Dropping the phone back in her pocket, she smiled at Calvin and said, "Looks like you better stick around."

After introductions, hugs, and welcomes, the examination was only a matter of ten minutes. Weight, blood pressure, heart rate, and a couple blood samples. Soon, Cal and Dydd were on their way.

But they had gone only two blocks before they met a pickup whose driver slammed on the brakes, skidded to a stop in the middle of the highway, and waved frantically to indicate that they should pull over. After they did so, the pickup made a U-turn and parked just behind them. From the driver's side emerged a tall, stocky man who trotted to the passenger window.

"Welcome home!" the man bellowed.

Calvin surprised Dydd by lowering the passenger window from the driver's side. Dydd stuck out his hand and said, "Thank you. It's good to be back."

"I'm Bartholomew Stondt," the big man said as he returned the handshake.

"We just saw your big brother," Cal said.

"The really big one?" Barth asked. Standing beside the pickup, he could only see Cal's lap but not his face.

Cal laughed. "The tiny one. Dydd, this is Doctor Ben's baby brother."

"So you're the vet?" Dydd asked.

Bartholomew nodded. "My dad used to talk about what a hell of a bronk rider you were. Have you been horseback yet?"

"Not yet," Dydd started to say.

Calvin cut him off. "No riding yet, Barth. His bones are brittle. Too dangerous."

Leaning down to peer across the cab toward Cal, Barth scowled. Then his face brightened and he asked, "Dydd, would you like a tour of the vet clinic? I'll take you back to Sam's place afterward."

When Dydd was situated in the passenger seat of the vet truck, Barth Stondt made another U-turn and continued one block until he pulled off the street and into the vet clinic parking lot. "There's the vet clinic," he said, pointing to the long, low concrete block structure. "Now are you ready to go riding?"

Dydd beamed an enthusiastic, "Yeah!"

Without even slowing down, Barth pulled through the lot and back onto the highway headed west out of town.

When they were saddled and moving away from the big barn that Dydd remembered as having belonged to his dad's cousin, Dydd asked, "What did Cal mean when he said Ben was your tiny brother? He's got a couple inches on me. And they tell me I'm five-ten now, even though the last time I remember being measured before, I was only five-eight. Maybe five-eight and a half."

Scoffing, Barth grunted, "Ben's only six-one. I'm six-six. And our oldest brother is half a head taller than me."

Dydd laughed. "You're kidding."

With a shake of his big head, the vet replied, "Over seven foot. He won't tell anybody how much over. Says nobody can reach up there to measure him. He's a mutant. I'm glad I'm tall—I can always see over the

91

crowd, I don't need a step stool to change a light bulb, and the kids love to sit on my shoulders at a parade—but I'm glad I'm not that tall. He has trouble finding clothes, pickups, horses, saddles, just about everything."

If Barth had planned to say anything more, he was cut off by his phone. Shucking his heavy glove, he fished the device from a pocket inside his coat. "Hello?" he answered. "Yeah. He's with me." To Dydd, he said, "It's Zeb. He wondered if you're riding the big dun gelding or the palomino mare. Zeb, he's on the dun gelding." The big vet listened for a moment. Then he laughed. "Well, I figured if I'd been cooped up that long, the first thing I'd want to do was get on a horse. Well, the second thing. But after all that time, the first thing wouldn't take very long. You want to talk to him?"

Dydd was shaking his head. "I can't take off my glove. My fingers are froze. Ask him if I can call later. And on my own dime, so I don't break you with long distance charges."

"I pay by the month. Unlimited nationwide plan," Barth informed him. "If I never turned on the phone or if I talked twenty-four/seven, it wouldn't cost anything different. I could call home or call New York City. No difference."

Shaking his head in disbelief, Dydd said, "Ask him what he wants."

Barth relayed the query. Then he replied, "Just calling to shoot the breeze. What, Zeb? . . . Okay."

He disconnected and said, "Zeb's flying up here tomorrow. They'll go to Stations of the Cross with us. I assume you're going?"

"Sure," Dydd enthused. "I used to carry the cross for Stations. But wait, how can Zeb fly? He can't get a flight medical with sugar diabetes, can he? Have they found a cure for it?"

"No. Why do you think he got married? He bought a plane and paid for her flying lessons." Barth slipped the phone back into the chest pocket on his coat. "And he said to tell you he has a couple horses to give you. You better feel pretty honored. He supplies all my horses, too, but I have to pay through the nose for them. His cayuses bring premium. Were you still around when his old man came up with the slogan 'Weller Broke Horses'?"

Dydd shivered. "Nope. But it's catchy."

"About the time Zeb started high school, David noticed that the highest selling colts at their sale were the ones Zeb broke. So he stuck Zeb on as many horses as he could. Last year at their sale, the top gelding was a four-year-old that brought an even sixty grand."

Dydd whistled. "Holy cow!"

"A PRCA bulldogger bought him. He's already made some money with him, too."

"I'm sure glad the PRCA is still around," Dydd said, as his teeth chattered.

Barth scowled at him. "I guess I better take you in. Skinny as you are, you could freeze solid out here in under an hour."

Dydd laughed, but he felt as though the prophesy had already come to fruition.

As they returned, Barth said, "And nobody says 'sugar diabetes' anymore. They just say diabetes now."

After the half hour ride and a bowl of soup at Barth's ranch, Dydd was dropped off at Devon's complex of offices. He entered through the main door and found himself in a cavernous lobby strewn with huge leather couches and adorned with magnificent paintings of western scenes. At the far side of the room was the desk where Marion Weller sat.

"Dydd! I'm so glad you've come. Are you here to see Devon?" she said as she came around the desk to give him a hug.

"Not particularly. I'm just taking in the local sights. Calvin said he'd be here this afternoon, so I figured I'd catch a ride back to Sam's house." He glanced around and indicated one of the huge paintings. "Where did Devon find these pictures? They're amazing."

Beaming with matronly pride, Marion said, "Zeb painted that one. And that one over there."

Jaw dropping, Dydd emoted, "You're kidding! I remember he was always a real good drawer. But I didn't know he could paint!"

"Painting funds his ranching operation. My goodness, your lips are blue," Marion crooned. "Would you drink some hot chocolate?"

She led him to the break room where he gawked around. "This is bigger than the kitchen where Sam cooks for a hundred people every day! Hey, is that a microwave? I remember seeing ads for them. I thought they were a lot bigger than this." He leaned over the appliance and squinted at the touch pad controls.

"They used to be," she explained as she popped open the door and heated his beverage. "When it's done, I'll show you some other marvels."

Armed with hot chocolate, they returned to Marion's desk where she demonstrated her basic office equipment. Copier. Printer. Scanner. Wireless mouse and keyboard.

The fax machine, she explained, was nearly obsolete in the age of emails and texts, its lifespan less than the time since Dydd's capture.

Of all the utensils on her desk, the one that most fascinated him was the electric tea pot. She heated a pot of water, slid in the infuser and, a few minutes later,

94

refilled his now empty cup with a strong brew of Darjeeling tea.

As she poured, she asked, "How are you getting along at the boar's nest?"

He chuckled. "Why do you call it that?"

She shrugged. "Well, I suppose I could share an abode with Sam. And Calvin. I couldn't stand Kevin for ten minutes."

"Why?" Dydd inquired.

With a most unladylike snort, she said, "He has a proclivity for infesting a perfectly fine conversation with something bawdy and vulgar."

With a smile, Dydd replied, "At least he hasn't changed."

"Exactly," she agreed. "But most boys stop being in junior high school before they graduate college."

"Marion, why do you think Sam moved back to Wyoming? There are stayers and goers. I always figured him for a goer."

"Your parents needed him," she answered in her sing-song Welsh cadence. "And he needed them. He was in hospital for over a year, you know. He was still very weak when he came home. He stayed at the ranch for several months. Then, when the twins agreed to move in with him, he bought the house in town and built on the restaurant."

"Aunt Marion, I'm sorry about Uncle David," Dydd offered.

Her brow furrowed. "Ah, Dydd, how kind of you to give condolences when you've lost so many. I'm surprised you're not overcome with so much grieving."

He shrugged. "Well, if I learned anything in the past forty-six years, I learned that wishing doesn't change things. Lamenting doesn't turn back the time. Or push it forward."

"How wise you are," she agreed. "You know, among you four boys, you're the only one who could've survived what you've been through."

Dydd studied her for a moment. As he refilled his cup, he inquired, "Why do you say that?"

"Over the years, I've read books about the Donner Party. About prisoners of war. Saint Petersburg under siege. Did you know that almost all the survivors of the Donner Party were women and children? One theory is that the men were so accustomed to being in charge, being in control, that they were mentally and emotionally crushed when events were out of their hands."

Dydd watched her, waiting for more.

Marion continued, "During wartime captivity, some lose their minds, others their wills. Those that today we might call control freaks had the worst time of it. Hiram and Kiel were strong-willed. They wouldn't have been able to tolerate incarceration."

"But what about Sam? He's a thinker," Dydd pointed out. "And there was a lot of time for thinking in the box."

"Aye," she agreed, "he is a thinker, but afraid of his own company."

Dydd seemed perplexed. "I don't understand what you mean."

Tipping her head to one side, she continued. "People have their phobias. I remember once when he was a little boy. He was taking a nap, so your mother and I walked outside to look at the garden. Sam awoke and ran out of the house screaming. Your mum rolled her eyes and whispered to me that he was afraid of loneliness. Dydd, it would have killed him to live it. It nearly kills him to even think of what you went through."

Unconvinced, Dydd said, "Humans are uniquely adaptable."

"Some of them are," Marion asserted. "But some are less so."

Dydd nodded slowly and after a moment, stood and said, "I'll be right back. If it's okay for me to grab another cup of hot chocolate."

"Certainly," Marion answered. "Help yourself."

When he returned, Dydd leaned his hip against the desk again. "Aunt Marion, can you tell me why my parents named us such weird names?"

She laughed. "Weird? And you're asking me, who named my children Justine, Zebekai, and Fiona?"

He grinned. "No, really. I mean, when I got out in the world, I realized there were no other Hirams or Dydds out there."

Marion leaned back and sighed. "Your mum was a creative woman. She was a poet. Did you know that?"

"Yeah. She used to make up rhymes and limericks." He chuckled. "I remember one time we were riding that northwest pasture looking for a bull with footrot. Mom, me, and Aunt Ruthie. So Ruthie and I are talking about school and stuff. And Mom pops up with this:

> Ruthie of the dell went down to the well
> To get her poor horse a drink
> When she got to the pumper,
> Thought a man tried to jump her
> So she slapped him, quick as a wink.
>
> She hit him and beat him and tried to unseat him
> And whupped him with sadistic glee.
> He said, 'Please excuse me
> But do not abuse me,
> I thought the durned water was free!'"

97

Marion nodded slowly. "But she wrote serious poetry, too. Beautiful work. I saw only a few of her pieces. Then one day—after her first heart attack—I drove by to check on her. She was standing by her burn barrel with her notebook, pulling out sheets a few at a time and tossing them in the fire. I asked her why she was burning her poems. She said they were too personal to have someone casually flipping through them when she was gone. Plus, she said they were words for a woman's soul. She had no daughters. Her daughter-in-law was gone. No granddaughters."

Dydd did not reply.

For a long moment, Marion stared into the distance, remembering her old friend. Returning to the present, she said, "But I do have a few of her pastel drawings, Dydd. Zeb made frames for them when he was in high school. When you're settled, I'll give them to you to decorate your new home."

Reggie Ellis, former major in the US Marine Corps and former commanding officer of a skinny kid from Wyoming, was digging into the back hall closet.

From the kitchen, his wife called, "What are you looking for?"

He grumbled a reply.

A minute later, she appeared, hands on hips, all five-foot-two inches of her, and said, "I hope you intend to put all that junk back in there like it was."

He looked at her across a rolled sleeping bag, a Coleman camp stove, and a folded waterproof groundsheet that reeked of mildew. "What the hell do you think your job is, woman? God invented women to keep house and look after kids. There ain't no kids left in this house, so all you have to do is straighten the place and dust. So give it a rest, for Christ's sake."

She sighed and scowled. "Are you going camping?"

"Yes. I'm going camping."

"It's the middle of winter," she countered.

"Jesus Fucking H. Christ. I can read the goddamned calendar. Here, carry this out to the car." He shoved the sleeping bag toward her.

With another sigh, she complied and followed him to the garage. As she watched him pitch items from the backseat—and knowing that she would be cleaning up that mess later, too— she said, "If you're going to sleep in the backseat again, be sure to flip those seat belt thingies under the seat before you load the trunk. Remember, it's easier to do that from the back side when the trunk is empty."

He swore at her and told her to shut up.

Twenty minutes later, he came back into the kitchen and began opening and slamming cabinet doors.

"Remember," she said, "not to spend too much. The tickets for our vacation are supposed to go on the credit card this month."

"I remember the damned vacation," he muttered. On the countertop, he assembled a jar of peanut butter, a box of saltines, and a few cans of pork and beans.

Her voice rising, she begged, "You will be home in time, right? I'm not missing my vacation because you aren't home from camping!"

"I'll be home. Besides, you'll enjoy your vacation more without me anyway, won't you?"

"Where are you going?" she asked.

"Wyoming," he muttered as he yanked a plastic grocery bag from the crammed drawer.

"Wyoming?" she gasped. "It's winter. It's cold in Wyoming."

"Yeah."

"Reggie Ellis, you aren't a spring chicken anymore. Good grief! Wyoming is next to Canada. You'll freeze to death."

He shot her a withering glare. But she didn't wither. "Good grief, woman. Don't you know anything? Wyoming is not next to Canada. It's next to Idaho. Idaho is next to Canada."

"You'll freeze to death! They have blizzards and grizzly bears in Wyoming."

"Yeah, and hot pots and volcanoes. If I get cold, I'll just sleep next to Old Faithful."

Raising and dropping her arms as in resignation, she said, "Well, I better pack you more food. Good grief. Why on earth are you going camping in Wyoming?"

He made no reply.

As she began assembling items from the shelf, she suddenly turned and peered at him through lowered brows. "Are you going to see that man who just got back from prison in Vietnam? Isn't he from Wyoming?"

"Yeah."

"Oh, good grief. Give it a rest, Reg. You don't even know the man. What makes you think he wants a bunch of old soldiers hovering around him?"

"I did know him. His platoon was in my command. The whole bunch of them was wiped out."

"Apparently not," she rebuked mildly. She clicked her tongue. "Camping in Wyoming. If you think winter is tough in Alabama, just you wait and see. There's liable to be five feet of snow there. You'll end up in a motel because it's too cold there to camp. But just you mind the cost. Remember the tickets for the trip are going to be applied to the credit card. Just remember that."

***

100

Calvin and Dydd returned to Sam's to find the parking lot full. Inside, Dydd glanced into the dining room from the kitchen and saw that it was the same. So he filled two plates in the busy kitchen and carried them to the quiet living room in the opposite end of the sprawling house.

"Thanks," Cal replied as he reached for the food. "You want to watch something on TV?"

Dydd glanced around the room. "Do you have a television?"

Calvin pointed a remote controller to a large black rectangle mounted on the north wall.

"Holy smokes!" Dydd emoted as the screen came to life. "That's like in a theater!"

"Yeah," Cal mused. "What do you want to watch?"

Dydd shrugged. "Whatever's on, I guess. Hey, speaking of movie theaters, what happened to the drive-in north of town?"

"Gone. I doubt there are a dozen drive-in theaters left in the country."

"Why?" Dydd asked, surprised.

"They were killed by the video cassette, which was replaced by the DVD. You can watch movies at home cheaper. And you can pause the action while you run to the can, refresh your beer, or make another batch of popcorn. By the way, you can make popcorn in a microwave now. Just takes a few minutes. What do you want to watch?"

"John Wayne is dead, I suppose," Dydd observed.

Cal chuckled. "About forty years. But hey, I know one you'll enjoy. It's the Duke using a bunch of little boys to move his herd to market."

Not missing the irony, Dydd grinned. "I hope they didn't take a forty-six year detour."

"It's called *The Cowboys*. I think it was one of his last pictures. Not the very last, but close." After pushing a series of buttons on the remote, Cal dropped the device on the end table and said, "There you go."

"What do you mean?" Dydd looked up at the screen and was mesmerized as the opening credits of *The Cowboys* began. "Hey! How did you do that?"

"Magic," Cal replied dryly. "You can get television programming on demand now. There's still regular programming, but you can watch just about anything anytime. If you pay for it. We're watching this courtesy of Amazon."

"Amazon?"

While the music blasted and the beautiful scenery passed by, Cal did his best to explain Amazon. He had to back up and explain dot-com. And the internet. And a computer mouse, though Dydd had earlier received a brief introduction from Marion.

"Boy, I sure missed out on a lot of stuff," Dydd said just as John Wayne appeared. "Especially the Duke. Man, I missed him!"

By the Entre'acte, Dydd had finished eating two more courses. Each time he left the room, Calvin paused the movie. And each time, Dydd shook his head and laughed at the frozen picture on the screen.

As the closing credits rolled, Calvin pulled a slender pocket-sized calculator from his shirt pocket and tossed it to Dydd. "It's solar-powered, so it never needs a battery. I have a drawer full of them at the office, so you can keep that one."

The device kept Dydd entertained for twenty minutes.

"Now that you've caught up to the late '70s, here's a little taste of the twenty-first century," Calvin said. From a pouch on the side of his wheelchair, he extracted a

102

smart phone in a hard plastic protective case. "This is your new phone. I put a piece of tape on the back and wrote your phone number on it. You can also find your number in the phone itself, but sometimes it's a challenge to find it if you aren't used to the technology. Once you memorize it, you can take off the tape. The phone has a calculator in it, too. But I like having the separate calculator, myself. So you keep both of them handy."

For the next hour, Calvin demonstrated the calling feature, the phone log and contact list, internet, email, and GPS maps. "And you have a video camera, of course. Here's a video Moffat sent."

Dydd squinted at the screen. The squint evolved into a scowl. "Is that me? That's the ship. Captain Tengut's ship. I didn't see any movie cameras there."

Holding up the phone, Cal said, "Someone took the video with a phone just like this."

"But how did Moffat get it?"

"Whoever took it sent it to Moffat. Moffat sent it to me. Flick of a button. Dead simple."

Shaking his head in disbelief, Dydd said, "Not even James Bond could have foretold all this new-fangled stuff."

With a chuckle, Cal said, "Right now, you're closer to Mayberry than the twenty-first century. But we'll catch you up. We'll catch you up."

Dydd inquired, "How come you never got married?"

Cal said, "Perhaps you haven't noticed, Cuz, but God made man with three legs. All three of mine are noticeably lame. But considering that I'm a seventy-almost-three year old guy in a wheelchair, I believe I will meet lots of women between now and my death. Doctors, nurses, and therapists of all kinds. Maybe a shrink or two."

"Why do you need a shrink?" Dydd asked.

Cal lowered one brow comically. "I've been rooming with my twin brother for almost fifty years. What do you think?"

Dydd grinned.

"But," Cal added, "one of these days he's not going to pass his flight physical. They'll yank his medical, and he'll lose his pilot's license. Then he'll be retired and be hanging around here all the time." In a mutter, he added, "And if that happens, maybe I'll just stay at the office like Devon."

"Where does he sleep?" Dydd asked.

"Devon?" Calvin snorted. "Probably sitting at his desk. You know, signing a sweet business deal gets him more orgasmic than a beautiful, naked woman could. I haven't seen him crack an emotion for decades. Not until you came home. But when the rest of us were shamelessly crying like a bunch of babies, he shed a single tear and let loose of one measly sniffle."

Dydd thought about that for a while. "Why do you suppose he's like that?"

Calvin replied, "He says he lost his soul in Vietnam. Maybe he did. I mean, he was always clever and shrewd. But he was different after he came home. He was more—I don't know how to describe it. I never really thought about it much. That's just the way it is. But I guess ruthless would be the right word."

"I figured," Dydd commented, "that if I ever got out, I'd come home and find you guys all married with a passel of kids."

"I guess you'll have to make up for the rest of us. But do me a favor, Cuz. Don't marry anyone you meet in the next couple months. Like Devon said, you're going to be a celeb for a while. There are a lot of people who would like to be seen on the arm of anyone who can get their mug on television."

Dydd nodded contemplatively.

Cal peered at him. "Are you starting to think about women yet? Because you know the old adage: if a man has enough to eat, he has a lot of problems. If he doesn't, he has only one."

Dydd shrugged. "I have plenty to eat now, but maybe I'll wait until I put on a few pounds before I start picking out a wife."

Blake Moffat was seated at his desk sipping his third cup of coffee when his cell phone rang. It was Constable Tran in Da Nang.

"Good morning, Lieutenant Colonel Moffat. I believe I am calling you in your morning, correct?"

Somewhat surprised to be hearing from Tran again, Moffat answered, "Correct. Good evening, Constable. Have you learned anything about the stowaway?"

"Yes. And I have a few questions for you." Tran spoke slowly, as though considering how his words would be interpreted by the bureaucrats he knew would monitor this call. "How long did the man say he traveled before he was placed on the ship?"

"He claims he doesn't remember leaving the cell."

"The cell?"

Moffat relayed Dydd's description of the room.

"I see," Tran replied. "I see. Please, Colonel Moffat, I want to be clear on something. I am considering you a part of my investigation team. That means if I learn something of interest, I will share it with you. If I have questions you can answer, you will share with me. However, I do not like to divulge information while my case is on-going. Therefore, I ask that you keep any information confidential between us."

105

"Absolutely," Moffat agreed. "That's how I prefer it."

"Ah, then. One more matter I will discuss." Tran paused for a moment, as though searching for the right words. "As you may know, the military and the police in Vietnam are not separate, as they are in the United States. I am a civilian constable. Therefore, I have certain, shall we say, jurisdictions. There are some records I can only access if I make a formal request to the military authorities. Do you understand?"

Though he wasn't quite certain he did, Moffat said, "I believe so."

"In other words, I don't believe there is a need to, shall we say, bother the military officials with this inquiry. At least not at this time. Do you understand?"

Moffat assumed that Tran was saying that if he began poking into old military records, he would likely lose control of the investigation. And if the case switched to military jurisdiction, the whole matter may quietly slip into oblivion. Moffat replied, "Yes, I understand."

"Good. Now, my grandfather knows a man who served as a guard in a military prison. Not Dong Phu, but he may have knowledge of the inner workings of Dong Phu. Tomorrow, I will talk with this man and see if he can tell me anything about that period of time."

"Good. Thank you." Moffat answered.

"So, here is what I have learned so far regarding this puzzle. First I assigned two of my. . . sorry, let me think of the word I want. . . people who work in my office, people over whom I have control."

"Underlings," Moffat said, stifling a smile.

"Yes. Underlings. I assigned two underlings to look into the event at the harbor. There are security cameras there. I instructed them to analyze camera footage from the area near the ship. Several hours before the ship left

106

the port, two unauthorized persons entered the ship. They were pushing a cart, like you would perhaps use to move garbage to the street when it is your trash collection day. You understand?"

"Yes, sir."

"The cart would be small for a person to fit into unless that person was, shall we say, folded. Uh, perhaps, legs and arms bent like a baby inside the mother. These parties were inside the ship for nine minutes. Then they exited. There is no way to know from the film if the cart was empty or full either on the way into or out of the ship. Do you understand?"

"Yes," Moffat replied.

"So then I asked underlings to look at footage in the car park. Oh, sorry. In America, I believe you say park lot."

"Parking lot," Moffat offered.

"Ah, yes! Parking lot. Sorry. I speak English, so I work with tourists here in Da Nang. Sometimes they are British, sometimes Australian, sometimes American, and so on. All of those places speak just a little differently, you see." Tran cleared his throat. He continued, still speaking deliberately, picking his words carefully. "So they found on the film where the same two unauthorized persons parked a car before they entered the ship. They extracted something from the boot of a car, but from the angle of the camera, it is impossible to see what they are doing when the lid of the boot is lifted. But it is obvious they took something from the car and placed it in the cart, which had been sitting on the walkway before they pulled into the park. Excuse me, parking lot."

Moffat was absorbing the information. Realizing Tran was waiting for some indication that he was following, he grunted, "Okay. So maybe the cart was left there earlier for the purpose of moving something heavy."

"Exactly my thought," Tran agreed heartily. "We are in the process of identifying the two people—one man, one woman. I will keep you in the loop, as you would say."

"Thank you." Given Tran's seeming helpfulness in this "puzzle," Moffat decided to throw him a bone. "I am emailing you the transcript of the interview I held with Sergeant Weller after I spoke to you on Wednesday and also a lab report I received this morning verifying that Weller was indeed drugged. In fact, the lab isolated at least four anesthetic agents. I spoke with a doctor who said that as slow as his metabolism was, it was not unexpected that he would be unconscious for such a long time."

Tran asked, "What is the problem with Weller's metabolism?"

Moffat explained the emaciation.

Tran hesitated. His voice was decidedly cooler when he replied, "Colonel Moffat, I would like to reiterate to you: I do not believe the government of Vietnam is involved in this case."

Tran wasn't finished, but Moffat broke in, "Thank you for your candor, Constable. We are in agreement on that point. However, I'd like to know where Sergeant Weller has been for the past forty-six years. And what he's been doing."

There was an awkward silence for several seconds. Then Tran suddenly said, "Ah. I have just received the copy of your transcript and the lab report. Thank you. I will be in touch with you soon, Colonel. It is sometimes difficult to manage with the time difference."

"Call me anytime," Moffat assured him. "This is my cell phone. I carry it with me at all times."

"Anytime?" Tran asked. "I do not wish to anger your wife."

"You'll likely never meet her," Moffat said mildly. "So leave that to me."

"I see. Have a good day, Colonel Moffat."

"Have a good evening, Constable Tran."

Though Dydd's eyes had cleared tremendously by Friday evening, he still couldn't see clearly enough to drive with any confidence, so he caught a ride to church with Bartholomew Stondt. On the way, Barth explained, "My wife is Lutheran, so I usually go to church with her and the kids. But their church doesn't do Stations of the Cross."

Nodding slowly, Dydd said, "Uncle Larry used to live where you live now. He was Lutheran, too."

"They were married."

Dydd pondered that for a block. Suddenly, he turned sharply to face the big veterinarian. "Your wife was married to Uncle Larry, you mean?"

Chuckling, Barth said, "May-December relationship."

Eyes wide, Dydd said, "May and December must've been about thirty years apart."

"More than forty. But Uncle Larry was a proven sire. Had two kids when he was over seventy. That should give you some hope. When you went in the box, you were drooling over high schoolers. When you look at a cute high school girl now, you don't know whether to date her or diaper her."

Dydd blushed and smiled.

The church had barely changed since Dydd had last seen it. The paint was new. The carpet was new. The altar was the same. Barth led the way into the sacristy and introduced the priest. "Dydd, this is my cousin, Father Loren."

"Nice to meet you," Dydd said warmly.

Loren shook Dydd's hand and gestured toward the cross leaning against its holder in the corner. "Welcome home. You can wear a cassock if you want, or you can carry the cross dressed just as you are."

"Really?" Dydd piped up. "I get to carry the cross?"

Before Father Loren could reply, Zeb breezed into the sacristy and gave Dydd a hug. Shaking hands with Barth and the priest, he grabbed a cassock from the cupboard and said, "Hope we're not late."

Slipping on his stole, Father Loren said, "Just in time. Boys, let's get 'er done. Barth, are you going to wear a cassock?"

With a snort, Barth said, "My wife says miniskirts don't become me. The biggest cassock in the closet quit fitting me when I was twelve. I was over six foot by then. It barely came to my knees."

"Oh, by the way," the priest informed them, "I had to bribe three kids who have been begging me since last fall to let them carry candles and cross this year for Stations. They relented this one week because it was for a good cause, but you guys will have to find a new gig next Friday."

For the first four of fourteen Stations of the Cross, the candle bearers cast frequent wary glances at their cohort. When they had cooked up this plan the previous day by phone, Zeb and Barth had worked out which of them would catch Dydd and which would catch the cross in case Dydd went down.

As youth, all three of them had shown off their strength and fortitude by holding the cross and candles high and steady. By the second Station, Dydd had quietly extended the pole supporting the cross so that it could rest on the floor. However, the candlesticks had no such option for extension. By the fourth Station, the candle holders—both of whom had suffered ruptured disks and fractured vertebrae in various livestock-related accidents over the years—were enduring spasms of their back muscles and sharp, piercing pains down a leg or arm. They fidgeted and squirmed more than would have been tolerated by their parents when they were little boys.

Finally convincing himself that if Dydd could do it after all he'd been through, he could make it through to the bitter end of the service, Zeb focused on taking deep breaths and managing the pain. Bartholomew came to more or less the same conclusion.

By the seventh station, Zeb stopped focusing on his own pain long enough to realize that Dydd, though he had no book to follow like the other parishioners, was reciting the prayers. For the most part, he knew all the words, and in the correct order. He even sang along with all fifteen *Stabat Mater* verses interspersed between Stations.

After the service, friends and family met at Sam's place where they welcomed Dydd home and enjoyed supper on the house. Many of the partakers had never known Dydd, but by the vagaries of social media, they knew about the offer of a free buffet at Sam's Restaurant, which was considered the best eatery in the region.

Before the evening ended, Marion sat at the piano and accompanied while everyone joined in on a series of old Welsh songs. Those who knew the lyrics in Welsh sang them that way. Others joined in with English. Then Zeb's wife Shiloh took the piano seat and played a round of big band songs, show tunes, and old country. Dydd knew most of the words to all of them. To his delight, two of Zeb and Shiloh's kids chimed in, hitting some fine harmonies.

After much cajoling, Dydd sat and played the "Maple Leaf Rag". As he had noticed at the base in San Diego, the concrete piano on which he had practiced for so long had been far out of tune. But the quality of his playing did nothing to dampen the enthusiasm of pianist and spectators.

Saturday, February 17, 2018

Dydd awoke shortly after Kevin the following morning. In the kitchen, he watched Kevin fill his coffee cup and marveled at the coffee maker with its digital display and automatic timer that yielded hot coffee first thing in the morning.

Removing a mostly defrosted burrito from the microwave, Kevin dropped onto a seat at the counter. "If you can be ready in time, I'll drop you off over at the office. Devon wants to talk to you."

"Okay," Dydd responded.

"He said come hungry. I told him to be careful what he wishes for. You eat like a family of four."

Sliding onto a bar stool, Dydd prompted, "Tell me about getting shot down."

Kevin looked perplexed. "Hell, you already know all about it."

"Not really. I was eleven when you got shot down. I never heard the story like you would tell a combat veteran. I only heard it like you would tell a little kid."

"Eleven?" Kevin scowled. "Really?"

"July of 1967. Right?"

Nodding slowly, Kevin pondered the date. "That's right. I'd forgot you are that much younger than me." He topped off his cup. "I'll tell you about it later. I don't like talking about it unless I can get drunk at the same time."

Dydd laughed.

Kevin did not.

After realizing perhaps Kevin was serious and that he was not going to tell the story now, Dydd disappeared to put on more layers under the sweats. When he reappeared, he announced, "I'm ready when you are. Does Sam know I'll be there?"

113

"You worry too much about Sam," Kevin stated. "He's a big boy. He can take care of himself."

"I'm surprised he never got married," Dydd mused. "Even if he can't talk."

Kevin lowered one eyebrow almost comically, and said, "Married? Are you slow?"

"What do you mean?"

Still staring at him, Kevin said, "Hell, he's gay. You knew that, didn't you?"

Dydd returned the stare. "What are you talking about?"

"He's queer. Come on. Surely you knew that," Kevin said, as though talking to a child.

Dydd's face was fixed in stark confusion.

With a shrug, Kevin added, "It's that way nowadays. You get to decide if you want to be a man or a woman or heterosexual or homosexual or gay or lesbian or transsexual or pansexual or asexual. Hell, some people won't even list a sex on their kids' birth certificate. Figure they'll let 'em grow up and decide what they want to be."

Calvin entered, took in the expression on Dydd's face, and said mildly, "What kind of cock and bull story is he feeding you? You look like you just swallowed a goldfish."

"I was just telling him Sam's gay," Kevin said nonchalantly.

Calvin snorted and shook his head. "Don't listen to him, Dydd. He's full of shit."

Kevin broke into a grin.

"But I heard that last part—I mean about people claiming to be gay, lesbian, transsexual and all that." Cal added. "Unfortunately, he is telling you straight on that. No pun intended. A couple years ago, there was a big flap about which bathroom people have to use. Some of

114

the gays said they should be able to use the bathroom for the gender they identify with, not the one whose anatomical parts they matched. I think that's mostly blown over now."

Cal turned to Kevin and posed, "By the way, did you tell Linda Sue that Sam was gay?" To Dydd, he explained, "Sam dated a gal named Linda Sue for ten, eleven years. They shared that room right back there," he nodded down the hall toward Sam's room. "And I don't think they spent all their time in there playing cards. Don't listen to Kevin, Dydd. You know he was always a jackwagon."

Kevin's smile widened. "She was something of an amateur shrink. She was convinced that Sam was mute because he didn't want to talk, not because he couldn't. Even the metal plate in his head didn't convince her."

Calvin agreed. "That part is true."

"But they weren't married?" Dydd pressed.

"Marriage is just about obsolete these days. People figure it's cheaper to move out than to get divorced," Calvin asserted.

Kevin stood. "You ready to go?"

When they pulled onto the road from the driveway at the residence end of the building, Dydd noticed a car leaving the restaurant parking lot. Something about it looked familiar, although all the new car models looked alike to him. There were new car manufacturers he had never heard of before, most with seemingly Asian names.

After they drove the four miles to Devon's office complex, Kevin pulled up at the main door but didn't shut off the engine or move to get out of the car. "I'm on my way to the airport. You'll have to push the door open since it's not a business day. The automatic gizmo is shut off. And you can have my bed for the next two

115

nights. I'll be in Seattle living it up on the boss's expense account."

With a wave, Dydd disembarked and walked up to the double glass doors. Despite Kevin's admonition, the doors did slide open automatically. When he entered, he saw Devon striding toward him across the cavernous lobby.

"How did you know I was here?" Dydd asked, knowing that two walls separated Devon's office from the main entrance.

Devon held out his phone. On the screen was a live view of the front entrance. "Smile. You're on candid camera. With this app, I can watch the doors and turn the automatic entry on and off. Now that you're here," the financier slid his finger across the screen to access the security settings, "I'll switch them off."

Grinning, Dydd said, "Jetsons. So where is the camera?"

"Right there," Devon pointed. "Little bitty thing. Come with me. You like French toast?"

Breaking into a grin, Dydd said, "Love it. Dreamed about it many times."

"I have the itinerary for next week." Devon cast an appraising glance at his younger cousin. "Your eyes are clearing up. Skin looks better. Who's giving you the eye drops?"

"I put them in myself," Dydd answered.

Cringing, Devon said, "I could pour a gallon of drops in my eye before I got a single one in without my lids slamming shut. The break room is back here. And there's an exercise room down that hall if you ever want to work out without getting frostbite."

"Where do you live?" Dydd asked as they walked.

"I have a house. A maid comes once a week. Usually, she was the last person there. I'm here most of the time. Or out of town."

"Must be a lot of work keeping up all those millions," Dydd smiled.

"I could afford to retire," he stated dryly. "But I'd be bored. Probably drill myself a third eye before the end of the first week. Have a seat there."

While Devon ate a slice of ham, Dydd smothered a slice of French toast with butter and syrup. Devon asked, "Did you think a lot about the war when you were in that box?"

With a touch of irony, Dydd replied, "I had plenty of time to think about everything. Why do you ask?"

"I try not to think about it much," Devon admitted. "I didn't see the whites of their eyes like you did. But I killed more people. Lots more. Granted, a lot of the bombs I dropped yielded smoliage, and not much more. But when I hit the jackpot, people died. Lots of them."

Confused, Dydd asked, "You yielded what?"

"Smoliage. Smoke. Foliage." Devon scowled at him. "You know. Shit. I hit shit. Accomplished nothing. Not a damned thing. Just wasted a bunch of bombs and jet fuel and time. And got paid for it."

Devon took another slice of ham. After wiping his fingers on a napkin, he pulled a brand new leather wallet from his shirt pocket and tossed it on the table. "This is for you. You have two credit cards in there. You can also use your phone to make purchases. Did Calvin show you how to access your bank account online?"

Dydd sighed. "This is all so Orwellian."

"Get used to it. It's the way the world works now. If you want to make purchases, you're going to use plastic."

Dydd stowed the wallet in the hip pocket of his sweats and, between bites, asked, "Do you still smoke?"

Shaking his head, Devon replied, "I had a heart attack before I turned fifty. That enticed me to give up the cancer sticks and lose forty pounds. Played hob trying to get back my medical so I could fly."

Scowling, Dydd said, "I didn't know you could get a medical ever again if you had a heart attack."

Devon gave a casual shrug. "If you have enough money, you can. Or you can do what I did for five years until I got reinstated. And what John Denver did until he died. You fly without a medical."

"John Denver died?" Dydd queried.

Nodding, Devon said, "In the cockpit. Crashed his Long EZ in the San Francisco Bay back in '97."

"What's a Long EZ?"

Devon pulled up a photo on his phone and explained the dynamics of the unique Rutan-designed plane. "Oh, and I cut back on booze. But I'm German, for Pete's sake. Couldn't give up booze entirely. Now Sam, he's only half German. He gave it up."

"Sam doesn't drink anymore?" Dydd inquired.

Devon studied him, scowling. "Same problem as Hiram. If he starts, he can't stop."

Unconvinced, Dydd said, "Kevin tried to tell me he was a queer, and now you're telling me he's a drunk."

"You know Kevin's full of shit. Always has been."

"Did you ever get married?" Dydd posed.

Devon shook his head. "All women want is my money."

"So share a little," Dydd grinned. "You have enough to go around, don't you? You could afford fifty kids and a thousand grandkids."

Shaking his head, Devon said, "Too much emotion. Most men are too emotional, for that matter. Why can't people just see things in black and white? Right and wrong?"

"Trust me," Dydd responded, "dim colors are boring after a few decades. Bright colors are refreshing."

Dismissing a subject that was too nebulous for his taste, Devon said, "The first bombing run I ever made, I followed the smoke the forward air controller had put down. On my way in, I saw little kids milling around outside the target. I pulled up and swung around and called the FAC and asked if he really meant for me to bomb a school house. He said just before I got there, he watched them lower one wall and drive a couple tanks inside. According to intel, there weren't supposed to be tanks in the area. But he was adamant. So I made another pass and made a crater out of all those little kids.

"I started thinking about all the little kids I knew in Whispering Pines. Thought about you. You could've been standing there outside that school and been blown to hell. But then I remembered what Colonel Chivington said. Nits become lice." He looked up at Dydd. "I felt like somebody had ripped out my soul. In a way, it never came back. Not the same way."

Devon continued. "You can talk about the politics of war all you want, but for me, it was about family. I knew Sam was down there somewhere during my first tour. In my second tour, it was Kiel and you. And I knew that every damned bullet or grenade or shell or gallon of gasoline that went down the Ho Chi Minh Trail was going toward an effort to kill one of you."

Devon took a long breath and let it out slowly. "In the late eighties, a woman reporter did a story about me for a national business journal. She called me cold and ruthless as a negotiator."

"You told her about the school you bombed?" Dydd asked.

119

"No," Devon shook his head. "But later, after that magazine came out, one of my financial officers came to my office, madder than hell. Slapped that magazine down on my desk and told me I should sue the publisher and the writer for defamation. I looked him dead in the eye and said, 'Truth is absolute defense.' At his retirement party ten years ago, he told me that those words shook him at first, when he realized I didn't mind being called cold and ruthless. But he decided to stay with me because he liked working for someone straight forward.

"Then in the nineties, some members of my team came to me with a business proposition involving a Vietnamese company. I told them flatly that I would need a damned good reason to do business with anyone in Vietnam. They gave me a long song and dance. They had done a lot of research and were convinced that the deal would generate a huge profit. Then they told me the names of the chief execs in the company. I recognized one of them as a member of the top brass at the Hanoi Hilton. You know, the prison camp where they tortured and starved our guys until the peace agreement finally came through. So I entered into the deal."

Dydd scowled. "I don't get it."

"The language of revenge for me," Devon stated, "is money. I made sure that I came out on the right side of that deal." He studied his cousin for a long moment to see if Dydd was reading him. In case he wasn't, Devon added, "I screwed them. Big time. Hundreds of millions. You remember what Grandpa Stondt used to say about business deals?"

Dydd quoted, "Be honest in all dealings. Unless there's a horse involved."

Devon nodded approvingly. "Except I don't deal in horses. So my mantra is: Be honest in all business dealings unless there's a former North Vietnamese torturist involved. Then screw the hell out of them."

"I thought you liked things black and white, right and wrong," Dydd reminded him.

With a shrug, Devon replied, "I just told you it was wrong. I freely admit it. It wouldn't be good for my business, however, if it were to become public knowledge."

Dydd smiled slightly. "Your secret is safe with me."

Neither of them spoke for a long time. Then Devon said, "One time on the carrier, I got sick. Bad head cold. Couldn't fly that day. Another guy volunteered to take my mission. When he was taking off, his nose gear collapsed. Plane burst into flames. Skidded off the end of the carrier. The carrier steamed right over the top of him. No part of plane or pilot was recovered.

"Sick as I was, I got lousy drunk. Forty-eight hours later, I was back in the cockpit. It could've been me, Dydd. Usually when I'm talking to a vet, I say, could've been you. But it was you. And on that note," again he changed the topic abruptly, "we will dine Wednesday evening at the White House. I requested the guest list be limited to twenty. That will include the President, some members of his immediate family, members of the Joint Chiefs and a couple of their spouses, a movie director who has made a couple of famous war movies, one of the actors who plays in those kinds of movies, and a country singer who has done a lot of patriotic anthems, the kind they use on recruiting ads. Do you want to say a few words, or would you prefer to be wallpaper?"

"I can speak," Dydd offered. "I've had plenty of time to perfect my public speaking. I have a two-minute account of my experience, a five-minute, a ten-minute, or a twenty-minute. You pick. But why movie stars and a singer? Why will they be there?"

"For a chance to meet you," Devon said simply. After a moment, he went on. "Unless I tell you otherwise between now and then, go with your five-minute spiel. The next day, we will appear together on the Caleb Chamberlain radio program. The day after that, we're in New York on Brian Wirth's television news show. As I told you earlier, you'll be famous for a week or two. After that, you can drift into anonymity. Is there anything you want to see while we're on the East Coast?"

"The Smithsonian," Dydd said without hesitation. "Did the space shuttle program ever pan out? I read where President Nixon signed paperwork to start research on it. A reusable space rocket! Unbelievable."

"The space shuttle program started, had a long run, and ended. We'll go to the aviation museum. Anything else?"

"Any leads on a ranch for me?" Dydd asked.

"Nothing yet. Land just doesn't come up for sale very often. You know that. Ranches generally stay in the family, though that's changed somewhat in the past few years because fewer young people want to remain involved in agriculture. They go to college, get interested in other fields, and take a job that lets them work forty hours a week with climate-control, a regular salary, and benefits."

"Sounds like prison to me," Dydd said with a broad smile.

Cal rolled into the break room. "Who's going to prison?"

"Me, if I took a job in an office," Dydd answered. "We were just telling war stories."

Cal sneered at Devon. "What would a squid know about war? Hell, I had a target one time on the beach, but I didn't have enough ordnance left to engage. So I called up a destroyer that was parked twelve miles offshore. Asked them to lay down a few bombs on the target. They asked me for coordinates. I said, 'It's right frigging there! I'm circling it! Can't you see it?' They said they could see me. But they needed coordinates. So I gave 'em some numbers. They fired some spotter rounds. Came close enough for horseshoes and hand grenades, so I told them go for it. They lobbed a bunch of shells and made the place look like the Fourth of July. Blasted the hell out of everything except the target. I radioed back and told them they missed by a half mile. They adjusted and fired again. Missed by a half mile the other direction. So I called back and talked to the guy on the bridge. He said he wasn't comfortable with the arrangement. That was that. They were done. Blew off fifty thousand bucks worth of powder, then took their ball and went home."

Devon retorted, "You were trying to direct anti-aircraft mortars to a fixed location. Destroyers aren't traveling at six hundred knots when they lob their shells. Their trajectory is different than an F-5. You can't tell them to shoot lemons if all they have is a pea shooter."

Cal shook his head. "See? You Navy squids don't even know what a bomb is. You sound like a green grocer."

Moffat answered the cell on the third ring. During the first two, he had been retrieving another beer from the refrigerator. "Good morning, Constable Tran."

"Good evening, Colonel Moffat. I trust I do not call you too late?"

"No, sir. I'm just cracking open my second beer. Your call is right on time."

"Ah, you are in an enviable position, the second beer. Today, I found further details in our mystery. First, I identified the man who helped roll the cart into the ship. He works at the harbor. In the security offices."

Moffat broke in. "He works with the security cameras, you mean?"

"Indeed. And so, you are thinking, he knows where the cameras can see and where they can't see. And so he knows where a person can park their car and retrieve something from the boot—sorry, I mean from the trunk—without being seen on the camera.

"I also have identified the woman as his sister. She is a nurse who works in a large medical facility." Tran waited while Moffat absorbed the last bit.

"Does she have access to anesthetic drugs?"

"You are following me very quickly," Tran praised. "Yes, she does. So I have underlings checking to see if any drugs are missing from the medical clinic. Next, I learned that the father of these two people died the day prior to this ship leaving the harbor. So I will do some checking tomorrow into the man who died."

"I see," Moffat said. He crossed his ankles on the coffee table a moment before he saw his wife slip out of the bedroom door down the hallway. His feet quickly returned to the floor before she re-emerged from the bathroom a few seconds later.

Tran continued. "Also, I spoke with the man who knew my grandfather. He first demanded that I give him money."

There it was, Moffat thought. They always wanted money. Whether it was really the grandfather's friend or Tran himself, he did not know. But he was not surprised. "How much money?"

"Thirty thousand US dollars," Tran relayed.

Moffat ground his molars but said nothing.

124

"I reminded him," Tran said carefully, "that it is his duty to respond to my questions. After a brief discussion, he agreed."

Moffat exhaled and waited and wished that the cat-and-mouse game did not always have to overshadow his dealings with the communists.

Tran went on. "He described to me the command structure of Dong Phu camp. You may not be surprised to learn that I connected the man who just died—father of the unauthorized persons at the shipyard—with the lieutenant who was second in command at Dong Phu. My grandfather's friend recalled that the lieutenant died sometime in the first half of 1972 because he himself was transferred to another unit in mid-June, and he said the lieutenant died a month or two before that. Or at least it was thought he was dead. Bombs struck a nearby village where his family lived, and he never was seen again. You see, Colonel Moffat, it is not only American bodies which were not recovered. Many of our people also were never accounted for."

"It is an unfortunate aspect of war, Constable," Moffat agreed.

Dydd entered the kitchen and found his brother simmering a huge pot of vegetable stock and signing fast to a woman with brassy purple hair and a stunning array of hardware in her ears, cheek, nose, and—as he learned when she tried to speak— her tongue.

Leaving the assistant chef to the soup, Sam led Dydd back to the residence end of the building. He gestured for Dydd to join him on the sofa, then he tapped into his phone and let it talk for him. "Are you looking for a ranch?"

"Yes."

Face furrowing, Sam tapped again. "Why? You can stay here as long as you like, you know."

"I know," Dydd replied.

With a look of frustration, Sam tapped, "You aren't a young man. In a couple weeks, you'll be sixty-two, Dydd."

When the phone pronounced his name, it sounded like *Did*. Frustrated, Sam knocked the device on his head and shot his brother an apologetic glance. As a boy, he and Kiel had endlessly tormented Dydd by mispronouncing his name.

With a chuckle, Dydd said, "I haven't heard that for a while."

Making a mental note to spell the name into his phone as D-e-e-t-h from now on, Sam typed, "Ranching is a young man's game. Do you think you are physically able to handle cattle and horses?"

Recalling Moffat's admonition that real people don't always say exactly what you expect, and relying on the immense patience developed in years of captivity, Dydd didn't answer right away. Finally, he said, "I can find someone to help me with the hard jobs. I assume there are still cowboys who like to work horseback."

"It's not that easy," Sam's phone relayed. "Not many people want to be a hired man these days. They like easier work. And the ones who are willing to do it don't work cheap. And they aren't always reliable. Trust me, I run a restaurant; I know about unreliable help."

"Ranching is a business, just like your restaurant. Your baby. This is what you always wanted, right?"

Sam sighed. Then he bobbed his head sideways.

"You don't like it?" Dydd asked curiously.

Again, Sam typed into the phone. "It's something I can do without a voice. I have a degree in psychology. But I can't counsel people. Running this place is a close

126

second. I'm like the bartender who listens to everyone's troubles."

"But you must like it or you wouldn't still be doing it," Dydd pointed out. "All my life, I've dreamed of ranching. It's all I ever wanted to do."

Sam sighed and stared at his phone. Disgusted, he tossed it on the coffee table and gestured for Dydd to remain on the sofa. Returning with a laptop computer, Sam dropped onto the couch next to his brother and typed, "I wanted to go to medical school when I got out of the Corps."

Nodding as he watched the words appear, Dydd said, "You wanted to be a shrink. I remember."

"But I moved back here when I realized I would never be able to speak intelligibly."

"Can you talk at all?" Dydd shifted his gaze from the screen to Sam's face. With a grin, he added, "I mean besides yes, no, and shit?"

Rolling his eyes, Sam typed, "You remember when Grandpa ran over Ruff's back end? You remember what he (I mean the dog, not Grandpa) sounded like when he was lying there howling?"

Dydd nodded.

"That's what I sound like."

"You sure can type fast," Dydd observed.

Sam gave a lopsided smile.

Dydd asked, "Why did you move back here? I never figured you'd come back to Wyoming."

"I was all they had," Sam answered.

"Mom and Dad?"

Sam nodded.

Dydd sighed.

Sam began typing again. "When Mom moved to town from the ranch, she kept the same phone number. After she died, I had that number wired into this place.

And when I upgraded to a cell phone, I had it switched to my cell."

Dydd scowled at him, not understanding. "You still have the old house number? Why?"

"Because you know this number," Sam explained. "If you ever made it to a phone, I wanted you to be able to call."

Sunday, February 18, 2018

The kitchen was busy with preparations when Dydd passed through at half past five in the morning. Holding up a hand to tell his assistant to stop talking to him, Sam waved to catch Dydd's eye and asked, "Hungry?"

Dydd looked contemplative.

Picking up his phone, Sam typed, "The Church recommends fasting for an hour before Communion. You can eat breakfast. Mass doesn't start until 10."

Grinning, Dydd said, "You talked me into it."

"Good," Sam tapped. "You don't need to fast. You need to eat." Setting down the phone, he signed fast to the assistant.

She relayed, "We don't have the buffet out yet, so go sit down and we'll bring you a plate."

"Okay. Thanks." Dydd sauntered into the dining room and sat at a table in the middle of the room. He noticed a couple sitting in the northwest corner and a man alone in the southwest. When Calvin rolled in a few minutes later, Dydd bade, "Good morning."

Cal smiled. "Good morning. Sam said he's bringing us plates."

Nodding, Dydd asked, "When does the breakfast rush begin?"

"We open at six."

"What time is it now?" Dydd inquired.

Checking his watch, Cal replied, "Quarter 'til six."

Dydd scowled. "Then why are there already people here?"

Without turning, Cal said, "The guy sitting behind me is Donovan Garrison. The couple over my right shoulder are Paul Richards and Jane Bellairs. Don and Paul are the ranking officers of Devon's security force."

"Body guards?"

129

"More than that," Calvin explained. "Don and Paul are both former Delta."

Dydd waited a moment, as though there was more. After a pause, he asked, "They used to be Delta airline pilots, you mean?"

"Army special forces. Jane is an Army-trained helo pilot. Her husband was a Ranger. He lost both legs in Afghanistan. Don's wife was convoy support in Iraq. An IED blew up the APC she was in. Killed the other three in the vehicle. She had brain trauma and now she can only walk with support. So she's in a wheelchair most of the time. Like me. Paul lost his readiness status because of a fib."

Dydd stared at Calvin. "What did you just say?"

Grinning, Cal asked, "Which thing didn't you get?"

"What's an IED?"

"Improvised explosive device."

"And an APC is an armored personnel carrier?"

Calvin nodded. "Right."

"And he got kicked out because he lied?"

"Atrial fibrillation. Like a heart murmur or something. So anyway, Devon likes his security guys to have military training. He instructs them to keep an ear to the ground for any personnel who would fit in with this group. Usually that means somebody who likes to hunt and fish and is tired of being deployed for months at a time. People with families. Hardship cases."

Dydd nodded slowly as he listened. He glanced again at the couple to his right. Squinting, he lowered his voice and asked, "Does he have a telephone wire sticking out of his ear?"

"Yep. The coiled wire is attached to a radio and earbud, so they can talk to each other across the room without yelling."

A waitress came from the kitchen and wordlessly set down two plates. Both men muttered a thank-you, but she was already gone.

Cal tasted the omelet. After he swallowed, he said, "Devon has probably spent more money helping veterans than any other private individual. Except maybe Ross Perot."

"Is he still around? Ross Perot, I mean." Dydd inquired.

"He is. And he's still helping vets," Cal asserted. "And you never hear about it on the news. You have to dig to find out how much either of them does. They like to keep it quiet."

"So the security guys come here for breakfast? Or are they just practicing having meetings from across the room?" Dydd asked.

"They're keeping the maggots off you."

Dydd smirked.

Cal went on. "Reporters are like maggots on a carcass in summer. Devon wants to keep the media off you until you've appeared on Chamberlain and Wirth's shows. After that, the reporters will forget about you."

"So those people are *my* bodyguards?" Dydd asked. "That must be costing a mint."

Cal shrugged. "The team loves it. They love having a mission, I mean. Those guys still train just like when they were on active duty. Of course, keeping strangers out of Central Wyoming in the middle of winter isn't too big a challenge. The nearest commercial airport with a car rental agency is at least four hours from here. And Devon owns the local airport. His team runs the FBO, so they don't grant permission to land without a flight plan. And they don't give you a flight plan if they don't know you."

"Did Devon build the new airport?" Dydd asked. "The one where we landed?"

"Yeah. You probably remember when the airport consisted of a grass strip carved out of a corner of old man Schleicher's pasture."

Dydd nodded.

"When Devon moved back here, he started from scratch and built an airport with a couple of paved runways and a real terminal."

Dydd laughed. "His new terminal is definitely an improvement over the old tin shack with a telephone in the corner."

Grinning, Cal replied, "There's also a training facility. That's the headquarters for the security guys. Trust me, if an unfamiliar face shows up in Whispering Pines in the next few days, they're gonna have some real-time, hard core, bad asses to deal with."

Somewhere in southern Missouri, Reggie Ellis pulled off the highway and turned onto a graveled county road lined with leafless trees. A quarter mile later, out of sight from the main road, he parked in a driveway that led into an empty field.

Shutting off the engine, he climbed out stiffly, stretched, and relieved himself against a tree. A glance told him it would be completely dark in less than a quarter hour. He had intended to make another fifty miles before he stopped but, though he hated to admit it, he no longer felt comfortable driving in the dark.

From the backseat, he pulled the sleeping bag and the sack of food his wife had packed. Tossing the bedroll over the back of the driver's seat, he peered into the bag. The only thing that caught his interest was a package of Fig Newtons. Dropping into the backseat, he opened the cookies and made a count.

It should take two and a half days to get where he was going, half a day to visit, and two and a half days back. Six days total. He divided the number of Fig Newtons by six to determine how many he could eat tonight.

Then he ate half the bag.

His wife had also packed bottled water. With a grimace, he recalled his last camping trip and reached under the seat.

Nothing.

Then he shifted across to the passenger side and again reached under the seat.

Bingo!

He unscrewed the lid and took a tiny sip of the bourbon. "Ahhh!" he belted aloud. Then he took a long swig. And another.

Then he grimaced and reached behind him to figure out what was digging into his back. That's when he realized he had failed to move the seat belt receptacles his wife had nagged him about moving.

Tuesday, February 20, 2018

Dydd slid off the couch where he slept and silently made his way through the big kitchen and into the dark, empty dining area.

"Good morning, Gunny," came a voice from a corner of the room.

Jumping sideways, Dydd collided with the wall and the light switch, which he flipped on.

"Sorry, Gunny. I didn't mean to startle you." The man in the corner took off his goggles and approached Dydd with his hand outstretched. "Lieutenant Jason Rodriguez. I was hoping to get to meet you. I wanted to shake your hand and thank you for your service."

Taking the offered hand, Dydd smiled. "Thank you for your service. And for scaring the shit out of me."

Rodriguez grinned. "Are you looking for a snack?"

"No. I was going to play the piano while there was no one here. How about you? You need something to eat?"

"I'm on my third pot of coffee. I'll be off duty soon, so I'll head home and eat breakfast with the family."

"Are you part of Devon's security team?" Dydd asked.

"That's correct. Don't let me keep you from your piano playing."

Instead of moving toward the piano, Dydd took a seat at Rodriguez' table and asked, "How do you like Wyoming?"

Rodriguez returned to his chair and grinned. "I love it. I mean, I was always a hunting and fishing nut. I kind of miss the action, you know? I was a SEAL for nine years. It was a little hard to leave it. But my wife gave birth to our third child, and he had cystic fibrosis. I couldn't leave her alone for months-long deployments, not knowing how long I'd be gone, not able to even communicate with her. So now I'm home almost every night. If I am out of town, it's only for a few nights. And we have a great support network here."

Dydd smiled. "Sounds perfect."

"It's pretty damned close."

"So were you just sitting here all night in the dark waiting for a reporter to break in?" Dydd inquired.

"I wasn't in the dark." Holding up the night vision goggles, Rodriguez said, "Bet you wish you'd had these in your day."

After a demonstration of the device, Dydd squinted at Rodriguez and said, "These could have saved my whole platoon."

"I wish they had, Gunny. Say, you're scheduled for an appointment at zero-nine-thirty, correct?"

"Eye doctor. She's supposed to make sure the infections are cleared up and then set me up with some glasses so I can see without squinting all the time."

Rodriguez said, "Kevin is flying this morning, Calvin will be in meetings, so one of my team will drive you there. Now, if you would indulge me, I haven't heard a good Scott Joplin song for a long time. How about it?"

Breaking into a broad grin, Dydd crossed to the piano and began filling the room with rollicking ragtime.

"So how did you end up being an eye doctor in Whispering Pines, Wyoming?" Dydd asked as he rested his chin on the ominous-looking apparatus in the dim office. "When I was a kid, we had to drive to Casper to get our eyes checked."

The late-twenty-something ophthalmologist smiled. With a very slight accent which, along with her dark complexion and straight hair, led Dydd to guess she was originally from India or Pakistan or maybe Sri Lanka, she replied, "When you were a kid, the population of Whispering Pines was tiny and declining. Then after

135

your cousin had a heart attack and moved his headquarters here, a lot of his staff followed. Including my dad."

"I see," Dydd said.

She flipped a lever that occluded his right eye, then she extended her right arm and asked, "Without looking to the side, how many fingers am I holding up?"

"Three," he responded.

"Good. And now?" She extended her left arm.

"Two."

"Good. When I graduated from high school here, I planned to get a degree in engineering and go back to India where my family lived until I was thirteen. But when I came back here for Christmas break during my last year of college, Devon invited me to his office."

Dydd interrupted. "I can see your fingers way out there in my peripheral vision, but I can't see your face when I look right at you. Not with this eye."

She scowled. "Hmm. Okay. I'll take a look."

Using a headlight and a lens that seemed to shine a bolt of light through the back of his head, she began examining his retinas.

"What did he want to ask you?" Dydd inquired. His left eye began to water.

"He said he was going to give me a plane ticket to go to India for a couple months after graduation. Then he said if I would come back to Whispering Pines and practice for at least five years, he would pay my way through medical school. There is a hole in your left retina. That's not the medical term, of course, but that's essentially what it is. A blank spot. I'm sorry, but it's not going to improve. Can you see straight ahead okay with your right eye?"

"Yep. So you went to medical school."

She smiled. "Yes, and by the last year, I realized I wanted to specialize in ophthalmology, not in general medicine. I very meekly approached Devon about it, and he said, 'Great.' And that was that. I got married the last year of my residency, have two kids now, and love my job. I work about twenty hours a week, and my mom watches my kids when I'm here."

"Cool," Dydd said. "What caused the hole in my eye?"

"Combination of low dietary plane and internal parasites."

Dydd pondered that for a moment. "Starvation and worms?"

"Exactly." She sat back in her chair and asked, "So how are you catching up on everything you've missed?"

"A couple nights ago—once my eyes cleared up enough so I could look at the surface—Calvin showed me how to look up stuff on his flip-top. So I've been reading up year by year. I made it through 1974 last night."

She regarded him with confusion for a moment. Then she brightened and said, "Laptop. Not flip-top."

"Oh, sorry. I can't believe Agnew and Nixon both resigned."

She laughed. "Just wait! Presidential politics gets a lot more interesting than that! Clinton was impeached."

"Really?" Dydd's eyes widened. "How come?"

"Sex. But I'll let you get to that on your own. Did you know Ronald Reagan was president?"

Dydd laughed heartily. "You're full of it! Ronald Reagan of B movies and GE Theater? Ronald Reagan who had second billing to a monkey? Give me a break!"

She shook her head gently. "He'll go down as arguably one of the greatest presidents of all time."

He scowled. "Why?"

"Because he said, 'Mr. Gorbachev, tear down this wall.' And not too long after, the Soviet Union crumbled."

"I knew about that. Cal and Devon were talking about it. But China is still communist. And Vietnam." The last part he added dejectedly.

"And North Korea," she added. "Now, let's see what we can do for you in the way of glasses. And I'm afraid your eyes won't adjust well to contact lenses. You have too much scar tissue on the surface of your corneas."

"I have no idea what you're talking about," he reminded her.

She smiled and clarified. "You will have to wear old fashioned glasses."

"I figured that. Will I be able to get a driver's license with that blind spot?"

"Sure. Just keep both eyes open when they ask you to read the letters in the little box."

Moffat hung up the phone and dropped his head to his desk. Five deep breaths later, he was sufficiently cleansed to place the next call.

The pleasant voice that answered belonged to a woman with some variety of British accent, though Moffat had never been adept at differentiating English from Scottish from Australian. He asked to speak to Devon Stondt.

A moment later, the billionaire answered. "Hi, Moffat."

"Good morning, Mr. Stondt. I have a little issue regarding Sergeant Weller's health care. Apparently, he wasn't supposed to leave the base in San Diego. They need to do more tests and evaluations."

"A little late to be telling me now," Devon replied tersely.

"Yes, sir."

His tone lighter, Devon said, "You just got your ass chewed, didn't you?"

"Can't even sit down. There's no padding left," Moffat admitted. "I was informed a few minutes ago that I have absolutely no authority to issue orders to a Marine regarding his housing or medical status. All that aside, can you get him back to San Diego ASAP?"

"I'll take care of it," Devon stated.

Moffat was silent a moment. Then he asked, "Does that mean you'll get him back to San Diego ASAP?"

"It means I'll bring San Diego to him. Next week. He has plans for the rest of this week. And I respect the wishes of a guy who's been to Hell and back for his country. Don't you?" Some referred to Devon Stondt as a negotiator. Others as a manipulator. Whatever the title, his means of communication was effective.

"I do. But I'm not sure the Secretary of the Navy does. That's who just flayed my ass over the phone."

"Sec-Nav, huh? Dydd is getting high profile status with the big brass. Listen, I'll call the Sec-Nav and explain things," Devon promised evenly. "They can send any doctors they want to Wyoming. We have a state-of-the-art medical facility, and our BOQ has a swimming pool. My dime. I'll even send a plane for them."

In the half full dining room of Sam's restaurant, Dydd sat eating a bowl of chowder and skimming through the major events of 1977 on a laptop computer when a man silently approached and stopped several feet from the table. He stood absolutely still for a full minute.

Without looking up, Dydd said, "Hi, Billy."

Grinning, Billy Sky pulled out a chair opposite Dydd's and dropped onto it. Over his shoulder, he called, "Sam, just bring me coffee. My missus will break

139

her skillet over my head if I don't come home hungry. How you doing, Dydd?"

"Good," Dydd replied as he reached over his late-afternoon snack for a handshake. "You're still playing Injun."

The seven-eighths-blooded Arapaho smiled. "I am Injun. Except for that nasty little German streak in me. But I always figured that did me some good. I could run fast because I was Arapaho. But the German part made me scared enough to run even faster."

Dydd laughed at the old joke he hadn't heard for nearly five decades. "So how long did you stay over there?"

"I served almost six tours, in all. Until some little gook shot me out of a tree. Came home with a bullet in my shoulder. It still bugs me when the weather is wet."

Tipping his head to one side, Dydd said, "I thought you were there for two tours, then you came home for good."

"I never have been very good at retiring. I went back and got in a CIA unit. We did stuff I couldn't have told you about until recently. We'd drop in by chopper and sit like crickets in the jungle watching and listening, and then come back in and make reports on what the gooks were up to. We had some high tech listening devices that sometimes worked and mostly didn't. So most of what we got, we got with our own ears and eyes."

"That's a long time to spend in war," Dydd said.

"That's funny coming from you," Billy said with a wry smile. Then he said, "I always wanted to be a warrior. My grandmother's father told me stories his grandfather told him. And it sounded like a hell of a lot of fun shooting guys and counting coup. But I figured it would be counter-productive to tackle the white population here around Whispering Pines. There's so

damned many of you. Besides, I wouldn't know which
eighth of myself to shoot or cut off. But I figured being
in the Army and later the CIA was a good way to
practice being a warrior. And get paid for it."

"So you're married? What do you do for a living?
And what does she do?" Dydd inquired.

"She puts up with me. And that's a full-time job.
After I left the Army, I worked for the BLM for twenty-
two years. Then I retired. Then I worked for the post
office for twelve years. Then I retired. Then I went to
work for my foster brother. You remember him? My
folks adopted him in—no, you wouldn't remember him.
He was eleven when they took him in. That was '83.
He's from down around New Mexico and Arizona."

"Navaho?" Dydd asked.

"He's a mutt. Even worse than me. His mama was
half Navaho and half Apache. And his daddy was white,
but he never met him, though the old man left him some
money. I'm sure he would've rather had a dad than a
lump of cash. Anyway, my foster brother worked for the
government for twenty-some years, then came back here
and started a school for mostly Indian kids, but there's
some whites and Hispanics, too. I teach history."

Dydd smiled. "I bet you're good at it."

Nodding slightly, Billy wasn't bragging when he
said, "Yes, I am. I've lived some history. I don't teach it
like it only happened in black and white on a page of
paper. I teach it like there were real live people living it."

"Maybe I can hire you to teach me current events.
Since 1972, at least."

Billy smirked and ran a hand over his spiky salt and
pepper crewcut. "You know all the presidents since
Nixon?"

Shaking his head ironically, Dydd replied, "I just
heard today that Bonzo went to Washington."

Billy laughed long and hard. "That's correct. Before him there was a peanut farmer from Georgia. They both did okay. Then after Bonzo was Bonzo's vice president. He did okay. At least he didn't get into too many scandals. During his campaign, he said, 'Read my lips! No new taxes.' And you just know that came back and bit him in the ass, so he was a one-termer. Then there was Slick Willy. He got lots done. Most of what he got done was ugly chicks. He had a whole string of them."

"Not married?" Dydd asked.

"Oh, he was married. Still is. After she was his first lady in Arkansas, she was his first lady in Washington. Then she ran for US Senate for New York and won. Then she ran for president against a black man. He won and made her his secretary of state. Then she ran for president again. And lost."

"We had a black president? That's good. I guess that means all the civil rights riots are done," Dydd observed.

"Guess again," Billy said sadly. "During his reign, we had a resurgence of rioting. If a black thug attacked a white guy and the white guy shot him, the president said the white guy was a racist. If a white cop shot a black guy who was trying to kill him, it was racist. There were riots all over the country. Not as widespread as in our day. But too many. The number of people on welfare has sky-rocketed since FDR and Johnson's days. My kids are eligible for handouts just because they have some Arapaho blood in them. I told them if they ever took free money from Uncle Sam—except for help with college tuition—they are out of my will. Here's my policy: if you want to eat, get a job. If you want a handout, move to another country. That's my philosophy."

"I'm surprised you don't work for Devon. It seems like everybody else here does."

Billy scowled at him. "I thought I did. Doesn't he own the post office?" He laughed as he stood. "I better get home before my pretty wife gets out that skillet. I'll come back in sometime to continue your history education."

"Is your wife Indian?" Dydd asked before Billy stepped away.

Billy leaned his hands on the back of the chair. Something outside the window seemed to catch his eye. He was distracted when he replied, "Her people are Greek. Skinnier nose. Lighter skin. Curlier hair." Returning his gaze to Dydd, he bid, "See you."

Billy crossed the room to a table in the corner where Jason Rodriguez and another man sat. Leaning toward them, he spoke for a brief moment, nodding his head toward the window. The man across from Rodriguez got up and disappeared into the kitchen.

After Billy left, a waitress breezed by and set down an ice cream shake before Dydd. "Thank you," he said as he looked up.

She stopped and glanced toward the kitchen to see if she was needed. Then she pivoted and dropped onto the same chair Billy had just vacated. Reaching her hand across the table, she said, "Welcome home, Mr. Weller. I'm Kaitlyn Holland."

"Nice to meet you. The name's Dydd. And thanks for the ice cream."

She wore a white button-down shirt over Wrangler jeans and roper boots. Slender and well-groomed, she smiled and said, "Calcium's good for your bones."

"That's what they tell me," Dydd verified.

The smile dropped. "Your body will preferentially store phosphorus in the osseous matrix if it's available in the diet in higher amounts than calcium. That can make bones soft and weak."

143

Dydd's brow rose in surprise. "I got all that from the first three doctors. How come you're waitressing if you're a doctor?"

She glanced again toward the kitchen. "I'm not a doctor or a waitress. I'm a rancher."

Scowling, Dydd asked, "How do you have time to do this job, too? And do you mean you personally ranch, or you ranch with your husband?"

"I'm not married. I was working for my dad. Well, not exactly." Her voice carried a bitter edge. "I was just working. Never got paid. I worked with the expectation of taking over the ranch. Until he notified me last year that he had sold the place. Didn't even tell me until a couple days before the deal closed. Nothing I could do about it. He never asked me if I wanted first chance to buy him out. When I mentioned that, he said he didn't think I could handle managing a ranch. He said I'm hired hand material, not boss material."

Dydd listened intently.

She continued, "I have a degree in livestock nutrition with a minor in ag business. I've kept books for Dad since I was twelve. I know livestock. I know management. The only thing maybe I lack is mechanical aptitude. I can weld, but I can't tear apart a tractor. I can install a new blade and guard on a sickle, but I can't rebuild a gearbox. I can build fence and develop springs." She looked over her shoulder and said quickly, "Gotta go."

Dydd waved absently as she darted off. A few minutes later, she was back. "It's slow this early in the evening. I asked Sam if it was okay if I talked to you when my tables are empty. He said it is."

"What have you worked out with your dad about your back wages?" Dydd inquired.

Jaw set, she stewed, "I haven't talked to my folks for a year."

"Oh, don't do that. I know you don't have to listen to me, but I'm telling you from firsthand experience that it stinks to miss out on talking to your folks. They know so much that you want to know. Family history, personal history. Just lots of stuff." Dydd dropped one eyebrow. "Wait a second, is your dad Dutch Holland?"

She nodded.

Scowling, Dydd asked without much hope, "Your mom is Leona?"

"That's right." Understanding his reservation, she explained, "My older siblings are a little younger than you. I was a change-of-life baby. I think my folks figured they couldn't have any more kids. Then they had me. Surprise."

"Ah," his face cleared. "So maybe your dad was just tired. Maybe he didn't want to face going through the ownership change, helping you buy out your older siblings, all the paperwork. Maybe he was looking at just getting out and walking away from it. He must be pretty old now, isn't he?"

"Seventy-nine," she replied.

He could tell she was thinking over what he'd said. "But," he added, "you and I have something in common. We're both looking for a ranch."

She cocked her head to one side. "You aren't going to stay here with Sam?"

"Nah. I'm not designed to live in town. Don't want to be in the restaurant business. I'm a cattle, horse, and tractor guy myself."

She smiled. "Good luck, then. I better get back to work. If you ever make it to the library, I'll see you there. I work there six days a week and in here evenings."

145

Suddenly, Jason Rodriguez was beside the table. Taking her cue to leave, Kaitlyn returned to the kitchen. Jason dropped onto the chair not across from Dydd but to his left, so that neither of them was in line of sight from the bluff outside the window.

"There's a guy who's been sitting over there on the bluff across the highway watching you."

"Why?" Dydd asked.

"Probably wants to get a picture of you to sell to some news agency."

Scowling, Dydd asked, "Wouldn't he be able to get a better picture if he came in here instead of taking it through a window?"

"Exactly. That's why we're keeping an eye on him."

"Is that why Billy talked to you guys? He saw something over there, didn't he?"

Smiling, Jason replied, "You're still a Marine, aren't you? Ain't no moss growing on you, Sarge."

The gymnasium was filled almost to capacity with spectators for the regional semi-final basketball game. It was so loud that conversation was possible only by leaning close and yelling. The Whispering Pines High School boys' team was ahead by three with six and a half minutes left in the game.

When Dydd started chuckling, Cal turned toward him and yelled, "What's so funny?"

"Their uniforms!" Dydd burst. "Whatever happened to shorts that were short? It looks like they're wearing skirts. What do the girls wear?"

"Same thing," Cal assured him. "What about the game? Does it look like you remember it?"

Dydd shrugged. "Basketball wasn't my game. If I had been in sports, I would have run track."

"Did we have a wrestling team when you were here?" Cal inquired.

Shaking his head, Dydd answered, "We had football and volleyball in the fall, basketball in the winter, and track in the spring."

"They have cross country in the fall now. And tennis. And golf."

Raising his eyebrows in surprise, Dydd merely nodded in reply. But a few minutes later, he inquired, "Since when do the refs allow traveling? Every time someone makes a lay-up, it looks to me like they're traveling."

"I don't know exactly when they changed that rule," Cal mused. "But you're right. We couldn't do that in our day."

Scowling, Dydd probed, "You were on that state championship team, weren't you? You and Kevin both, right?"

Cal nodded.

Dydd wondered if it made his cousin sad to reminisce about his once able legs that were now withered and nearly as thin as his own.

After a moment, Cal yelled, "Devon played that year, too. He was a freshman. We were juniors. I think that was the only year he played."

"It was," Dydd verified. "He started working at the lumber yard. And the dry cleaners. And I think he kept books for the gas station, too. The one that used to be on the south end of town."

The opposing team rallied and got ahead by one point. The noise of the cheering doubled. Then Whispering Pines got two three-pointers in rapid succession and pulled ahead by a comfortable margin.

Cal cast a glance at Dydd who had suddenly become intent on someone in the crowd on the opposite side of the gym. After a moment, he asked, "What are you looking at?"

Dydd blinked several times. "Who is that across the way? Just sat down in the second section, third row up. I can't make out a face, but I recognize the walk."

After a full minute and further description of clothing, Cal nodded slowly. "Gloria Adkisson. I can't remember her maiden name."

"Hoelscher," Dydd supplied. "Gloria Hoelscher."

With a sigh, Cal said, "Yeah. That's right. Her grandson plays center for the other team. Did you have a thing for her once upon a time?"

Dydd chuckled. "She knocked me off the monkey bars in third grade. Sixteen stitches."

The man perched in the notch on the big bluff facing the restaurant fought to keep his eyes clear. Between the dry wind and the cold and the long hours of peering through the exquisite lens, he was having trouble seeing people inside.

He reached for the Thermos and refilled his mug. *Damn this cold!*

Wait! There! It was a clear shot. But Weller slipped past the window too quickly.

The man cursed aloud. Then he cursed again even more loudly. To hell with being quiet. Who was going to be out in this weather anyway? Who would be crazy enough to sit out here, waiting to freeze to death?

Suddenly it occurred to him that Weller would have to pass by one of the windows again.

So he waited. And he watched.

And he blinked to clear his eyes yet again.

***

Reggie Ellis woke with a start when the farmer outside his car started not only knocking on the window but yelling, too.

"Hey! Buddy! Wake up. Are you dead or deaf? Come on, man."

Reggie blinked, ran a hand across the stubble on his chin, then rubbed his eyes. Yawning, he sat up and stared at the man's khaki farm coat and blue stocking cap. After a moment, he rolled down the window and growled, "What do you want?"

The farmer seemed slightly taken aback. "What do I want? For starters, I want you to move your car so I can get back to the creek. I mean, you're parked on private property. My property. So I'm not real sure why you're snapping my head off, man. Maybe I should call the sheriff."

"Fuck off," Ellis barked back. He climbed out of the backseat and, without bothering to straighten his stiff back, shuffled to the front door and slid behind the wheel.

Head pounding, making him ponder if this was what a stroke felt like, he drove ten miles to be sure he was out of range of the farmer with the chip on his shoulder. Again, he pulled off the main road and onto a tree lined lane.

He rummaged around for a bottle of the water his wife had packed, poured most of one over his head, and took a sip of what was left. Making a face, he reached into the back for the bottle of bourbon. Utilizing the theory of the hair of the dog, he took a couple swallows, put the car back in gear, and returned to the main highway.

149

Wednesday, February 21, 2018

Twenty minutes before take-off, Dydd Weller stepped on the official scale in the doctor's office. One hundred four.

Dydd peered at Ben Stondt and asked, "I've been eating like a horse. What's up? Shouldn't I be gaining more weight?"

With a scowl, Ben answered, "I spent several years working in developing countries. Areas with a lot of malnutrition. Sometimes when you introduce food to a digestive system that is unaccustomed to it, there is a lag in absorptive capacity."

Dydd grinned. "Are you telling me my guts are out of practice?"

Returning the smile, Ben said, "Once you knock the rust off your innards, you should start packing on the pounds."

"Maybe I should drink some WD-40," Dydd smirked. "It's good for taking off rust."

Ben's smile faded. Tapping the lab workout he had just interpreted for Dydd, he said, "I don't know how you hung on for as long as you did. Your fat reserves are nonexistent. Your immune system was taxed to the limit fighting infections and parasites. You couldn't have lasted even a few more months like that. At most."

Dydd picked up the smile Ben had lost. "I was already dead to all of you. No one would have known the difference if I had checked out in the jungle in '72 or in a box in '18."

For security reasons, Devon was not allowed to land his personal helicopter on the White House lawn, so they arrived in a huge black SUV.

After a guided tour given by the President's fourteen-year-old son, they met up with the others in the dining room. In time, they were seated and, after an opening toast, were served the first course.

As most were finishing dessert, the President leaned toward Dydd and asked, "Would you mind saying a few words, Sergeant, or would you prefer not to?"

"I'd be happy to speak, sir," Dydd replied easily.

The President—who had been a kindergardener the day Dydd Weller was captured in Vietnam— stood, held up a hand, and waited for silence. He said a few words, introduced Dydd, and then took his seat.

Standing on the historic carpet, Dydd thanked the President for his introduction and then invited four guests to assist him. First he called Nathan, the presidential son who had guided him and Devon through the White House. Then he asked Carlton, the movie actor to come up. Next was Darrell, the movie director. And finally Steve, the tall, thick-set country singer. Dydd placed each of them so that they formed a rectangle, toes facing toward him in the center.

"These gentlemen represent the four corners of the box where I was held," Dydd began. "Nathan and Steve are five feet apart and represent the south wall. It was composed of steel, with a steel inset door. I never saw that door open. At the bottom of the door was a slot two inches high by eight inches wide. The top of this wall was about nine feet high. Attached to it was the thatch roof. On this end, it was fairly waterproof." He stopped and grinned. "Carlton and Darrell would not be so lucky if it were to start raining right now."

Dydd moved toward the actor and director. Standing between them, he extended his left hand over his head and jumped as high as he could. "This wall was one inch higher than that. I couldn't quite touch the top of it.

151

These three walls were concrete with a six inch gap on top separating them from the frame that held up the thatch. At the bottom of all three concrete walls was a two-inch gap."

Dydd stood toe to toe with Carlton. "The concrete floor sloped slightly to this corner. So this was the bathroom. Anything that didn't drain out on its own was kicked under the wall. The pigs and chickens outdoors were the sewage treatment system."

There were a few snickers as he crossed the rectangle diagonally. "Here at Nathan's feet was where I slept. When I woke in the morning, I started walking. For two hours, I walked. If you ever try to walk laps inside a five-by-eight rectangle, you will quickly become dizzy. So I alternated directions. Twenty-five laps to the left; twenty-five laps to the right. At first, I counted seconds to know that I had walked for the full two hours. But after a while, I just knew.

"Then I sat over here in Darrell's corner and waited for chow. If I made a peep or a move, no food. So I waited very quietly. Before I ate, I said Grace. After I ate, I began recitation. I recited poems, stories, books, movies, speeches, scriptures, the Preamble, and anything else I could think of. I also made business deals. I followed my own stock exchange, buying, selling, and trading. Then I practiced the piano. And I never hit a wrong note. Not once." Here he stopped and gave a sheepish smile. "When I actually sat down at a real piano last week, I found out that the concrete piano wasn't tuned all that well."

Again, there were a few chuckles.

From near the end of the table, Devon sat nursing his fourth drink of the evening. He was not watching Dydd but rather the other guests. They were riveted.

In his businessman's brain, Devon was pondering how he could help Dydd capitalize on this speaking phenomenon.

Dydd continued. "Then I did a few calisthenics. But never sit-ups. If you weigh ninety pounds, sit-ups on a concrete floor are not a good idea. Then I prayed."

Here, he paused slightly. Brilliant timing, Devon observed.

"I prayed every prayer I knew. And made up new ones. Then I asked God to bless my family— my mom and dad, my brothers and cousins, grandparents, aunts, and uncles— and not let them forget me." Again, he paused.

From the end of the table, Devon noticed that all of the women at the table began dabbing at their eyes.

"Then I prayed for my country," Dydd went on softly. "And prayed that they would not forget me."

This time the hesitation was, in Devon's mind, no less than artful.

"Then I waited for sleep." Turning to his four corners, Dydd smiled and said, "Thank you, guys, for being props. The box is gone now. Please have a seat."

While he had been studying the guests at the table, Devon had missed the fact that all four of the "corners" of the make-believe cell were also swiping at their eyes and noses.

Dydd waited until the four were seated. Then he concluded. "You may not remember my name after this evening. You may not remember my story. But I hope you remember one thing.

"The next time you pour yourself something to drink, be grateful.

"The next time you sit on a chair or lie on a bed, be grateful.

"The next time you put on clothes, be grateful."

Again, Dydd paused ever so slightly. Voice lowered, he said, "And the next time you see the people you love, thank God."

The room was deathly silent for half a minute. Then Dydd said, "Thank you for inviting me here this evening. God bless."

No one spoke for a long moment. The first to move was the Secretary of the Army. He stood and began clapping slowly and loudly.

At the end of the table, Devon Stondt swallowed a lump in his throat and stood with the others. Impatiently, he swiped at a tear and, turning his back to the others, quietly blew his nose.

The President stood and pumped Dydd's hand. Leaning toward Dydd and keeping his voice low, he said, "I will, Sergeant. I will. Thank you."

Reginald Ellis, who considered himself a mechanical genius, had no idea why the car suddenly stopped. With barely enough momentum to make it to the shoulder, he slammed his hand against the steering wheel and cursed.

Lifting the hood, he stared at the engine and went through a mental checklist. He had just filled the tank fifty miles ago. He hadn't heard any funny noises. Oil level was fine at that last stop. Couldn't be spark plugs. What the hell would cause the car to shut down so abruptly?

Before he had time to ponder further, a farmer pulled off the highway and parked behind him. The man appeared to be nearing sixty. An old man, Reggie thought to himself.

Then he remembered he himself was past seventy.

"Howdy. Having car trouble?"

Anyone who lived north of Interstate 70 would consider the farmer to have a slight southern drawl. But to Reginald Ellis, native of Alabama and the United States Marine Corps, the man sounded like a Yankee. "It just quit. No warning. No nothing. Just died."

"Hmm," the farmer mused. "Could be the coil. Could be the timing belt. Unless it has a timing chain. Which is it? Do you know?"

Ellis shrugged. "Hell if I know. It's never broke before."

The farmer leaned over the engine compartment and squinted. Then he returned to his pickup and brought back a handful of tools. A minute later, he said, "Yep. Looks like a belt. And it's busted. Let me call the parts store and see if they have one. What year is your car?"

It took an hour for them to drive into town, buy the new belt, return to the disabled car, and install the new part. It took another hour to adjust the timing. During the encounter, Ellis revealed the cause for his trip. Going to see an old friend from the service. Served in Vietnam together.

"What branch of the service?" the farmer asked.

"Marines."

"I served in the Air Force myself," the farmer stated. "Never saw combat, but I qualify for membership in the Legion because I was in during the Grenada invasion."

"Were you involved in it?" Ellis asked.

"Never set foot in Grenada. But my wife and I go to Legion meetings every month. Pot luck."

Before he pulled back onto the empty highway, Ellis pressed a ten dollar bill into the farmer's hand and said, "Thanks for the help."

"Good luck," the man replied as he folded the bill into his pocket. "Have a nice trip."

Thursday, February 22, 2018

When Moffat took a call from Constable Tran, he thought the investigator eight thousand miles away sounded tired. Sensing that Tran was not in the mood for idle talk, Moffat said, "Good evening, Constable Tran. Do you have more information?"

"Today, Colonel, I learned that drugs like those used to sedate Sergeant Weller were missing from the inventory at the medical clinic where the daughter works. When I interviewed her, she first acted like she didn't know what I was talking about. After more than an hour, she began to break down in tears. She claimed that she and her brother did at times wonder if their father had a human captive. Finally, she admitted that even though their father always forbade them going near the cell, they sometimes crept there. She said they heard someone talking, and she thought sometimes it sounded like he spoke French. She also said that sometimes they put their faces to the ground and watched his feet."

"My god," Moffat murmured.

"She said she and her brother didn't know what to do without causing their father disgrace. After their father passed away, they argued. She claims that after they placed Sergeant Weller on the ship, her brother had second thoughts and said they should have killed him and disposed of the body. I have arrested her. So far, I cannot even count the charges against her. She will not be out of prison for many years, I think."

"What about her brother?" Moffat inquired.

"Ah, now, that is another matter," Tran replied. "We have not located him thus far."

To Moffat, it seemed more was forthcoming. But Tran said nothing. Finally, Moffat asked, "Constable? Do you have some idea where he might be?"

After another hesitation, Tran replied, "His cell phone was last noted to place a call from Hong Kong."

"So he could be on his way to the States to finish off Sergeant Weller," Moffat mused.

Tran took a long breath and swallowed audibly. "Colonel Moffat, what I found today is very disturbing to me. Once, when I was a young officer, I helped to free three women who were chained inside a—what is the word you would use? A dungeon, I think. They had been there for a long time. And they did not fare well after they were released. Two of them, last I knew, had taken their own lives. It was a very unfortunate thing."

Again, Tran paused. Finally, his voice lower, he said, "I went today to the home of the man who died the last day of January, the father of the man and woman who— I believe—placed Sergeant Weller into the ship. I made several discoveries that will be very difficult for me to erase from my memory.

"First I found a—sorry, I cannot think of the word. A collection of his own writing. A diary, maybe?"

"Journal?" Moffat offered softly.

"Yes. That is what I mean. I found several volumes of his journals. Some of them are from the 1950s. Those I will read later." He hesitated, then added, "Maybe. But the others I have here before me, and I will begin this journey tonight and well into the dark hours.

"Inside one of the journals whose entry dates begin shortly after the time of Sergeant Weller's capture, there was a hiding place where all pages had the center cut away, such that there was a compartment inside. Do you understand what I mean?"

"Yes," Moffat answered.

Tran continued. "Inside the hiding place I found identification. I think you would say dog tags. They are inscribed with the name D.E. Weller.

"But what I found the most disturbing was a structure behind the man's house, perhaps a four or five-minute walk. The path was well worn. Colonel Moffat, I can barely speak. You see, I have a son who is sixteen years old. This is very difficult to me. In some ways, becoming a parent ruins a man."

"I understand that sentiment," Moffat said, partly to give Tran a break, as the report was obviously troubling the investigator. "Life does not become full until you realize how precious it is. And that cannot happen until you hold your own child in your arms, at which point you realize that life is not only precious, but also tenuous."

Tran let out a deep breath. "Yes. That is true. Colonel, the structure was exactly as Sergeant Weller described it. Steel wall. Cement walls. It was very, what is the word? It was very terrifying. Creepy. I took many pictures inside and outside of both the home and the cell. And I also took samples. Some of these I have posted to you. The others I reserved for my own lab to examine. I hope I can implore you for a DNA profile from Sergeant Weller, so that it may be compared to the samples."

"Of course. As soon as I have the profile, I will forward it to you." Sensing that Tran had said all he had to say, Moffat stated, "Thank you, Constable. I appreciate your diligence in this matter. But may I make another request? Please go watch something mindless on television for a while, and then go to bed. Don't read those journals tonight. They'll be there tomorrow. And you'll sleep better." As an afterthought, Moffat added, "I hope."

"Colonel, tell me, please. How is Sergeant Weller doing? Is he going to be okay? I don't know how a person can be—normal, after what he experienced."

158

It was Moffat's turn to pause. "Constable, I've made a profession out of studying the lives of POWs. There is no way to determine beforehand which of them will come through okay and which will not. Some trends are there, for sure. Farm boys—like Sergeant Weller—are historically more likely to survive captivity. The theory is that they spent their childhood outdoors doing hard physical work, sometimes not eating on a regular schedule, not quitting until the work is done, knowing that they are at the mercy of something larger than themselves—like weather and markets. They are typically well adapted to military service—especially combat—for the same reasons, although some people now think that this may no longer be the case, as farming and ranching is not as strenuous as it once was."

Moffat added, "I will see him tomorrow. I will let you know."

Leaving their hotel two hours before the start of the radio interview, Devon drove them to a side street and parked. "You ready for a little walking?" he asked.

"Sure," Dydd said. "Are we near the Smithsonian?"

Devon stepped out of the rental car and stood, stretching. "We're not near anything. That's why we're walking. Parking is a nightmare in the city."

In nearly a mile of walking, they talked about the highs and lows of the stock market since 1972, the trade embargoes, the assassinations, the terrorist attacks, the wars, and what had become of a girl Dydd had been sweet on.

Shaking his head, Devon replied dryly, "Married three times, six kids with several different fathers, and weighs about three-fifty. You dodged a bullet there, my friend."

Dydd laughed at the deadpan delivery. Then he squinted and asked, "What's that up ahead?"

"It's called The Wall," Devon answered as they neared the long, low black granite memorial. "I'll show you your name. You and Kiel are very near each other."

They approached, keeping their voices low to match the somber mood of the other visitors. When they reached the correct section, Devon did not speak. He merely pointed.

Dydd knelt and gently rubbed his fingers across his brother's name. Then he looked at his own name and grinned. He stood and whispered, "You suppose I should call whoever carved these names and tell them I'm not dead anymore?"

They turned and walked for several minutes toward where they had left the car. Finally, Devon spoke. "I don't know many people who can stand there and not be affected."

"It's pretty powerful," Dydd agreed.

"Really?" Devon turned and studied him. "You seemed rock steady."

Dydd shrugged. "I've been there and back. Death doesn't scare me." A minute later, he added, "Marion asked me if I've been grieving a lot. But I haven't. I learned you have to accept whatever comes. Sure, I'd have liked to talk to the folks again. And Grandpa. And my grandmas. And Uncle David. And Hiram and Kiel. But there'll be plenty of time in the next realm."

While Dydd bantered live on Caleb Chamberlain's nationally syndicated radio show—usually forgetting he was talking not only to the guy across the table from him but to millions of listeners around the world—Devon guzzled coffee and fidgeted with an ink pen, rapidly twirling it over and under his fingers in an intricate pattern.

Ten minutes into the interview, Caleb Chamberlain posed, "Those of us who have been here all along have seen steady changes in the world and in society. To you, those changes may seem far more abrupt. What is different in the world since you were captured in 1972?"

Without hesitation, Dydd replied, "When I left the country, most of the kids I knew had a mom and a dad who lived in the same house and had the same last name. When I left the country, a kid came of age and decided which church they wanted to go to, not which gender they wanted to be. When I left, there was maybe one chubby kid in each class at my school. Now there might be one skinny one, and all the rest are fat. And when I left, you could call a fat person fat without being called out for it.

"When we were at war in Vietnam, we were fighting for a defined territory against an enemy generally in a recognizable uniform—though that wasn't always the case, of course. Today, your war is with a philosophical group anywhere in the world and wearing whatever clothes they happen to be wearing. They might be dressed like the Sheik of Arabia or the guy who works in the office next door.

"When I left the country, I thought I was going overseas to help bring freedom and democracy to the rest of the world. When I came back, my country had traded liberty for a life of ease and luxury."

"Whoa!" Caleb reacted. "You just tossed a hand grenade into the conversation. Would you care to elaborate?"

"Sure. Everyone carries a cell phone. I'm told that the cell phones communicate with satellites that track your location. So Big Brother knows exactly where you are all the time. You carry all your money in credit cards that can be stolen physically or by computer. Peoples' lives are stored on little bits and bytes. I'm told that the government ag office knows how many cows everybody has, how many acres they plant into each crop, when they harvest, and how much the crops yielded. Shoot, when a steer arrives at the packing plant, it can be traced back to every place it has ever been, clear back to the ranch where it was born."

Dydd waited a second for comment, but Caleb was oddly silent. Having been warned against dead air on the radio, Dydd continued.

"In 1972, girls could be secretaries, nurses, or teachers. Now they can be everything. And now instead of wearing shorts to play basketball, they wear dresses. And so do the guys. When I left, our pants stayed up. And sometimes our pants were plaid."

Caleb Chamberlain was grinning. "And do you think that was a good thing?"

Dydd laughed. "No. Plaid pants were never good. But I liked watching girls play basketball in short shorts."

"Who doesn't?" Caleb laughed. "Keep going. What else?"

With the air of someone who had given the question a lot of thought, Dydd continued. "When I left home, just about everybody I knew went to church. Men wore a suit coat and tie. Ladies wore dresses. Last Sunday at Mass, I saw two men in ties, one lady in a dress, and more than half the folks were wearing blue jeans. When I left home, the only kinds of jeans were Levis, Wranglers, and us kids wore Tuffskins, you know, with the doubled knees. When I left, nurses wore white dresses, white shoes, and those little white hats. Last week at the medical clinic, everybody was wearing the same thing. Doctors, nurses, x-ray people, janitors, secretaries. Everybody was dressed like they were ready to do an operation on somebody.

"And that lady that I saw in the dress in church? She reminds me of a couple other changes in fashion. When I left, women were shaped like humans. Now, some of them are shaped like Barbie dolls. Bigger on top, if you follow my drift. And when I left, I knew five or six old guys who had tattoos. All of them were Navy or Marine vets of foreign wars. Now everybody from the teenager checking out your groceries to the grandma giving out communion in church has a tattoo. When I left, my mom's generation thought that if a woman had pierced ears, she was a hussy. Since I got back, I've seen people who look like they were in a car wreck while holding an open tackle box on their lap. Men and women both."

Caleb chuckled.

Smiling, Dydd continued. "If you wore a hat indoors, somebody would knock it off your head and give you a dirty look. Now there might be fifteen guys sitting in the dining room of any nice restaurant, and half of them are wearing grubby caps. Electric plugs had two prongs; now they have three. Paying at the pump meant handing cash to the guy who pumped your gas, washed your windshield, and checked your oil when you pulled up to the station. And you didn't have to rob a bank to pay for a tank of gas.

"Every ranch family I knew had a milk cow. Televisions had wood cabinets and legs, and it took two big guys to carry them. Now people carry tiny little televisions in their pockets. Back then, if you wanted to buy something, you pulled money out of your pocket and paid for it. And the money looked different than it does now. A postage stamp cost eight cents. Cars and pickups didn't ding when you opened the door or left the lights on or the keys in the ignition. Tennis shoes were comfortable, but nothing like these running shoes. These new ones are definitely an improvement.

"When I was a kid, our grocery store had staples in it. I mean, you could buy the ingredients and go home and cook something with those ingredients. Now, they have a deli with ready-to-eat meals. The first time I saw a mango was when I went through Hawaii on my way to Vietnam in 1971. Now there is a whole bin of them in the grocery store in Whispering Pines, Wyoming. There is another bin next to it with kiwis. Until I ate one the other day, I thought kiwi was slang for somebody from New Zealand. There are pineapples and papayas and eggplants and a bunch of stuff I never heard of before. Stuff I never thought I'd see in the middle of Wyoming in the middle of winter.

"There were four TV channels in the country," Dydd started on a new topic.

Devon waved a hand and mouthed something to him.

Dydd corrected himself. "I mean television networks. We could get one of them at our place if the weather was right. But the picture was always snowy. And if you were lucky, you might have a transistor radio to listen to in the barn. Now in the palm of your hand you can have a whole library, a record collection, the New York Stock Exchange, a travel agent, and a photo album. And probably a lot of other stuff that I don't know about yet."

"What do you think of computers?" Caleb inquired. "Certainly, technology must present one of the most profound changes in society."

Shaking his head with a mixture of dismay and awe, Dydd said, "They're great. And annoying. Keep in mind that hand-held calculators were being talked about when I left, but nobody had one. Now everybody seems to have a computer glued to their hand or their head. I suppose it's like a lot of things, though. My parents thought us kids were going to be mentally retarded because we watched too much TV and sat too close to the screen. Now everybody says kids will be vegetables because they play on their phones all the time. Shoot, back in Mozart's day, the parents thought Amadeus would warp their kids and make them crazy. I guess every generation is pretty sure the next one won't make it."

Caleb went to an ad break. When the interview resumed, he asked Devon, "What is it like for you, Devon, and other members of your family? Because you've essentially welcomed home someone who was dead to you."

Belying the caffeine and the fidgeting, Devon calmly responded, "Dydd said it best himself. He went to sleep with Rip van Winkle, traveled through the Twilight Zone, and woke up in the Jetsons. And the Rip van *Wrinkle* can't be overemphasized, here. I was in Vietnam from July Fourth of 1969 to July 12, 1970 and again from August tenth of 1971 to September fifth of 1972. For years after I returned, I continued to learn of events that occurred in my absence. Births, deaths, weddings, birthday parties, car wrecks, sports events, murders, divorces, foreclosures, weather anomalies. You name it. I'm sure it still happens for those who are deployed but to a lesser extent due to improved communications. But Dydd can't possibly ever learn about everything he's missed, no matter how diligently he tries. He will continue to be amazed by changes in society, family, historic events, technology, and the world in general."

"Let me ask you this, Dydd," Caleb posed. "Are there any inventions that you might have expected that haven't come to fruition?"

Dydd laughed. "This sounds like a trick question. I've only been back for a little over a week. When I answer your question, you might tell me that it has already been invented. But one thing I expected was some kind of portable nuclear power cells. Something that would hook into your house or barn and create power wherever you are. I thought electric transmission might be conducted without power lines. I also expected some kind of implant in cattle that would communicate with satellites and tell you the location, body temperature, and maybe even health status of the critter. For instance, if your cows are out of their fence or if a cow is calving, the satellite system would automatically call your phone and alert you."

Caleb looked at Devon. "Does that exist?"

"Not completely," Devon replied. "But it's close. There are Radio Frequency Identification ear implants for cattle. When the animal is in the chute, a wand is waved over the ear and picks up a signal which is then communicated to a computer that stores information useful to the livestock producer, such as what the animal weighed each time it came through the working facility, movement history, and medical records. Some systems also measure feed intake, feed conversion, average daily gain, et cetera."

Dydd's eyes were alight. "No fooling?"

With a chuckle, Caleb stated, "Wow. I had no idea cows were so high tech. Dydd, what else did you expect?"

"I still have to wait for hot water at the tap. Just having water is amazing, by the way. But I figured hot water would be instant by now."

Together, Devon and Caleb said, "Point source water heaters."

Devon explained. "I had them installed in all the bathrooms in my office building."

Dydd said, "I figured cancer would have been cured. The common cold and the flu and pneumonia would have been ancient memories. I never dreamed that bacteria and weeds would develop resistance to antibiotics and herbicides.

"Now it's my turn to ask a question," Dydd spoke. "What happened with the debate about atmospheric heating from supersonic aircraft?"

Caleb scowled and pointed at Devon, indicating that he should answer the query.

After a second of dead air, Devon nodded slowly. "I'm trying to recall that debate."

While Dydd responded, Caleb's assistant searched the internet and spoke into Caleb's earpiece.

Dydd said, "Some scientist predicted that the increased vapor in the stratosphere would lead to ground heating and a decrease in ozone production."

Caleb announced, "My producer tells me that the theory was debunked, but not before it gutted the government's supersonic research program."

"I see," Dydd replied. "I figured there'd be a high-speed train system all across the country. I thought tires would be flat-free. I also thought that farming would be more automated. I figured tractors would be robotic and pull huge equipment so that fields could be covered in just a few passes."

Again, Caleb looked toward Devon, who replied, "Robotic tractors are in the experimental phase. But a lot of farming is done by satellite guidance. The driver merely sits and makes sure everything keeps working properly while the satellite steers. At present, most automated systems still require the driver to turn the implement around at each end of the field. But some systems have accounted for that now, too."

"How about automatic cars?" Dydd asked. "I figured cars would drive themselves by now, and people would just go along for the ride."

"That's coming, too," Caleb stated. "Prototypes are being road-tested."

"How about colonies on the moon or Mars?" Dydd asked.

"We've sent probes to most of the planets," Devon answered. "No colonies, yet. But we have data regarding the composition of soil, temperature, and atmospheric conditions for several planets."

"Well, gentlemen, we're almost out of time," Caleb said. "Devon, my listeners are already familiar with you on the show, and I'd like to extend an invitation to you, as well, Dydd. I would love to have you on the program when you can make it."

Jovially, Dydd said, "That sounds just fine, Caleb. I find that as I grow older, I can talk to anybody about any topic—"

Devon broke into a rare smile and finished the sentence in unison with Dydd. "As long as they want to talk about ranching."

Devon clarified, "Our grandfather was fond of that saying. He had a whole series of great quotes, such as: I don't want all the land in the world, just what adjoins me."

Dydd added, "Always be honest in all dealings. Unless a horse is involved."

With a glance at the big digital clock on the wall, Caleb said, "Gentlemen, thank you for coming on the show today. We're about out of time, but I believe I speak for all of my listeners, Dydd, when I say: Welcome home."

***

The timing belt held fine in Reggie Ellis' car. But when his bald tires hit the frost on the westbound interstate in southern Nebraska, he lost control and spun abruptly into the median. By the time the car came to a rest, it was eastbound on the snow-covered grass.

Leaning his head on the steering wheel, he took several deep breaths to calm himself. After he lowered his heart rate, he gently pressed the accelerator to see if he could ease back onto the highway. Two minutes later, he was on the road again.

But something didn't feel right. The car kept pulling to the right. He would get it checked out when he got home.

If he ever got home.

This trip, reflected Reginald Ellis, was beginning to feel accursed.

Friday, February 23, 2018

Paul Richards slipped through the kitchen, nodded to Sam Weller who was washing a large pot in an oversized sink, and moved soundlessly into the dark dining room.

Without looking up at him, Jane Bellairs said softly into the otherwise empty room, "Our guy is back on the rock face outside the east window. Two hundred meters. Sector Seventeen."

Barely breaking a grin, he asked, "How do you know he's a man and not a woman?"

"Because I don't know any women who pee standing up," she returned. "I got bored during the night, so I did a FLIR scan and picked up his heat signature. He has a bunch of chem packs that heat up when you activate them. But I bet his ass is still frozen to that rock he's sitting on."

Taking up the infrared binoculars, Paul scanned the hillside. "Looks like he's all alone. And it looks like his chem packs are wearing out. He better get a new supply before he turns solid."

"I haven't detected anyone else in the area. What do you want to do with him?"

With a humorless chuckle, he said, "I wonder if he knows Sergeant Weller is on the East Coast."

She yawned. "Maybe he's not after Sergeant Weller. Maybe he got a bad steak, and he wants to take out the chef."

Wryly, he smiled at her. "Have you ever had a bad steak here?"

She returned the smile. "Never. If you have this under control, I'm going home. I just have time to make my famous French toast for the kids before school."

Leaning back in his chair, Paul said, "If he's a reporter, he'll leave as soon as the sergeant appears on television. After that, the story'll be leftovers. The American public has a very short attention span."

"Tell me about it," Jane replied dryly. "And if he doesn't leave?"

"Donovan ran a check on his license plate. Car is registered to a woman in Nebraska. We'll have a chat with him later today and make sure all he's planning to shoot is photos."

Blake Moffat crossed the tarmac at the general aviation terminal and shook hands first with Devon Stondt, then with Dydd Weller.

"How long do you need him, Lieutenant Colonel?" Devon asked.

"A couple hours should suffice, Commander."

"Nobody calls me that. Not for years," Devon scoffed. Then he said, "I have four or five hours of meetings. Can you entertain each other that long?"

"Will do, sir" Moffat answered. As he led the way to the drab government-issue car, he asked Dydd, "What are you hungry for?"

Dydd laughed. "Whatever you like is fine with me."

As they climbed into the car, Moffat asked, "Is it different for you to wear a seatbelt now? They weren't really a thing when you were last on this continent."

"They were at our house," Dydd replied. "My mom was a big fan of seatbelts. The car didn't move until everybody was buckled in. Dad didn't care so much. And we boys thought it was great to get away with not wearing them. Until the day Sam got his license and took us for a drive and wrecked. Nobody got hurt bad, but it made a seatbelt believer out of me."

"Are you warm enough?"

Dydd shook his head. "I haven't been warm since I got back."

As he turned out of the parking lot and onto the access street, Moffat adjusted the heater controls and observed, "Looks like you've gained a little weight."

"Twenty pounds, so far," Dydd replied, sounding disappointed. "My doctor says I'm not absorbing nutrients as well as I should. He's also my cousin's son, by the way."

"Of course he is," Moffat replied dryly. "You come from the most inbred place in the country outside Arkansas."

Dydd laughed. But he was serious when he relayed, "I cracked a joke and told him my guts are out of practice. He said it wasn't a joke. It's true."

"We'll get you some practice," Moffat said as he picked up his cell phone. A moment later, he said, "Hi, Sweetheart. Good news. I'm fixing dinner. Would you mind calling the Pizza Slab? We'll pick them up. . . No, order two larges. You remember when you told me you'd like to meet Dydd Weller? Well, I'm bringing him home with me. . . Okay. Turn the thermostat up to eighty-five, so you two will be comfortable. I can strip down to my BVDs and sweat. See you soon. . . Love you, too."

After he disconnected, Moffat asked, "So what else does your doctor say about your health—and keep in mind that I can't officially ask that as a government representative. I can only ask as a friend."

"I heard about the patient confidentiality boloney," Dydd replied. "In 1971, the newspaper listed everybody who was in the hospital and why. You could call up the nurses' station and get somebody's room number and status report. And if you were sick or needed an operation, they kept you there until you got better. Now, I'm told, you can break your leg in the morning and be home in a cast by suppertime."

Blake nodded. "True."

"As far as my health," Dydd went on, "my bones are still brittle. Ben—that's my cousin, the doctor—said I should avoid any activity like running or jumping. I can't remember how he stated it."

"High impact exercise," Moffat offered.

"Yeah. That's what he called it."

Glancing at his passenger, Blake observed, "I had a buddy in officer basic who loved horses. He said sometimes the only way he could get his head straight was to go riding. Took me out to his farm one time and put me on a horse. I gotta tell you, it terrified me. But he loved it."

Dydd smiled.

Moffat asked, "So I guess you aren't supposed to do that either, are you?"

"Well, let's just say there's a difference between what you're supposed to do and what you do."

Moffat laughed. "So you've gone horseback riding."

"First day home," Dydd confessed. "It was great, but I almost froze. Ben's brother took me out. He threw a couple layers of sheepskin on the saddle to cushion my bones."

While they stood in line to pay for the pizza, Moffat said, "I heard you on the radio. You sounded quite professional."

Grinning, Dydd responded, "I've had a lot of time to polish my public speaking skills."

A sixty-ish man in front of them turned around and blandly took in Moffat's uniform. Then he glanced at Dydd and did a double take. "Hey," he blurted, "I'm sorry to eavesdrop, but are you that guy who just got back from Vietnam?"

Dydd stuck out his hand and introduced Moffat, then himself. "Are you from here in Chicago?"

173

"Yeah," the man stammered as he pumped Dydd's hand. "Wow! I can't believe I just happened to run into you in the Pizza Slab! Man, welcome home. Welcome home."

"Did you serve in the Armed Forces?" Dydd plied.

Seeming surprised that a bona fide celebrity was actually talking to him, the man replied, "Yeah. I was in the Coast Guard for seven years. Right after high school."

"A puddle pirate? That still counts," Dydd smiled. "Thank you for your service."

The clerk behind the counter, adorned with several rings in her lips, a tattoo on the side of her face, and another impressive set of hardware in the ear opposite the tattoo, said, "Yo! Buddy, you want to pay for your pizza, or what?"

The Coast Guard veteran turned and fumbled in his pocket for a phone with which he paid for his order. Taking his receipt, he turned again and said, "I'm so glad I got to meet you. I'm telling you, my buddies will be jealous. You take care, man. Okay? I mean it. You get some meat on your bones and enjoy being home."

"Thanks," Dydd replied warmly.

Moffat paid for the pizzas and picked up the twin boxes. "I'll carry these," he said. "You get the door. Unless you're too busy signing autographs."

In a typical suburban house in a typical suburban neighborhood that looked like all the others surrounding it, Blake introduced his wife to Dydd. Once she saw that the returned POW was even thinner than he appeared on television, she suggested they eat first and talk later.

Blake Moffat draped his uniform jacket over the back of an empty chair, removed his tie, and kicked off his shoes before they sat at the dining room table. And before the first slice of pizza was dispersed, Linda asked

Dydd to lead the prayer. He recited the Catholic meal prayer, complete with the sign of the cross before and after.

When the first pizza was gone, Blake looked at his wife and said, "Guess you can go watch that movie you've been dying to see."

"I've been dying to see a movie?" she asked.

"Yeah. You can go now."

"Oh," she took the hint. "Mr. Weller, it's been a great honor to meet you. Thank you for your service to our country and for your sacrifice. And come again anytime. You're always welcome."

When Linda Moffat stood, so did Dydd.

As he watched his wife leave, Moffat commented, "We've been happily married for twenty-three years because I don't tell her about my work, and she doesn't tell me about hers."

"What does she do?" Dydd asked as he returned to his seat.

"She's a shrink. You want anything else to eat before we get started? Want a Coke? I have some on hand just for you. I'm a coffee and beer man, myself. She drinks coffee and wine, mostly. We don't consume much soda."

With a wry smile, Dydd admitted, "Doc said I better lay off the pop until my bones build up more calcium. Pop has a lot of phosphorus in it—so does rice, he said—and it replaces calcium in your bones if you get more phosphorus than calcium in your diet. Or something like that."

"Your skin looks better," Moffat offered.

"All except the bony parts," Dydd answered. "I slept on concrete for a long time. No padding on my bones. Some of those sores are stubborn to heal. But for the first time in a long time, I'm not itchy."

175

"The Navy docs want to have another look at you. In San Diego, preferably. They'd like to do more blood work, a bone scan, and some psych evals. The results of the latter will help them prepare other GIs in case they end up in a similar situation."

Dydd pursed his lips. "With all due respect, Colonel, I feel like I've given enough time to the United States government, the Marine Corps, and the Vietnam War. I just want to live my life now."

"Understood," Moffat said. "But remember you're still on active duty. This isn't a request. Uncle Sam let you get reacquainted with your family, but be prepared to spend at least a couple weeks in California."

Dydd sighed.

"So now that we've covered your health, how's everything else going?" Moffat asked.

With a reticent shrug, Dydd said, "Well, it's time for me to find my own place. Devon has his real estate team looking for ranches, but nothing close to town is going to shake loose anytime soon. Ranchland doesn't change hands very often. Usually doesn't leave the family."

"Why don't you just stay with Sam and Cal and Kevin for a while?"

Letting out a long sigh, Dydd stated, "You know, when we were kids, us Weller boys always kind of drifted into pairs. Hiram and I had a bond. We both wanted to be ranchers. Sam and Kiel had a bond, too. They both wanted to get out of Wyoming as soon as possible.

"When Hiram got drafted, Dad tried to get Sam to take Hiram's place and help out. But Sam flat refused. The minute he graduated—and he even graduated a year early— he couldn't wait to get out of town. And Kiel never was any good with livestock, had no interest in tractors or farming. So I figured Hiram would come back and take over the ranch when Dad retired. Part of the reason I went to war was so I could get it over with and get back home and help him."

Dydd sipped his water. "Sam and Cal and Kevin have been rooming together for years. They have a routine. A rhythm. You know? They get each other."

"So you feel like a fifth wheel," Moffat offered.

Dydd nodded. "Sometimes I say something, and I think Sam takes it the wrong way. And I don't know much sign language. It's awkward for him to type into his phone so it can speak for him. Especially when he's cooking. Don't get me wrong, I love him. He's my brother. He's been awful good to me. It's just that I don't fit in at the restaurant.

"Kevin is still working full-time as chief pilot for Stondt Industries—that's Devon's company—so he's not there much. And Cal is semi-retired, but he still works ten hours a day for Devon. I don't know how many hours he put in when he was full-time. He's an IT guy. I guess you know what that is."

Moffat nodded.

"He got me a phone. He's been trying to teach me how to use it. To me, a phone is for calling people. I'm still figuring out how to use it as a slide rule and a post office."

Blake snickered.

"Me, I always loved numbers. Devon offered me a job. But I don't want to play with other peoples' numbers. I want to play with my own." Dydd got up and refilled his water glass from the tap. Over his shoulder, he said, "After Hiram left and Sam wouldn't help and Kiel was more or less worthless—with ranching, I mean—I became Dad's shadow." Dydd took a long drink and sat again. "I mean, from the time I was maybe eight, I used to sit on his lap watching him do the bookkeeping at night. He said I should become an accountant someday. Said it would be helpful to know that kind of stuff when I had my own ranch."

"How old were you when Hiram was drafted?" Moffat asked.

"Twelve." Dydd chuckled as he reminisced. "Sam and Kiel always told me I was an accident. My birthday is nine months after Dad's. So the boys always said Dad got drunk on his birthday and forgot he wasn't supposed to touch Mom."

Shaking his head with disdain, Moffat muttered, "That's why my wife and I had one kid. Siblings can be such assholes."

"Yeah, you mentioned before that you had a kid. Said something about knowing a lot about snot."

Blake nodded. "She's in college. Architectural engineering at Drexel."

"Where's that?"

"Drexel University. Philadelphia. Big bucks. We're going to go broke getting her a good education."

Without pause, Dydd mused, "When I was a kid, my science teacher explained the law of entropy. He said if you pulled your finger out of a bucket of water, the water instantly filled in. It was like your finger was never there. That's how I feel sometimes. Like the dent I left in this world closed up. Everybody got used to me not being here. Now I don't know where I fit. Or if I fit."

Nodding slightly, Moffat assured him, "You'll find that spot. Everyone does. But give yourself some time. You have a hell of a lot of adjusting to do."

After a moment, Dydd said carefully, "The first time we talked, Colonel, you seemed kind of, well, I don't know how to say it. I think you thought I was lying to you."

"I did, quite frankly. For years, people have been tossing around conspiracy theories about POWs still being held by the Vietnamese government. I've never bought into that. For one thing, I've been boots-on-the-ground in Nam several times. I've talked to a lot of people on both sides of the Pacific. There's no evidence that compels me to believe it. But I've been receiving information from a police officer in Da Nang that corroborates your story. We'll get to that in a minute."

Out of the blue, Dydd said, "My nephew, Neil, is living in sin with a woman. I hear that's not unusual now. My mom would die if she knew."

Moffat nodded slightly. "It's common practice. In fact, it's getting almost unusual to get a wedding invitation these days."

Shaking his head sadly, Dydd said, "But something good has come of my being home."

"A lot of good has come of your being home, I should think," Moffat offered.

Dydd smiled. "Neil's girlfriend came to the restaurant the other day to see me. She said ever since she's known Neil, he's been gloomy. Depressed. She said it's like he's always been under the shadow of his dad.

"But she said when he got back from San Diego, he gave her a big hug and started crying. She'd never seen him cry before. She said it was like someone lifted the world off his shoulders. Then he got down on one knee and proposed to her."

"That is good news," Blake said.

Nodding, Dydd said, "Yeah. It is."

Moffat refilled his wine glass and set his briefcase on a vacant chair. He stacked the empty plates and shoved them to the far end of the table along with the leftover pizza. Then he extracted a thick file from the briefcase

179

and set it on the slick, polished surface. "I have some things to show you."

Dydd stared at the file incredulously. "Is that all about me? Or does it include all the MIAs you are looking for?"

Moffat rolled his shirt sleeves to the elbow before he slipped on a pair of reading glasses. Looking at Dydd over the top of the rims, he said dryly, "This is just part of your file. There's more at the office. I didn't feel like lugging around a whole file cabinet."

Dydd's brows rose appreciatively.

From the folder, Moffat extracted a color printout of a satellite map. Sliding it across the table, he asked, "Do you recognize that?"

Dydd studied the print for a full minute. "Is this where we were ambushed?"

"It is. Now look at this one." The second sheet depicted the same map but with hand-written notations and symbols.

"This is where you found them?" Dydd asked. "Douglass. Saunders. And over here—how far away was that? Looks like a hundred meters."

"That's about right."

Voice dropping, Dydd said, "And Dieterman. Damn. They all died there?"

Blake Moffat nodded. "Twice a year, I travel to Vietnam to look for remains. There are four members of my team, and we travel with four officials of the Vietnamese government. They only allow us to look for remains of those on our list, a list they must pre-approve. And we have to know the exact location—or at least a pretty tight area— where those remains are expected to be. Seven years ago, I went searching for your platoon."

"How do you know where to look?" Dydd inquired.

With a wry face, Moffat said, "Oh, it's a piece of cake. In this case, a Brazilian national was working as a civilian contractor for a Belgian company that studies plants to use in new drug research. He hired some of the locals in the area. Made friends. Some of the village old-timers told him about a battle that happened essentially in their backyard. These were tribal people, mind you, and very suspicious of the Vietnamese government.

"So a couple old guys took the Brazilian out to the site and showed him where they'd found bodies. They said they had covered the bodies at the time with a thick layer of vegetation instead of burying them because they were afraid the NVA soldiers might return and retaliate. While they were poking around, the contractor said he found some bone fragments—probably part of a hip or tooth because the acidic soil and high rainfall in the area degrades osseous bone fast—along with a metal button that he thought might be from a uniform.

"So the Brazilian talked to the US Embassy and gave them the button. They sent me the button. It turned out to be from a Marine uniform. So, based on records of the approximate location of your ambush, I submitted your name and the names of your platoon to the Vietnam authorities and asked to add you to my search list. Six months later, they informed me that there had been no battles in that area. So, very politely and politically correctly, I appealed and asked again. Six months later, they told me they had sent a party out to look for remains but had found nothing. The Brazilian got word to me—we couldn't contact each other directly out of concerns for his safety—that the government officials conducted their search without consulting any locals or him. And they searched five klicks away in the wrong canyon. So again the Vietnamese government informed me that there were no remains, there had been no battle, and the case was closed. Shortly thereafter, the Brazilian lost his visa and was basically kicked out of the country."

Moffat took a sip of wine. Then he continued. "Two years later, I re-applied to search the valley for you and your platoon. They approved the request. Different day, different bureaucrats, I guess."

Dydd smiled. "Piece of cake. Are all your searches like that?"

With a shrug, Moffat said, "I've acquired a lot of patience."

He returned the maps to his file and extracted a report from which he read, "The morning after the ambush, April tenth, Greshan made it back to a US camp. He had four bullets in him. Phipps and Madison found an American unit forty-eight hours later; they were also both shot up. Carlton was captured and taken to Dong Phu, as you were. He ended up being transferred a couple times, then wound up at Hoa Lo Prison Camp, also known as the Hanoi Hilton. The prisoners there were released in four waves after the peace treaty in 1973. The first captured were the first released. Doug Carlton was in the fourth and final flight out. They landed at Clark Air Base in the Philippines and were transported to the hospital to get checked out. Carlton died there during the night."

Dydd listened intently.

Moffat continued. "Greshan reported that he never saw you after the shooting started. Phipps was certain he saw you get shot in the head, but he was at a bad angle. Madison said you got hit in the head, but not by a bullet. He said part of Saunders's skull struck you. He was pretty sure you were dead. Both Phipps and Madison were certain you weren't wearing your helmet when they saw you get hit. Neither knew why."

Moffat slid out another page. This one he did not offer to show Dydd. "My predecessor personally interviewed your CO twice. His predecessor interviewed him once. All three times, Major Ellis was adamant that you never told him you were underage and that he had no idea your brother was in the combat theater."

Dydd scowled but said nothing.

"After I spoke with Captain Tengut the first time, I called up Reginald Ellis and chatted with him again. He still vowed he didn't know you were sixteen and that you never mentioned having a brother serving in combat. I've submitted paperwork to the JAG. They could mount an investigation, but there's probably a statute of limitations on whatever charges they might be able to press."

Moffat let out a long breath and put away the report. "Now for the interesting stuff. When I first contacted the Da Nang authorities about you, I figured I'd get the usual red tape run-around. I gave them the facts I had. They said they would call me back. I figured they wouldn't, but to my surprise, I got an update two days later.

"They started at the shipyard. Surveillance from a security camera showed a man and a woman rolling a cart—a cart big enough to hold a very skinny American—onto the Indonesian freighter. Tengut's ship. The footage was good enough to identify the car they were driving, which led to their identification, a brother and sister. Anyway, the investigators learned that their father had just died the day before. So they searched his place, looking for the structure you described.

"In the meantime, they found the woman and interviewed her. She beat around the bush but finally admitted that she and her brother suspected their dad

183

kept a captive. But she said they didn't know what to do about it."

"What did the brother say?" Dydd inquired. "Did he admit to knowing about me, too?"

"They haven't found him yet. Last known whereabouts Hong Kong." Shaking his head dismissively, Moffat went on. "The investigators also found your dog tags and the old man's journal which should provide some answers. And they took swabs inside the cell. The box, as you call it. They're sending me some samples for DNA analysis here in the States. The results will prove that you were in that cell. And the constable in charge sent me these photos."

On his computer, Moffat pulled up first a photo of Dydd's dog tags. He turned the screen so Dydd could see. Dydd's only reaction was a slight nod.

The next picture showed the interior of the cell, brightly illuminated by a camera flash. Again, Moffat turned the screen so Dydd could see.

The reaction was not what Moffat expected. And he instantly regretted showing Dydd the photo.

All the air left Dydd's lungs at once, causing him to emit a gasping, choking sound. He spun and lunged to one side, almost coming off the chair. His chest began heaving forcefully as his eyes went vacant.

"I'm sorry," Blake Moffat said as he slammed the computer shut. "God, I'm sorry, Sergeant. I shouldn't have shown that to you."

Dydd's breathing was rasping, gasping, as he clung to the edge of the table with one hand and the back of the chair with the other, his knuckles going white. He began pitching forward and backward as though retching.

Blake jumped to his feet. "Linda?" he called into the next room. "Hey, come here a minute."

Linda Moffat trotted into the room and immediately knelt beside Dydd, putting one hand on his back and the other on his arm. She caught Blake's eye and nodded toward the trash can at the edge of the kitchen. She mouthed silently, "He may vomit."

Blake quickly slid the can between Dydd's knees.

"Dydd, it's okay," Linda said soothingly.

Blake's finger was hovering over his phone, ready to summon an ambulance. "Linda?" he asked softly. "What should I do?"

Instead of answering her husband, she spoke to Dydd. "I hear the weather has been pretty cold in Wyoming. I bet it's hard to stay warm, isn't it? I'm like you, always cold. It seems like I can never really get warm in the winter."

For an instant, Dydd's eyes focused on her face. Then he swung his chin toward Blake. He burst, "I can't go back there!"

Shaking his head in the negative, Blake assured, "You're not going to. You're home now. You're home to stay."

Taking in a sharp breath, Dydd dropped his head and took three choking sobs. "Why? Why? *Why?*"

Blake slid around a chair opposite Dydd, glad for an opportunity to sit as the adrenaline rush subsided and left his knees weak. "You're okay, Dydd. You're home."

Dydd looked up at him, tears suddenly streaming. Voice terse, he demanded, "Why did he steal my life? The wife I would have had? The children I would have had? The ranch I would have had? Why did he take all that from me? *He didn't even know me!*"

When he finished the words, he seemed to sink on the hard chair, as though the shock, the pressure, the very air had been siphoned from him. He looked into Linda Moffat's eyes and softly said, "I'm sorry. I'm so sorry."

"You're okay," she smiled as she rubbed his back, her fingers bumping along between ribs and over vertebrae. "It's okay."

His countenance registering something between terror and exhaustion, he cast his gaze toward Blake Moffat and begged, "What's happening to me? This has never happened before. I really am happy to be home."

"We know you are." It was Linda who answered. "That was a panic attack. Sometimes something triggers a painful memory. You're not alone. I work with soldiers every day who have been in combat. Sometimes it's hard, some days are harder than others, but as time passes, it'll get easier. You'll come through this okay." She looked up at her husband, and he could tell she wasn't sure she was telling the truth.

She continued talking to Dydd in a soothing tone. "This happens sometimes. But it doesn't happen all the time. And it will happen less and less after you've been home with people you love. You'll see."

Donovan Garrison, dressed in desert camo and nearly invisible unless he moved, stood motionless between the rock wall and the aging car with the Nebraksa license plate. When the man came into view, Donovan let him stagger twenty feet toward the car before he spoke.

"Kinda cold out here for camping, isn't it?"

The man looked up, startled, but quickly regaining control.

Donovan asked, "Do you know whose land this is?"

The man grunted.

"What's your name?"

"What's yours?" the man asked insolently.

"I asked first. And I do know who owns this land. And I know that you're trespassing. And I know that you don't have a permit to camp here. And I know that no one by your description is registered in any local hotels."

"Sounds like you're pretty smart," the big man replied. "So why ask me who I am? You probably already know that, too."

"Just being polite. I imagine your name is Marjorie because that's who this car is registered to."

"It ain't stolen," the man retorted. He appeared to be in his late sixties or maybe early seventies. His hair needed a trim, as did his beard. He wore several layers of mismatched and rumpled clothing. Over his shoulder was the strap of a battered camera bag.

"What's your name?" Donovan's voice lost some of its civility, announcing that it was now time to get serious.

The big man squinted at him, as though sizing up the smaller, younger man. Finally, he said, "Jerome Bradley."

"Mr. Bradley, what is your business here?"

"None of yours unless you got some credentials. All I see is military clothes. Ain't seen no badge."

"I can have a badge here in five minutes or less, if you'd like. Is that how you want to play it?" Donovan asked.

The older man emitted a quick, humorless chuckle. "That's right."

"No worries. He's on the way." For the next three minutes, Donovan didn't move; he merely stared. Then a pickup emblazoned with County Sheriff pulled up and parked behind the car.

The man who emerged appeared artificially stocky due to a heavy down-filled coat and the Kevlar vest below it. If Jerome Bradley had stopped in at the local Catholic Church, he would have noted a striking similarity between the priest and this man.

187

Sheriff Lon Stondt asked all the same questions Donovan Garrison had asked. The answers were substantively the same except that Bradley further identified himself as a freelance photojournalist.

"Who do you work for?" Donovan pelted.

Sneering, Bradley snapped, "None of your business."

Lon sighed patiently. "He's a sworn deputy of this county, sir. But if you prefer to hear it from me, who do you work for?"

"Whoever bids highest."

"And who would that generally be?" Lon pressed.

"NewsNet. America Today. Whoever has the deepest pockets."

Donovan chortled. "NewsNet and America Today? That's like telling me you make a living selling jalapeno ice cream. NewsNet is about as right-wing as they come. And America Today is so left-wing, it's practically communist."

"Like I said," Bradley reiterated, "whoever has the deepest pockets."

"Do you have some ID on you, Mr. Bradley?" Lon asked.

"It's buried in the car," Bradley replied evenly.

"I'll wait."

Bradley simply stood and looked down at the shorter man. Finally, he pushed himself off the side of the vehicle and opened the passenger door. After five minutes of rummaging and placing half the car's contents on the cold rocky ground around their feet, he stood up and began patting himself down.

"Oh. Had it here all along." He extracted his driver's license from a wallet retrieved from an inside coat pocket. Then, keeping the document faced away from Donovan, he handed it to the lawman.

The expression on Lon's face was hard to read. But it was obvious he wasn't happy. "Donovan, why don't you follow us down to the courthouse in his car. Sir, you'll need to answer some questions for me. Starting with why you lied about your identity."

***

The weather in Whispering Pines, Wyoming, had deteriorated during the day. A winter system had descended from the Arctic and sagged down over the Northern Plains. After they stepped into the cabin of Devon's private jet parked on the Chicago tarmac, Devon asked, "You want to stop in and see Zeb and his family?"

Still shaken from his encounter at the Moffat's, Dydd shrugged. "Whatever you think."

"I think the weather in Whispering Pines sucks," Devon stated clearly as he leaned a hip against the back of a passenger seat and ducked to glance out the cabin window. "Right now, it's a balmy forty-four in Tyler County, Kansas."

"Better call ahead," Dydd recommended.

Devon straightened and pointed to Dydd's pocket. "You call. You have a phone now."

"I keep forgetting," Dydd returned with a wan smile.

"Maybe you don't remember turning thirty, but you must have. If you were a kid, you'd just start punching buttons on that thing until it did whatever you wanted it to do. Here, give me that." Devon took the phone and pressed a button on the side. "That's how you turn on the screen. Here, press that to get your contact list. But first go get buckled in."

Devon followed Dydd into the cockpit and took the left seat. This was a smaller jet than they had flown from San Diego. It was rated for a single pilot and, as Kevin was currently flying a contingent of Devon's employees to Japan, Devon was the single pilot.

Before he slipped on his radio headset, Devon said, "Kids are intuitive with computers. If I figure out how to do something on my computer in ten steps, I'll watch some pipsqueak junior staffer do the same damn thing with one keystroke. Makes me feel like a dumb old fart."

"Cal drives a pickup. Kevin has a car. What do you drive?" Dydd asked.

"Car," Devon answered. "Well, SUV. Better clearance than a car. Seats eight. Four-wheel-drive. And as you know, sometimes the weather where we live makes four-wheel-drive a necessity."

"What's an SUV?" Dydd inquired.

"Sport Utility Vehicle. Like we took from the airport to the White House. Like the old Chevy Suburbans. Most manufacturers have a comparable model now. Wait a second." Devon spoke to the traffic controller, listened to the response, and made a reply. Then he returned to Dydd. "Speaking of computers and gray hair, let me give you some hard-learned advice. When you go to WalMart, always note the row where you parked before you walk away from your car."

"WalMart?" Dydd asked.

Devon shook his head. "Jesus, you've been gone a long time."

With a chuckle, Dydd turned to look out the window at the bright glow of Chicago. Devon's comment about being gone a long time reminded him of the conversation with Moffat.

The panic attack.

The fear.

More than fear of the panic attack itself was the fear of it happening again.

It took several minutes of sliding his finger around the screen before he remembered how to place a call. By the time the phone began ringing, they were taxiing toward the runway.

Zeb's wife, sounding harried, answered on the fourth ring. "Hi," Dydd said simply. "This is Dydd. Is Zeb home?"

"Hello, Dydd! How are you? Are you coming for a visit soon?" Her voice switched in an instant from frazzled to friendly.

He chuckled. "Maybe sooner than you'd like. Devon is flying me out of Chicago right now, and the weather back home is sketchy. We wondered if we could crash at your place." He caught himself. "Let me re-word that. How about, we wondered if we could stop in?"

"Of course you may! What time will you be here?"

"I have no idea," he replied honestly.

"Give a call when you're a half hour out. I'll send Zeb to the airport to pick you up."

When Devon swung open the hatch at the airstrip in Tyler County, Kansas, Zeb was standing on the tarmac just outside. As he had done two weeks earlier, he bounded inside like a school boy. "Boy, is it good to see you!"

Devon reminded Zeb, "Be gentle."

Laughing, Zeb asked Dydd, "How long can you stay?"

Dydd sighed. "If you promise the temperature will stay above zero, I might stay until spring."

They stood chatting in the warmth of the cockpit for several minutes before Devon announced, "Zeb, if you have this under control, I'm going to head on to Dallas. I have a meeting there tomorrow afternoon. You'll already have a full house without me spending the night."

"All right," Zeb said as he squeezed Devon's hand. "Thanks for bringing him. Don't hurry back."

Devon smirked. "I see where I stand."

Despite the "balmy" forty-degree evening, Dydd was completely chilled by the time they reached Zeb's ranch.

Chilled, but not unwelcome.

Willa, the youngest, met them on the porch and gave Dydd a hug. "It's good to see you again, Uncle Dydd." She winked at her stepfather and added, "Because when you're around, nobody calls Dad skinny!"

Zeb guided them toward the door, saying, "Let's get inside where it's warmer. We have a fire going. Have a seat over there, Dydd."

No one went to sleep until a couple dozen old Welsh songs had been sung, most of the leftovers in the refrigerator had been eaten, and Dydd had regaled the family with tales of Zeb getting into trouble as a youth.

When Reginald Ellis crossed the state line into Wyoming, he let out a sigh of relief. His muscles were tired from fighting the limping car. His eyes were tired from squinting against the sun glinting off the thin layer of snow on the ground. And he was just plain tired of driving.

He pulled off at a service station in Cheyenne and found a folded map of the state. Donning the reading glasses he reluctantly carried in his shirt pocket, he scoured the map for a town called Whispering Pines. After a solid five minutes, he waved his hand to attract the attention of the clerk who had wandered to the far end of the counter to straighten a display.

"Hey. Where is Whispering Pines?" Reggie asked.

The teenager shrugged and continued chomping his gum. "Beats me."

Stifling the urge to bark at the kid, Reg held out the map. "I can't see the fine print here. What are the coordinates?"

"The what?" the kid asked as he approached.

"There's a letter and a number," Reg replied in what he guessed was near enough to a patient tone. "Tells where the place is on the map."

"Oh." Leaning over the map, the kid ran his finger down the list of towns at the edge of the big sheet. "Whispering Pines. D-7."

Opening the map fully and resting it unevenly on the cluttered countertop, Reg found the letter D on the left side and the 7 on top. "There it is. How long does it take to get there from here?"

The kid glanced at the point designated by the big gnarled finger. "Well, looks like it's maybe two hours past Casper. So four hours, give or take."

"Four hours?" Reggie spluttered. "Four more hours of this god-forsaken fucking desert?"

Several people turned their heads toward him. One mother put a hand on the side of her young daughter's head and nudged her toward the door.

With a deep sigh, Reggie folded the map and asked, "How much for the map?"

"They're free," the kid snapped back. "And this is a family joint, you know? You can watch your mouth, old man."

Saturday, February 24, 2018

While Dydd slowly ate breakfast, Zeb sipped his sixth cup of coffee for the morning and asked, "So what do you plan to do? Mom said you were looking for a ranch."

"Yeah. The old home place sold."

Zeb nodded. "Twice. The folks who bought it from your parents recently sold it. The deal only closed a couple months ago. You just missed it."

"I've just missed a lot of things," Dydd grinned.

"When you finish eating, we'll take a drive," Zeb suggested. Taking his coffee cup with him and picking a livestock magazine from a rack on the wall near the hallway, he disappeared toward the bathroom.

Shiloh dropped onto a seat across from Dydd and asked, "So how has your digestive system reacted to reintroducing food?"

With a wry smile, Dydd replied, "The grilled cheese sandwich and milkshake Sam fixed me the first night I was back tasted like heaven. But an hour later, my guts were twisted in a knot. I thought I was gonna die for sure!"

Shiloh grinned. "Too much dairy all at once, huh?"

"I guess so. I can't eat very much at one time. But I can eat almost constantly." He laughed. "Now that there's a lot more going in, there's a lot more going out. But I figured I'd put on weight faster. Dr. Ben said half the weight I've gained back is water. He said being drugged made me dehydrated."

Nodding, Shiloh changed the subject. "I knew Zeb for four years before he told me about you. Until then, I'd only seen him cry if his blood sugar was out of whack. And that's not very often. But he had trouble talking about you going missing."

194

A soft smile crossed Dydd's face. "Zeb's three years younger than me. We were always doing stuff together. Riding. Roping. We used to—" Suddenly, he burst out laughing. "We used to practice team roping on Uncle David's milk cow! He drove in one day when it was real windy, and we didn't hear him coming. Boy, did we catch hell!"

"What'd I miss?" Zeb said as he returned and went to the coffee machine for a refill.

"Your fourth pot of coffee," Shiloh ribbed gently.

"Well, I better catch up," Zeb returned jovially. "Dydd, let's go for a drive."

If Zeb or Shiloh noticed a change in Dydd's manner since his previous visit, neither mentioned it. But he was different. Quieter, more circumspect. Jumpy.

He did not tell them about the encounter at the Moffat home. Nor did he plan to tell anyone.

Ever.

Though unbeknownst to Dydd, Blake Moffat had already reported the incident.

At the end of Zeb's driveway, they turned north and took a lane that progressed from a narrow dirt road to a narrower, rutted two-track trail. Four miles north of Zeb's headquarters, they turned west onto a well-maintained county road.

On the south side of the road was a huge hay yard with thousands of big round bales in long, triangle stacks. On the north side was a rambling ranch house on the west side of the farmstead and a smaller, older home down a lane to the east. Zeb pulled into the drive and parked.

"Want a tour?" he asked.

Dydd scowled. "Is this the dog house where you stay if your wife is mad at you?"

195

Laughing, Zeb stepped out of the pickup. "Come on. I'll show you."

Using a key from the same ring that held his pickup key, Zeb unlocked the front door and led them inside the empty domicile. The first room was a small entryway with a coat closet and a built-in wardrobe along one wall. Beyond the ceramic tile flooring in the entryway, they entered an expansive carpeted living room.

"It looks better with furniture," Zeb commented. He continued through the house, pointing out the hall bathroom, the three huge bedrooms, and the master suite with its own oversized bathroom. Then they entered the combination kitchen and dining area with its adjacent laundry room. "Kitchen was just remodeled a few years ago. What do you think?"

Dydd nodded approvingly. "It's nice."

Zeb opened a door and ushered his cousin to the basement where they walked through a room with a ping pong table, a pool table, and a foosball table. Beyond that was what might have once been a sewing room but was now empty. As they returned to the stairway, Zeb chuckled. "She took everything except the gaming tables. Said she didn't want the foosball table, the ping pong table took up too much room, and the pool table was too heavy."

"It doesn't even look like a basement," Dydd observed. "The walls are all finished and painted up nice."

Zeb grinned. "It's better than concrete walls, isn't it?"

Somberly, Dydd agreed. Then he asked, "Why did the owner sell? Why didn't she rent the place out and keep making money off it?"

Zeb spoke slowly, picking his words carefully. "There was a murder near here. She didn't want to stay on. Didn't want the memories. She came to me and asked if I'd buy the place. Shot me a number that was ridiculously low. I wouldn't have felt right stealing it from her when she was vulnerable. So I advised her to consult an appraiser. She came back with a new number that was a little over ten percent higher than her original figure. Would you ever live in a place where someone had been killed?"

Dydd shrugged. "Ghosts don't bother me. I've known a lot of them."

Zeb snapped his fingers as he suddenly remembered something. "I've been meaning to ask you. When we did the Stations of the Cross, how did you know so many of the words to the readings? And the song?"

"Recitation," Dydd replied. "One of the things I did to pass time was to remember things. At first, I'd recall a scrap of this or that. Then more words would come to me over time. Eventually, I'd get most of it. Then by the time I'd recited it a million times, it was set in stone."

They ascended the stairs and returned to the empty kitchen. Zeb asked, "So, what do you think of the house?"

Again, Dydd nodded and, with a shrug, said, "It's a nice place."

"Some people think the living room is too big."

Dydd laughed aloud. "A gymnasium wouldn't seem too big to me."

Zeb made a wry face. "You sound like Shiloh's brother. He said we could rip out the carpet and use it for a basketball court. So what do you think? The place is yours if you want it. Big barn. Nice working corrals. Good roundpen. There's enough hay across the road to last you ten lifetimes. Plus there's two sections. Good fences. Mostly grass with four hundred-plus acres of bottom-fed hay ground."

Dydd stared out the big picture window. "I can't tell you how many times I dreamed myself to sleep picturing the silhouette of the Wind River Mountains, Zebekai. I'd stared at it so many hours from horseback or a tractor when I was a kid that I had it memorized. And, son-of-a-gun, it was still just like I remembered it when I got back. I figure no place else will ever feel like home."

Zeb mused, "I still miss the Wind River Range, myself. Lived in South Dakota for a few years. Then Scotland. Now here. But a pile of rocks doesn't make a home. Home is where you find the people you love."

Breaking into a big grin, Dydd said, "Well, if you find me a wife to keep house here, maybe it would look better."

Zeb laconically stated, "You must be getting enough to eat now if you're starting to think about women."

His brow furrowing, Dydd asked, "Did you live with Shiloh before you were married?"

Scowling, Zeb responded, "Hell, no. She would've decked me if I'd suggested it. Why would you ask me that?"

"I keep hearing that no one gets married anymore, and that everybody just lives in sin," Dydd replied.

Zeb scoffed. "Well, maybe some people do. But some of us still fear Hell. We better get going. Devon will be at the airport in less than an hour."

Blake Moffat had just stepped off the exercise bike when his phone rang. "Good evening, Constable Tran."

"Good morning, Colonel Moffat. I call to thank you for your advice. I got a fresh start on the old man's journals today. And I slept much better last night."

"What did you learn?" Moffat asked as he ruffled his sweaty hair with a towel.

"First, I found that the old man's wife, a schoolteacher, was killed by bombing in the American War in 1969 when the schoolhouse was destroyed. He wrote that the schoolhouse was used to house tanks, and the enemy learned of it. After her death, he built his backyard prison and began to pester his nephew—recall, please, the nephew was the second in command at Dong Phu prison camp— for a prisoner of his own. Over the next few years, the nephew continued to deny his request because, he explained, the captives were valuable to the government. They were officers. Men who knew how the American military system worked. Men who knew the locations of bases and troops. Knew how the planes and ships and tanks worked. Knew the hierarchy.

"But when the old man went to his nephew to repeat the request on April twelve of 1972, the nephew made him a deal. There was an enlisted Marine who was considered of little value. The nephew agreed for his uncle to have the captive for five days. That would have been from April nineteen to April twenty-four. The nephew was killed on the third day of the arrangement, April twenty-first."

Moffat absorbed the story, wondering how much of it, if any, he would ever relay to Dydd Weller. Considering the conclusion of their last meeting, he wasn't sure Weller could handle it.

Tran went on. "Another finding of interest was that the old man was terrified of his captive. He wrote in his journal that he took the unconscious man's clothes to prevent him using them to devise a means of escape. And he wrote that the American was two meters tall and weighed one hundred sixty kilogram. Would you like me to convert that to your units?"

"I have a pretty good idea," Moffat said. He made a quick calculation and came up with six-six and

199

something over three hundred fifty pounds. A giant, for sure.

Tran continued. "The old man lived in fear for the first couple of years. He was afraid the American would break out of the cell and kill him and his children while they slept at night. He was afraid his children would discover the man and tell someone. He was afraid someone might happen to pass through the jungle and find the man—and he worried even more because the man sang and talked in the afternoons. But after a few years, he rarely mentioned the man in his journal. Feeding him just became another chore that he did without much thought. Like feeding the dogs and the hogs and the chickens or sweeping the floor or washing the clothes. He was convinced at first that the American would soon die of starvation because he fed him what he himself ate. And because the American was so huge, he certainly could not survive long on those rations.

"One question that still remains for me," Tran posed, "is why the captor didn't serve in the military. I think perhaps it was because he was mentally incompetent. And now that I have solved this puzzle for you and for me, I will turn my findings over to my supervising officer. This will make its way through channels, as you say, and will land in the hands of my military counterparts. This means that I will no longer be your person of contact on this side of the Pacific."

"Have you located the brother?" Tran asked.

"Not yet, I'm afraid." Tran took a deep breath. Then he asked, "Please tell me, Colonel Moffat, how is Sergeant Weller doing?"

The vision of Dydd Weller lunging sideways from a chair in the Moffats' kitchen popped into the colonel's head. "I think time will tell, Constable. This is nothing any of us have ever dealt with. The best we can do is to be supportive. I've seen men who went through less who crashed and burned. And I've seen men who went through hell and recovered. Relatively speaking."

In his mind, Moffat pondered that the two easiest men to talk to in the Stondt-Weller group were Calvin and Dydd, arguably the two most affected by the war.

"I will pray for him," Tran said softly.

"You know, Constable Tran, when I first heard this story, I was certain the man couldn't really be Weller."

"Did you know of Weller before?"

Moffat explained about his trip to Vietnam to search for the remains of Weller and his platoon.

"Is it common that you come to this country, Colonel?" Constable Tran inquired.

"Twice a year for the last fourteen years," Moffat replied.

"Ah," Tran said. It was obvious he was smiling. "Then please do me the honor of dining in my home on your next trip, Colonel. If you can fit me into your schedule, that is."

Returning the smile, Moffat said, "Constable, how about seven weeks from tonight?"

The man who had called himself Jerome Bradley had not been seen in town since he had stood in front of the local judge and promised to return for his hearing scheduled for next month.

He had then walked casually from the courthouse and driven out of town.

No one had seen him since. And, after Bradley saw Dydd Weller on the front of *People Magazine*, no one in Wyoming would ever see him again.

Across town at a body and repair shop, Reginald Ellis swallowed his reaction and did not slam his big, arthritic old hand on the countertop when the mechanic told him that the frame of his old car was bent.

Bent.

Totaled.

"*Damn!*" Ellis muttered with feeling. "So where can I find a car that ain't gonna break me?"

The mechanic said, "I got a car in the back I could sell you. Belonged to an old lady. It ain't pretty, but it runs. I mean, when I say it ain't pretty, it ain't new or fancy. But it's clean. Runs good." He mentioned a price.

Ellis groaned.

An hour later, after talking the price down by a thousand, Reggie Ellis drove across town in a nondescript, gutless, four cylinder, ten-year-old beige car with an In Transit sign taped in the back window.

He had not yet given up the notion of this trip being cursed.

Especially when he realized he had forgotten to retrieve the replacement bottle of bourbon from under the seat of his old car.

It was too late to try to find Weller tonight, so Reg pulled in to a park near the edge of town and was in the process of figuring out how he would sleep in the backseat that seemed a foot shorter than the backseat in the old car and how he would keep from freezing to death.

He was not far into his ponderings when a black car pulled in behind him and two men emerged. The taller one who had been driving asked, "Sir, you mind telling me what you're doing in town?"

Reggie was about to tell him it was none of his business, but instead, he said, "I come to see somebody."

"And who would that be?"

Squinting, Reggie asked, "And why would you care?"

"I'm Donovan Garrison, head of the security team protecting Dydd Weller."

Reggie's scowl deepened. "Why does Corporal Weller need protecting? Are the fucking gooks over here trying to take him out? Hell, they could've done him in over there if they'd wanted to."

"Do you know Weller?"

"Hell, yes. I was his CO. I came to see him, to welcome him home," Reggie drawled.

"What's your name?"

Reggie told him.

Donovan nodded slowly. "Give me your cell number and tell me where you're staying. We'll check your story and if everything is above board, we'll arrange a meeting with the Gunny."

"I don't have a cell, and he ain't a gunny sergeant."

"He is now," Donovan answered simply. "Hotel?"

"I'm sleeping in the car."

Donovan glanced at Jason Rodriguez. Turning to Ellis, Jason said, "Sir, it's going to be below zero tonight. I wouldn't recommend sleeping in your vehicle."

"Well, last thing my wife told me on the way out the door was not to break us. She's got some damned vacation planned, and she don't want me to tip the credit card over the edge before her precious tickets get covered on it."

With a slight grin, Jason said, "We'll find you a place to sleep, sir. Follow us."

"Where we going?"

"We'll get you a hotel room," Donovan answered. "You have provisions?"

"Yeah. But I'm tired of peanut butter and crackers. Might find a restaurant and have a decent meal."

"No, you won't. You will stay clear of Sam's Restaurant. And it's the only place in town that's open right now. Better get used to peanut butter and crackers."

That night, for the first time in days, Reginald Ellis took a hot shower and slept on a real bed.

Monday, February 26, 2018

Seated at the breakfast table with Dydd were Bartholomew Stondt and his veterinary partner, Kyla Schleicher. Dydd asked her about being a woman veterinarian.

She explained that her female predecessors in the field had paved the way. In fact, though she had heard stories about women having difficulty with chauvinistic clients, it was rare nowadays.

"My cousin Zeb's wife is a vet, too," Dydd pointed out.

"Before that, she was a farrier," Kyla said knowingly. "She said when she first started shoeing, she had some trouble with men. Not many, but a few. She tells a great story about conveniently whacking a guy in the crotch with a rasp handle."

Barth's face screwed up. "She never told me that."

Kyla laughed. "She figured you'd get that look on your face like you have right now. Anyway, she said the guy had made a number of rude and insulting comments to her. So without even looking up, she shifted her toolbox and made sure the protruding rasp handle made him a temporary soprano."

"Shiloh?" Barth asked with surprise. "She's too nice to do that."

There was an evil edge to Kayla's chuckle. "Apparently not. But she said after she became a vet, the only chauvinism she ever encountered was from a guy who had been drinking a lot. He said he couldn't understand how a little thing like her could work with great big cattle. She reminded him that he uses a headgate to work cattle, same as she does. It's not like he goes out and grabs a tonner bull and tosses him on the ground."

205

"I treated one of Zeb's bulls that way," Barth said. "Without a chute, I mean. The bull was so gentle, we walked right up to him in the pasture and treated a wire cut. I figured we'd get killed. But the bull just stood there like he was enjoying the attention."

"Did you know our waitress is a rancher?" Dydd inquired after Kaitlyn breezed past their table.

"Kaitlyn Holland," Kyla responded. "Sure, I know her. She's a hell of a hand."

The profanity surprised Dydd, but he realized that if women could be veterinarians and ranchers, they could cuss along with the men. He vividly recalled the one time he had heard his mother swear. She had come in from the chicken house to find that the boys had engaged in a pillow fight that had knocked the cuckoo clock to the floor, scattering tiny pieces of it across the living room floor.

She had said, "*Damn it!* What's wrong with you boys? Were you raised in a barn?"

"I tried to hire her," Barth said quietly. "After her old man pulled the rug out from under her. But she had already taken the jobs at the library and here by the time I found out about it."

"Hey, Barth," Dydd asked suddenly, "who is the general manager of the Stondt Family Ranch these days? When I left, it was your grandpa."

"Luke Stondt. Before him, it was Aunt Ruthie."

Dydd's jaw dropped. "Ruthie? Really?"

Nodding slightly, Barth replied, "She was GM for over twenty years. Did a good job. She retired eight years ago. Now Luke runs the show."

Dydd nodded slowly. "Who does he belong to?"

"Steve's boy. Steve married Charlene Mueller. Did you know her?"

"Sure," Dydd responded.

Barth continued with the family lore. "Their first set of twins are now Sheriff Lon and Father Loren. Then they had another set of twins. Luke and Linn. Linn married a rancher from Kansas. Lives a hundred miles from Zeb. Do you remember Ronnie Schulmann?"

Again, Dydd nodded, though he was having trouble following.

"He had two little boys—must've been about five and seven—when he and his wife died in a wreck. In fact, at the same intersection where my sister-in-law got killed. Anyway, Steve and Charlene took in those two boys. They were five years or so younger than Luke and Linn. Grandpa said Steve and Charlene raised three sets of twins. But the third set was born two years apart."

"Where are those boys now?"

"They're in Kansas, too. Same county as Zeb. One of them works for Devon. He translates documents. German. French. English. Maybe Spanish. I don't know. I never could read and write German worth a damn. Just speak it. But he's the opposite."

Scowling, Dydd asked, "Why'd they all end up in Kansas?"

Shrugging, Barth said, "I don't know. It's a hundred fricking degrees there all summer. It'd melt the paint off the barn. I'll stick here where I can wear a shirt all summer without dying of heat stroke."

Shaking his head slowly, Dydd asked of no one in particular, "How am I ever going to catch up?"

After the vets returned to their practice, Dydd opened the laptop Cal had acquired for him. He stared at the black screen for several seconds. On her way by, Kaitlyn said hello.

Without taking his eyes from the blank screen, Dydd lifted his hand in a wave. She slapped the hand and kept moving.

Looking up, his face perplexed, Dydd saw Sam chuckling in the kitchen. Sam fingerspelled, "High five."

"High five?" Dydd repeated slowly.

Finished with the morning rush, Sam came around and pulled out the seat Kyla had vacated. He reached for Dydd's laptop and turned it on.

"Oh. That's how you do that," Dydd said as he watched. "Couldn't remember where the switch was."

After the machine booted up, Sam typed, "A high five is like a handshake. You raise your hand HIGH and slap another hand (FIVE fingers). Get it?"

"Got it," Dydd replied. "I thought Kaitlyn worked in the library during the day."

Sam typed, "Library isn't open Mondays."

After she had cleared her last table, Kaitlyn disappeared to the kitchen for a few minutes. Then she returned with a plate. "Mind if I sit here with you guys?"

Sam nodded and gestured to the empty chair.

"Thanks."

"So Kaitlyn, what kind of cattle did you run with your dad?" Dydd asked.

She held up a finger until she swallowed. After a sip of coffee, she replied, "Before I was born, it was all Herefords and a few Shorthorns. Then when I was in diapers, he got his first continental bull. Charolais. After that, he used Limousin, Saler, Maine-Anjou, Simmental, and a couple of Chianinas. By the time I got out of high school, his cows were averaging almost sixteen hundred pounds. So on my suggestion—and against his better judgment—he started using Black and Red Angus bulls on those big girls. Three years ago, we had two hundred sixty head of moderately framed, moderately milking twelve hundred pound cows. We were getting ninety-four percent conception rates breeding fourteen-month-old heifers at sixty-five percent mature weight and had lowered our average birth weights from ninety-six to seventy-five."

Dydd was impressed. This was the kind of conversation he'd had many times in the box, with his own brain supplying both sides of the conversation. But the speaker in the box had never been a woman.

She continued. "We also selected for low maintenance energy and switched calving from February to May, so the cows—who didn't enter third trimester of pregnancy until late winter—could manage on stockpiled grass. We didn't have to start offering supplemental hay until late January or early February most years. Unless, of course, there was heavy snow cover. Which, as you know, isn't common in this part of the world. Those smaller cows were producing more beef and grading better than the huge ones. And eating a lot less. Oh, wait! Mandatory coupling of beef grades came along after you went to Vietnam. In 1974, in response to trade embargoes, a bunch of cattle were held on feed for more than a hundred extra days. They were all grading prime on the rail, but they were yield grades four and five, so the USDA required mandatory grade coupling."

She stopped and looked at her listener. Then she broke into a repentant smile. "Maybe I better shut up and eat. You look like you're suffering from information overload."

Dydd shook his head. "No, no. I'm having a ball. You're the smartest person I ever met."

She gave a self-deprecating laugh. "If I were so smart, I wouldn't be working here. No offense, Sam. But the most important money you put away for retirement or a major life purchase is the money you save in your twenties. Well, I spent all my twenties working my butt off with the expectations of getting a ranch I didn't get. Shows how dumb I am."

Glancing at Sam, Dydd asked, "Could I hire her away from you for a couple days? There's a ranch I want to look at. And she might be handy to have along as a consultant."

Sam grimaced and signed, "You sure you don't want to stay here?"

Correctly interpreting the signing, Dydd broke into a broad smile. "You're the stayer, remember? I'm the goer."

Sam looked toward the front entrance as a trio of strangers entered. To Dydd, he signed, "Looks like you're about to be a goer."

Dydd turned and surveyed the uniformed officers. He stood as they approached.

"So you're the long, lost POW," a short blonde woman said as she offered her hand. "I'm Lieutenant Commander Stewart." She introduced the other two.

Both doctors.

Taking the outstretched hand, Dydd asked, "What can I do for you?"

"Plenty. You'll need to come with us to the clinic."

Dydd glanced over his shoulder toward the table where Jason Rodriguez had been sitting just a moment ago. But Jason was now standing right behind him. "It's legit, Gunny. They're here from San Diego to check you over. If you want, I can come along to keep you out of trouble."

Unaware of the conversation between Devon and the Secretary of the Navy, Dydd was convinced this visit was related to the panic attack.

He was not completely incorrect.

After some begging during the afternoon session, Dydd convinced the medical team to allow him to return to Sam's for the night. After all, he plead, he had survived sleeping there so far.

They agreed, as long as he reported to the medical facility by nine the next morning.

When Kevin walked into the house that evening, he tossed his tie on the lampshade, dropped his coat on the back of the recliner, and nodded toward Dydd. "Hey. Looks like the docs didn't kill you. What are you up to?"

"Trying to stay awake long enough to read this stuff on the computer." Looking up from the screen, Dydd added, "I sure miss paper books. But everything is right here. If I could just keep my eyes open."

As he finished speaking, it was clear Dydd was giving up the battle. He closed the computer and set it on the couch beside him.

"I'll be right back," Kevin said.

By the time Kevin returned five minutes later carrying a bottle and a glass, Dydd had moved the computer to the coffee table and was stretched out on the couch.

Dressed in baggy running shorts and a t-shirt, Kevin propped his bare feet next to Dydd's computer and poured himself a glass of whiskey. Without preamble, he said, "I was involved in a rescue. Two guys had been shot down right near the coast. The back seat guy ejected and landed a couple miles inland. He was never seen again. Still listed MIA." He tipped the glass toward Dydd. "Like you."

Kevin drained the glass and refilled it. "He was never seen again by any round-eyes, anyway. The front seater landed right on the beach. There was all kinds of Triple-A flying around, but we were keeping them pretty well harassed while the jolly green came in. You remember jolly greens?"

211

"Big green choppers," Dydd offered with a yawn.

"How about Triple-A?"

"Anti-aircraft artillery," Dydd supplied.

Kevin nodded and held out the bottle. "You want a blast?"

"No thanks," Dydd chuckled. "I drank once. I was thirteen, five inches shorter, and weighed twenty pounds more. I better wait until I have some meat on my bones."

"That's for sure," Kevin snorted. He took a long drink and again refilled the glass. "Two of the chopper crew got hit. No fatalities there. Then I got hit. Somewhere near the tail. I felt it, but the gauges didn't show anything wrong. At first. Then another pilot radioed and told me my ass end was on fire. So I banked and pulled out over the water. I still had good hydraulic pressure. For a little while. Figured I could make it back to a base in the south."

Again, he emptied the glass. And again, he refilled it. "Then all of a sudden the pressure started dropping like a rock. The whole plane started rocking and bucking. I figured it would break apart. So I ejected."

Emitting a sudden humorless laugh, he said, "They trained us for ejection. Trained us how to cut some lines on the chute—but sure as hell not the main lines. How to inflate the life raft. But they didn't prepare us for the fact that ejecting breaks your fucking neck."

He took another long drink. "I was knocked totally unconscious. When I woke up, I was dangling from the superstructure of a goddamned destroyer."

He looked over at Dydd, who was mesmerized by the tale. "As least it was an American destroyer."

Dydd grinned.

"How the hell do you hit a ship out in the middle of the whole goddamned big ocean?" Kevin wondered aloud. "That's where I woke up. Dangling from a con tower. Or whatever they called it. If I hadn't hit that goddamned ship, I'd have drowned. Nobody on the ship had any idea how to get me down. Guys down on the deck were yelling at me. I was half-conscious. They finally got a jolly green out there. He was trying to hover over a ship that was bouncing on the waves. Lowered a chair down to me. He was talking to me on my radio. I could hear him, but I was too goofy to get into the chair and ditch the chute. I couldn't move my left arm at all. My legs were numb, but they were still kind of responsive. Finally the chopper sent a PJ down the cable.

"The second worst pain of my life was when he strapped me into that chair. They reeled us both up. Then I found out what real pain was when they pulled off my helmet. Thought my head was gonna come off with it. *Jesus!* Thought they would rip my freaking head right off with it. I spent almost a year in a halo cast."

Kevin refilled the glass. Speech slurring, he tipped his head back against the chair. "You know, Calvin was stationed in Germany at the time. They wouldn't let two of us fly over there at the same time. So I figured after I had a chance to talk to him, he'd stay in Germany. Nope. The dumbass *volunteered* to fly in Nam.

"The only thing he learned from my story was that ejecting was a rough ride. So instead of punching out after he got all shot up, he tried to nurse his Phantom in with its hydraulic system blown to hell." Kevin let out a long sigh. "I saw pictures of the wreckage. Hell, the biggest piece left of it was him and his seat. There wasn't anything else there bigger than a breadbox. They probably cleaned off the landing strip with a whisk broom."

Dydd watched his cousin drain the glass one last time and wondered if there was anything left in the bottle.

213

Kevin looked directly at him and seemed to have trouble focusing. "But he remembered what I told him about the helmet. He told them to be careful with the helmet. Before they took it off, he could move his feet. Afterward. . . nothing."

From the kitchen end of the room appeared Jason Rodriguez. "Excuse me, guys," he broke in softly. "Sergeant Weller, are you up to company? Your old CO is here to see you."

"No," Kevin answered simply. "He's beat. Calvin said the Navy docs tested the shit out of him today. He's no good for company. Tell the major he can sit tight."

Wednesday, February 28, 2018

In his office at Stondt Industries, Calvin placed a call to Lieutenant Colonel Moffat. "Good morning, Blake. How are you?"

"Fine. Is everything okay there?" Moffat asked with concern.

"We've had a few developments I thought you might like to be apprised of. I'm handing the phone to Donovan Garrison, head of security."

Donovan took the phone and introduced himself.

"Pleasure to be talking to you," Moffat returned. "Your reputation precedes you, and it's not every day I get to talk to a bona fide hero."

"Thank you, sir," Donovan said. Then, cutting right to the chase, he began, "First, the son of Sergeant Weller's captor landed in Seattle early this morning. My sources tell me he fled Vietnam despite the desire of authorities there to interview him."

"Okay," Moffat responded.

"We will keep an eye out for him or any potential associates of his. Secondly," Donovan continued, "a man who called himself Jerome Bradley had the diner under surveillance. Turns out that's not his real name. His ID said Marcus Anderson. He's a part-time free-lance photographer, part-time drug dealer, part-time pimp, and full-time scumbag. He was charged with a couple misdemeanors and, so far as we know, has skipped town.

"The third person of interest is a Reginald Ellis. He used to be—"

"Reggie Ellis is there? In Wyoming?" Moffat broke in.

"Yes, sir. Is there anything I should know about him?"

Moffat was slow to answer. "No. Uh, well. . . no. Not at this time. Just keep an eye on him."

"We intend to. He showed up late Sunday, sir. We intercepted him and told him to stay away from Sam's until we checked him out. We put him in a motel where he's been guzzling cheap booze ever since. Monday night after the gunny underwent debriefing and medical testing all day, he was too wiped out to talk to Ellis. And last night, the docs kept Dydd in the hospital. He was weak, and they were afraid he might fall and break a bone. Maybe get hypothermic waiting for an ambulance. It's pretty cold here."

"Roger that," Moffat agreed. "A little chilly here in Chicago, too. Thanks for the update, Master Sergeant. Is there anything else for me?"

"No, sir. That's all for now." He hung up the phone and peered at Calvin across the desk.

"What do you think?" Calvin asked, correctly reading in Donovan's expression that the security expert was thinking hard about something.

Pursing his lips, Donovan said, "I wish I knew what Moffat was thinking. He's not telling me something about Ellis. What do you know about him?"

"Not a thing," Calvin admitted.

Wrapped in a blanket, Dydd was sitting cross-legged on the hospital bed when a man with curly, shoulder-length blond hair and a thick beard stopped in the hallway just outside the door.

"Good morning, Sergeant," he said. Muscular and fit, wearing civilian clothes, he had to tip his head to duck through the doorway. "Mind if I come in for a minute?"

"No problem," Dydd responded expectantly.

"How are you doing?"

Dydd shrugged. "I thought I was doing pretty well until all these doctors got a hold of me. But I guess I don't know much."

"Most people don't know their capabilities," the man stated. "They either don't have the confidence to perform to their potential, or they overestimate their abilities and get themselves into trouble."

"I'm happy to visit with you," Dydd said, "but I'll just warn you that somebody will probably be in here pretty soon to haul me off for some kind of test."

"Actually, you're with me for the morning. My name is John." He leaned down and offered a giant hand.

Taking the hand, Dydd asked, "And what kind of doctor are you?"

"I'm not a doctor. I train military personnel in a program known as SERE. That stands for Survival, Evasion, Resistance, and Escape. The program was started by a former POW from your era.

"I've interviewed a thousand former captives, POWs, and detainees. I learn something from every one of them, and every one of them has a unique story. I'm hoping to get ideas from your story to improve the training and help captives in the future."

"Is that all we're going to do?" Dydd asked. "Just talk?"

John nodded.

Dydd tossed off the blanket and suggested, "How about we walk while we talk, then? Just as soon as I find my clothes."

With a gentle smile, John said, "Sure."

Dydd opened a couple of cabinet doors before he found the USMC sweats. While he dressed, John said, "Gunny, you impress me."

Scowling, Dydd looked up from tying his running shoes.

217

John went on. "You did exactly what you would have learned to do if you had been through SERE training. You learned to have a routine. To do the same thing every day."

"Every day," Dydd agreed.

"Every day. And you stuck with it. When a captive stops caring enough to keep to the schedule, they lose heart. They lose faith. They lose touch. I'm also impressed that you know four languages."

"How do you know all this about me?" Dydd inquired as he led the way out into the hallway. "By the way, there's an indoor track down this hall. It's the best place to walk without running into somebody."

Falling into step beside the smaller man, John said, "I've read Moffat's report."

Dydd sighed. "So you know I lost it at his house."

John's reply was not immediate. Several strides later, he said, "If that's the worst it gets, you're blessed. So what are your plans, Sergeant? Do you know what you will do in the future?"

"In the short term, I'd like to find some jeans that fit. In the long term, I'd like to find a ranch."

"Sounds like you've given it some thought," John said.

"For a long, long time," Dydd answered. "Do you know who else is working me over today?"

"Sorry, no."

"So who qualifies to take your training course?" Dydd asked.

Feeling like the interviewee instead of the interviewer, John smiled slightly as he answered. "We train anyone who might be at increased risk for capture. Pilots, flight crews, combat rescuers."

"Are you military or civilian?" Dydd probed.

"I'm a master sergeant in the Army." He grinned down at Dydd. "And I'm supposed to be asking *you* questions."

Dydd returned the smile. "Mom always said you can learn more with your ears than with your mouth. For a long time, I had to do all the talking."

"Roger that. I've also read a report from your former CO. He said you were pretty smart."

"Major Ellis?" Dydd asked.

John held open the door that led to the walking track. "Said you were always reading and talking about books, encyclopedias, articles in science magazines."

"How would he remember that after all this time?" Dydd mused.

"The report I saw was made in 1974. You are a fast walker," John observed. Then he added, "For a little guy."

Dydd laughed. "How tall are you?"

"Six foot eight. And most of it legs. So I don't often compliment short guys for walking fast."

Letting out a long breath, Dydd avowed, "It's nice to be able to walk more than a couple steps without hitting a concrete wall. So how do you train guys for survival and all that?"

"Well, let's just say that most of the students who've seen me in SERE wouldn't invite me over to their house for a beer. Not unless they thought they could poison me and dispose of my big, gangly body without getting caught."

Dydd scowled at him.

John clarified, "We have to make it real. We have to make it rough."

Nodding knowingly, Dydd mused, "Dong Phu. It was rough."

***

Three hours later, Dydd was perched on the edge of the bed eating a meal someone had brought over from Sam's. Wearing a scowl, Calvin entered and took in the room in a glance. "Are they done with you?" he asked without preamble.

Dydd finished chewing and swallowed. "I don't know."

"How are you feeling?"

"I'm recovered from yesterday. I guess. I was doing okay until they took a bone sample. That hurt like hell. And I bled more than they expected."

Cal let out a long breath. "You want to go see Zeb?"

Dydd shrugged. "Sure. If I'm allowed to go."

With a snort, Cal asked, "What are they gonna do? Bust you back to lance corporal? Get your gear. We're gonna blow this popsicle joint."

Hesitantly, Dydd offered, "I think there's some other doctors who need me this afternoon."

Breaking into a broad grin, Calvin revealed, "Actually, they need you for two more days. But they don't have the equipment they need here in Wyoming, so we're gonna fly you out to San Diego next week. You're off the hook for a couple days. They don't want to see you again until you're sixty-two. Don't forget your phone."

"Got it," Dydd tapped his pocket. Doing so reminded him to call Kaitlyn. She had agreed to accompany him to Kansas to render an opinion on the ranch Zeb wanted to sell him.

The SERE trainer who had called himself John was sitting hunched over his cell phone in the security wing of the airport terminal when he sensed more than heard someone approach behind him. He turned and asked, "Yes?"

Extending his hand, Donovan Garrison quietly introduced himself and briefly outlined his operation. Then with a smile he added, "And at one point in my life I wanted nothing more than to castrate you and feed you your nuts."

John grinned in reply. "You're not alone."

Donovan chuckled. "It was good training. There's not a day that goes by that I don't recall something I learned in SERE."

"Glad to hear it," John stated. He knew Donovan had something on his mind. He was patient.

Donovan cleared his throat and looked around to be sure they were alone. "Do you know the name Reginald Ellis? Former Marine?"

John's face revealed nothing. "Why do you ask?"

"Because he's here in town. Says he wants to see the gunny and welcome him home. I talked to Moffat earlier today. He wouldn't say much, but I got the idea he wasn't necessarily in favor of the idea."

John looked contemplative. "Do you have kids?"

Donovan replied, "Three."

"Married or divorced?"

"Married. Why?"

"I know a former operator, a guy like you, who got divorced. Lost custody of his kids. No visitation, even. He'd had some issues with PTSD. Alcohol. Domestic abuse. But he got himself cleaned up. Dried out. Went through a lot of counseling. And after a long court fight, he got supervised custody. That means that when it was his weekend, he had to have a state employee hanging out with him and his kids."

Donovan's face was still for half a minute. "Are you saying that Ellis should only have supervised visitation with his former corporal?"

John shrugged and replied, "I have no idea what you're talking about. I've never heard of Major Reginald Ellis. I've never been to Wyoming. And I've never met you."

Donovan shook his head. Wryly, he said, "Spooks."

Thirty minutes after Dydd and Calvin left the hospital, Kevin and Dydd were secured in the cockpit of the Stondt Industries Cessna Citation with Kaitlyn buckled in the main cabin.

As they climbed out of the broad valley, Dydd glanced at his new watch and chuckled. "You know, the last time I bought a watch, I was in Saigon. It had glow-in-the-dark hands. I thought it was pretty up-town. When I got captured, it was the thing I missed most. Even more than my clothes and boots. But now I have a watch that reads signals from space, measures my blood pressure, and alerts me if there's a pretty girl nearby. I like this one a lot better."

Kevin grunted and adjusted something on the control panel.

"Is it okay if I go back and talk to Kaitlyn?" Dydd asked.

"You can do whatever you want with Kaitlyn. As long as I get to watch."

Dydd shook his head and unfastened his seat belt.

Kaitlyn looked up when he approached. "I need to thank you. I went to see my folks a couple days ago. You know, I hadn't noticed how old they were. But I think you were right—Dad was just tired. Long story short, we're on good terms now."

"That's great news," Dydd relayed.

She shrugged. "Still doesn't mean I have a ranch."

"Nope. But at least you have parents," he offered.

Their chauffeur from the Tyler City, Kansas, airport to the ranch was Shiloh's oldest son Foster. He explained that the rest of the family was taking catalog photographs for the spring bull sale that would be held next month. The job entailed catching each nearly two-year-old bull in the headgate, brushing off the larger chunks of debris, then turning him into a pen and trying to get a photo of him in a flattering position.

Bulls, Foster stated dryly, do not always feel like standing still, let alone standing still in a flattering position.

They arrived to find Shiloh brushing bulls in the chute. She wore goggles and several pounds of dried manure and bull hair. "Happy birthday in a few days, Dydd!"

He held both palms toward her and, with a grin, said, "Thank you, but please don't hug me until you have had time to shed all that extra hair."

Two kids maneuvered the bulls through a series of pens until they were ready for the photo pen where Zeb stood with a long stick, alternately enticing the bull to move a step or two, giving advice to the teenaged photographer, or opening and closing gates to let out the last bull and let in the next.

Dydd made quick introductions at the chute and left Kaitlyn there to help Shiloh. Before he sauntered toward the photo pen, he said, "At least you'll have the upwind side of the chute, Kaitlyn."

Dydd gave a high five to the kids as he passed. Then he turned and looked back the way he had come.

"If you're looking for Foster, don't bother," Willa said with saccharin sweetness. "He's gone back in the house to play on the computer. He never helps with cattle work. He's afraid he'll get dirty."

With a sideways grin, Dydd said, "Maybe he'll have a restaurant someday."

"He wants to be a lawyer."

"I hope he gets his wish," Dydd said with meaning.

Willa laughed. "Actually, he's in the house putting these photos in the new catalog. Molly takes the photos out here and sends them in there to him. By the time we finish up out here, the catalog will be finished inside. Then we hit a button and send it to the printers."

"Amazing." Dydd continued strolling down the alleyway until he was standing on the outside of the photo pen. To Zeb, he called, "I thought I was here to look at a ranch."

Zeb's moustache twitched with a grin, but he said nothing. The bull was standing perfectly, and if he moved or spoke, it might spook. When the girl carrying the camera nodded, Zeb opened the gate. Then he called out, "What took you so long? You left Wyoming two hours ago!"

Dydd chuckled and leaned on the fence. "How long does it take to drive that far?"

"Ten hours, depending on your bladder," Zeb replied.

"And on how many Thermoses full of coffee you have with you," said the photographer dryly. "It takes two tanks of diesel and twelve pots of coffee to get Dad from here to Grandma Marion's house in Wyoming."

By six o'clock, the fence shadows lined the ground across the whole pen. Zeb said, "We're done for today. If we took pictures now, people would think we were selling zebras, not bulls."

To utilize the last of the light, they sent the kids inside to fix supper while the adults drove four miles north to the ranch Zeb had shown Dydd earlier.

They started their tour in the barn. At the far end of the huge enclosure was a roundpen. "That'll be handy when it's blowing a gale outdoors," Zeb pointed out. "Or when it's muddy or snowy."

"Or hot," Kaitlyn pointed out. "Dr. Stondt says it's outrageously hot here in the summer."

To their right were three box stalls. Crossing the floor, Kaitlyn glanced inside them in the waning light. "Wow. These are really nice stalls. I wouldn't usually put a horse in a stall unless it needed medical treatment. Or maybe if I was gonna need it early the next morning. But these are sure fancy."

"Sometimes we put the dog in a stall if he's 'helping' too much with cattle work," Shiloh offered.

"No!" Dydd snapped. As he stared at the stall gates, he began absently backing through the dust toward the barn door. "I wouldn't lock an animal in a box under *any* circumstances."

In an easy tone to abate the sudden tension, Zeb said, "They make good tack rooms and feed rooms. Don't have to worry about a critter breaking in to chew on your saddle or tear open feed sacks."

Dydd had backed nearly to the entrance. Zeb put a hand on his back and gently turned him, leading the way outside. "Let's have a look at the machine shed. There isn't much in there right now. I hauled the tools and equipment down to our place to prevent it walking away."

During the short walk across the packed gravel, Kaitlyn stayed slightly behind Dydd, watching him warily.

Thursday March 1, 2018

Twelve hours later, Zeb parked on the tarmac at the airport and pushed open the door but remained in the seat. "Looks like we have some time to kill. So what do you think, Cousin?"

Dydd grinned. "I think I'd sure like it here if you could move the Wind River Mountains a little closer."

Pursing his lips so that the massive moustache stuck out comically, Zeb said, "It's not mountains that make a home. It's family. If you need some kids around, you can borrow ours anytime. Cheap."

Shiloh chuckled. "You can pay their college tuition, too."

Dydd stared across the runway and the barren plains beyond. Then he lowered the window and, sticking his head through it, stared straight up into the sky and emoted, "God! That feels good."

Kaitlyn had barely spoken since Dydd had backed away from the box stalls in the barn the previous evening. Now her brow wrinkled as she stared at him.

"What feels good, Dydd?" Shiloh inquired.

"The sun." Still peering, eyes closed, toward the warm sunshine, he asked, "Zeb, is there a good implement dealership nearby?"

"Custer. Forty miles. Good parts desk. Helpful fellas in the shop."

"How about furniture stores?"

Shiloh answered that query. "A couple of them. With free delivery."

Sucking in a huge breath, Dydd leaned back inside the pickup and turned to face Kaitlyn, who was seated behind Zeb. "Are you available full time? I'm going to need help."

Her face seemed frozen for several seconds. Then she replied, "Sorry. No."

"Okay," Dydd mused, "You know anybody looking for work, Zeb?"

"You can always check at the vocational schools or the university ag department in Custer."

"I might have a couple leads for you," Shiloh offered. "I know a guy who works for his uncle. He might be available at least part time."

Turning back toward the window, Dydd squinted toward the north. "Here they come. Right on time."

Zeb snorted. "Half hour late."

"What's time to a pig?" Dydd grinned, reciting the punchline to an old joke they had shared as boys.

Pushing open his door, Zeb stepped out onto the pavement. "I have to go check the tires on the north side of the hangar."

Dydd followed him. "I didn't know there was an outhouse on the north side of the hangar."

"There is now," Zeb replied. When they were out of earshot from the pickup, he asked, "What made you change your mind? Don't get me wrong, I'm thrilled you'll be nearby. But I thought your umbilicus to the Wind River Range wouldn't stretch that far."

Dydd let out a deep breath. "It's all so confusing."

Scowling, Zeb asked, "What is?"

"All the people. Did you know Ronnie Schulmann got married? And that he and his wife died?"

Zeb nodded as he pulled up the zipper tab on his jeans.

"Well, I didn't. And I didn't know that Steve's twins became a priest and a sheriff. And I didn't know that Old Dutch and Leona had a change-of-life baby. It's like I'm trying to catch up on forty-six years of reruns and everybody else has seen them."

227

"What's up with Kaitlyn?" Zeb inquired. "I figured she'd take your job."

There was no hesitation in Dydd's answer. He was very matter-of-fact when he replied, "Lots of people figure I'm crazy. She's one of them. Maybe I am crazy. I've had a couple bad moments. Like last night in the barn. I don't know why I backed away from that stall. I mean, I know why I thought what I thought and said what I said, but I don't know why I backed up like that. It was like somebody was pushing me."

Dydd lowered his voice and added reluctantly, "I had a panic attack last week. I don't know what's going on with that. The Navy doctors tell me I have PTSD. I'd never heard of it until this week."

"They used to call it shell shock or battle fatigue."

"I just wish people could back off a little. You know what I mean?"

With a nod, Zeb said, "I know exactly what you mean. After we open presents and eat Christmas dinner, I have to go outside to do chores. Even if I don't have any chores. I get edgy after a while with all the folks and commotion."

Dydd said softly, "Same here. When I was a kid, I loved it when we had company. But I always bugged out after a couple hours. I know it sounds dumb when I spent all those years by myself. But I need a little solitude."

"You've been surrounded by people since you got back," Zeb agreed. "But I promise you one thing. There's plenty of time and space for thinking here in Kansas."

Having finished the newest bottle of bourbon the night before along with a hamburger one of the security guys had delivered from Sam's, Reggie Ellis woke with a pounding headache. The motel served breakfast, but nothing on the buffet looked enticing.

So Reggie sat in the lobby that was decorated with stuffed heads of large game animals, antlers, snowshoes, and other hunting paraphernalia. He had half a cup of coffee with a double shot of bourbon as a chaser.

He watched people come and go and wondered when he would be allowed to see Weller, and while he stared at a series of framed prints of various hunting rifles, he started drifting back into the history of his life.

Vaguely, he wondered if his memories were reshaped at all by the booze.

No. He was clear as a bell. Perfectly lucid.

But those rifle photos got him thinking about the old days.

And that got him thinking about the last conversation he'd had with Weller.

He went over it again and again.

Of course he hadn't known Weller was underage. The kid had talked like a college professor. Read everything he could get his hands on. Argued like a damned lawyer.

Reggie had had no idea the kid was sixteen. No way to know. Not until the Marine Corps told him. And that was after the platoon was lost.

Wasn't it?

He heard the conversation again. And again.

It began to change. The words morphed from the version he had remembered all these years—the version he had reported to those MIA investigators, the version he had planted in his subconscious.

How had he reported the brother's death? Had he sent for Weller? Or had he hunted him down in camp? Where had they talked?

Reg couldn't remember. It had been so long ago.

229

So long ago.

The kid was too skinny to be a man.

He was too eager.

Too naïve.

His headache was getting worse. His brow furrowed with concentration.

Had the kid told him he was underage?

Jesus!

Former Major Reginald Ellis's heart began to pound.

And then he remembered it. The conversation where the scared little boy confessed to being only sixteen years old. Right after he'd been informed of the death of his older brother.

How had Reggie managed to block that out all these years?

Who else knew about that conversation?

No one could know about it. No one but Weller himself. Would anyone believe Weller now, after all he'd been through?

The lines in Reg's forehead grew deeper as he ruminated. No. No one would believe him.

Wait.

No one would believe him? Or no one would believe Weller?

Reg pulled the bottle from the bottom of his pant leg under the table. With a quick glance to be sure no one could see him, he refilled his coffee cup.

What if they *did* believe Weller? What would happen to Reggie Ellis? Would he be charged? Could they throw him in the brig? Take away his pension?

Suddenly, Reggie Ellis felt sick.

Friday, March 2, 2018

Donovan Garrison entered the residence door and made his way through the nearly deserted kitchen, bidding a good afternoon to Sam as he strode through. In the dining room, he dropped onto a chair at the table where Jason Rodriguez and Jane Bellairs were playing cards.

"Strip poker? Deal me in," he said. "Seen anything of Ellis today?"

"Nope," Jason said as he dropped an ace on the pile.

Jane groaned. "Jeez. Not again."

Grinning, Jason played an eight and said, "Clubs. And I got your message about the old man's son being picked up in San Fran."

"They'll question him at the Naval Base in San Diego and figure out who has jurisdiction. They'll eventually ship him back to Vietnam once their government and ours agree on how to go about it." Suddenly, Donovan looked around. "Hey, where is the gunny?"

"He's in the house," Jason replied with a grin as he watched Jane draw several cards.

"No, he's not," Donovan said, getting to his feet. "I just came through there."

Jason dropped the cards on the table and followed the other two through the kitchen.

A look of concern washed over Sam's face as Donovan and Jane trotted past him.

Jason stopped and asked, "You know where Dydd is?"

Sam jabbed a finger toward the residence and fell into step beside him.

A quick search yielded nothing indoors.

"Any ideas where he might go?" Donovan asked Sam.

Sam shook his head in the negative.

Donovan bounded off the back step and jogged across the parking area and into the sparse pine timber while Jason darted left. Jane took the right.

Sam yelled, "Hey!" His voice cracked. He tried again and smacked his forehead with his palm when the sound came out reminiscent of a dog howling.

A minute later, Donovan turned toward the back door. With a wave, he said, "Jason found him. He just went out for a walk."

Sam sighed and dropped his head to his chest.

"I'll tell him he needs to let one of us know when he goes off on a hike," Donovan grimaced.

Trotting up, Jane countered, "He's an adult. As far as he knows, we're here to keep the maggots off him. Not to keep him from being a free man."

Unconvinced, Donovan snapped, "Ellis is a maggot. A maggot with military training and with maybe a loose screw." Into his mic, he asked, "Lieutenant, where are you?"

Sam shot an inquisitive look at Donovan while the latter listened.

Aloud, the team leader assured Sam, "They're coming."

Forty meters behind the house, out of sight from the back porch, Jason crouched on a boulder. "You doing okay, Gunny?"

"Yeah," Dydd replied.

"I'm just curious why you're sitting on the edge of a cliff."

Turning to engage him, Dydd said, "I'm not going to jump, if that's what you're worried about. I just needed some time. You know? Sounds dumb because all I had for a long time was time."

"I get it," Jason assured him. "Like I said, I'm a hunter. Fisherman. An Army helo pilot once told me the dumbest thing he ever did was teach his wife to hunt deer because before he did, hunting was the only time he ever got to be alone. I get it, Gunny."

Jason leaned forward and tried to determine how far down Dydd would fall if he went over the edge. Impossible to see from his vantage. "So what are you thinking about?"

"Wondering what kind of cattle to stock my range with. Zeb raises blood stock. Purebred stuff. Lots of paperwork and hassles. I'm thinking three-way cross. I can buy my bulls from him, but I want crossbred cows."

Jason relaxed slightly. "Is that ranch gal going to work for you. Kaitlyn. Is that her name?"

"That's her name. And no. She thinks I'm going to flip my lid. Or maybe she just doesn't want to leave Wyoming. I don't know which."

"I'm a little surprised you want to leave Wyoming when you just got back," Jason prompted.

Dydd didn't answer for a time. Finally, he said, "I think a transplant would do better in fresh soil."

With a snort, Jason, who had been working his way closer to Dydd's position, said, "That sounds like something my college lit professor would say. Then I'm supposed to figure out what the hell he meant."

Dydd chortled.

Still edging nearer the cliff's edge, Jason asked, "How far down is it from there, Gunny?"

Dydd leaned forward and looked down between his feet. "About four feet."

Letting out a giant sigh of relief, Jason asked, "You mind if I sit there with you?"

"Nope. It's a big rock. Plenty of room. You can trespass along with me."

"We're not trespassing. This is Sam's rock."

Looking around, Dydd commented, "He needs to get a few goats to browse this scrub."

"What did you think about your old CO?" Jason asked.

"Major Ellis?" Dydd asked. "He was big. Red hair. Gruff. I don't think he liked me much."

"Why do you say that?"

With a shrug, Dydd replied, "I guess he was just doing his job. Trying to keep us alive and doing our jobs." They stared out across miles of open country. After a time, Dydd added, "I know he lied to Colonel Moffat."

"How so?"

"Told him I never said I was underage. I did. When Major Ellis told me Kiel was dead, I admitted I had lied about my age."

"What did he say?" Jason probed.

"Exact quote? He said, 'Pack your shit, you little bastard, and get on the next fucking flight to Saigon. There'll be an investigation, and I hope they nail your scrawny ass to the wall.' But he must not have told my sergeant that because Sargeant Dietermann came to get me for patrol later. That's the night he died, and I got captured."

Sunday, March 4, 2018

Sam baked all day Saturday and part of Sunday morning. By the time Dydd returned from church—driving his brand new pickup, wearing his brand new glasses, dressed in his brand new suit coat over a button-down shirt and jeans, and carrying his brand new driver's license along with the brand new credit cards in his brand new wallet—the restaurant was filling with people. This time, it was not just the general rabble looking for a free meal, but a group assembled by special invitation from Sam. For the first time in many years, the restaurant was closed to the public.

By the end of the party, which started winding down in mid-afternoon, Dydd had consumed his share—and more—of the many cakes and pies and confections. He found Sam in an unusual position—sitting in the dining room instead of laboring in the kitchen. "I can't believe you made me a birthday cake for every birthday I've missed!"

Sam beamed a big smile and picked up a plate sporting a slice of three-layer fudge cake. With a flourish, he wafted it before Dydd.

Putting a hand on his belly, Dydd declined. "I'm going to explode inside if I even look at that. But give me five minutes. Then I can eat it."

Seated beside Sam, Devon asked, "Have you seen your old CO yet?"

Dydd scowled. "My old CO?"

"Ellis," Devon answered.

Still scowling, Devon shrugged. "Not since April 1972. Why?"

Devon nodded across the room to where Donovan Garrison stood scanning the crowd. Donovan approached the table on cat-like feet. "Sir?"

"Where is Major Ellis?"

"Haven't seen him today," Garrison replied.

Devon looked contemplative. "Did he check out of the motel?"

"No, sir. He was there this morning." Donovan stepped away from the table and began checking with his operators.

Jason Rodriguez had only come on duty an hour earlier. He had not seen Ellis since yesterday. Jane Bellairs had gone home after Jason reported in. She had been at the restaurant for the duration of her shift.

Paul Richards was keeping an eye on Ellis. Earlier in the day, he had watched Ellis hand his credit card to the owner of one of the local gun shops to pay for a new hunting rifle with an exquisite scope.

"What is he planning to hunt?" Donovan probed rhetorically. "Where is he now?"

Via cell phone, Paul replied, "Sleeping it off. He came back to the hotel after his shopping spree."

"Are you the only one there?" Donovan inquired.

"Yeah. Sitting across the street in the grocery store parking lot."

With a glance out the window toward the bluff where the photographer had previously perched, Donovan said, "He could slip out the back door and get to Sam's on foot without you spotting him."

"He could," Paul admitted, though given his previous observations of Ellis, he was unconvinced. "You want me to go find him?"

"Yeah. Report back to me."

In under two minutes, Paul breathlessly announced, "He's gone. I'm on my way to the restaurant."

Donovan slipped out the little-used door on the side of the residence end of the building, a door obscured by a rambling shrub.

"Paul, report."

There was no reply.

As per protocol, Donovan sent a preset text to Jane ordering her to return to the field of operation. At the same time, he called into his mic, "Jason, report."

Jason Rodriguez' voice was low when he replied, "I'm on the west side of the restaurant, detecting movement on the bluff, sector seventeen, near where the photographer was stationed."

"Can you cross the highway and get to the foot of the bluff unseen?"

Jason replied, "No chance."

"Get your rifle," Donovan ordered.

"Roger."

"Paul, report," Donovan repeated. Still, there was no answer. But as he scanned the bluff opposite, Donovan's attention was aroused by two different movements.

The first was a glimpse of the dull red of the shirt he had seen Ellis wearing previously. It was visible for only a fraction of a second as Ellis ducked behind a boulder.

The second was a hand movement. Paul Richards had managed to work his way to within a few meters of Ellis. Too close to report verbally without giving away his position.

Donovan heard the piano inside the restaurant. It wasn't ragtime, but it seemed familiar. It took him a moment to place the tune.

Then he recognized it.

Amazing Grace.

He leaned back and glanced through the window to determine that it was Sergeant Weller at the keys. As long as he stayed where he was, he would be out of range of a potential shooter.

But Donovan was uncertain why Ellis, who had waited patiently for days, would suddenly begin stalking Weller.

Donovan edged toward the front of the building and eased his head forward in order to see around the corner of the native stone wall.

Immediately, he saw a flash from the cliff, quickly followed by the sound of broken glass tinkling to the floor inside.

Then he heard the report of the shots.

Then all hell broke loose.

The first shot shattered both the inner and outer panes of the big picture window near the restaurant's main entrance. The bullet struck Sam Weller's upper right arm, causing him to lose his grip on the wineglass. Merlot and blood splattered on the floor, the piano, and the wall.

The wineglass itself became so many shards added to those of the broken window.

With amazing quickness, Dydd dove and tackled his brother, knocking Sam to the floor.

Then they were both scrambling behind the cash register counter.

From the corner of the building outside, they heard five rapid shots from a rifle. Across the draw came several more blasts, also from a rifle but one with a decidedly different report.

Then all was quiet.

A few seconds later, Paul Richards' voice soared across the valley, "All clear!"

Using his bony, talon-like hands, Dydd applied pressure to the entry and exit wounds on Sam's upper arm. "It's just a flesh wound. Might get you a few nurses, but it won't get you a purple heart."

With a rush, Donovan was suddenly beside them. "Sit rep?"

"Situation report, sir," Dydd snapped in his best Marine lingo. "One casualty. Flesh wound, upper arm. He'll live."

Don squatted beside Sam and assessed the injury at a glance. Then he scowled at Dydd. "And you, Gunny?"

"Right as rain. Thanks," Dydd replied.

"You're bleeding," Paul pointed to Dydd's wrist.

With barely a glance at the inconsequential wound, Dydd shrugged and replied, "I must've cut myself on the glass when we scooted back here behind the counter. It's nothing. Who fired the shot?"

Glancing out the broken window, Donovan saw Paul and Jason hovering over the body across the road on the bluff. It was in the same location where the photographer had perched. "What's the status on the shooter?"

The reply that came through Donovan's ear piece was loud enough for Dydd and Sam to make out. "Dead. It's Ellis."

Dydd's face went quiet.

"Your former CO," Donovan said with feeling. When his words seemed to make no impact on Dydd, he added, "The one who didn't send you back home when he found out you were sixteen years old. The one who let you go back out there and get captured. The one who, as far as I'm concerned, was responsible for letting you rot in that goddamned jungle cell."

His face growing cold, Donovan peered back out the window. Into his mic, he said, "Kill the bastard again."

Across the narrow valley came the echoes of two more lonely shots.

Tuesday, October 9, 2018

The phone rang four times before it was answered. Then a voice said, "Hang on, let me get out of the wind." After thirty seconds of wind interference on the line, Dydd Weller said, "Okay, I'm here now. Hello?"

"Hey, *Mister* Weller. I just came across a notice that says you are now officially separated from the United States Marine Corps."

Dydd laughed. "You're a little behind, Colonel Moffat. I got officially separated three months ago."

"How's it going out there in the Wild West?" Moffat probed.

"Great. We weaned calves last weekend. Got a little rain shower two weeks ago to wet the dust. Good weather since then. Raised one hell of a hay crop. I never dreamed I could get that kind of tonnage in a single cutting. How about you? What's up in Chicago?"

"It's windy, like they say," Blake replied.

Dydd laughed. "Fifty-four miles an hour here yesterday. Cry me a river! I don't care if they do call it the Windy City, you got nothing on the High Plains when it comes to wind. What else is going on?"

Blake hesitated. "Well, I received an invitation that I was asked to extend to you. I didn't commit to anything. I wanted to talk to you first."

"What kind of invitation?"

Speaking carefully, Blake asked, "Have you ever heard of Andersonville?"

After a long breath during which he searched his memory, Dydd asked, "Wasn't that a Confederate prison camp during the Civil War? In Virginia, I think?"

"Georgia. Andersonville is now a National Park. It is also the National POW Museum. They tell the story of POWs from the Revolutionary War to the present."

Moffat was silent for a long time.

Finally, Dydd asked, "So what kind of invitation did they make?"

Again speaking carefully, Blake said, "They would like you to come to a gathering. They'd like you to speak. If you want to."

"Sure. What's the date?"

"Really?" Blake asked with surprise.

"Yeah."

"Okay. Well, I wasn't sure if you'd want to rehash your experiences."

Standing in his shop, Dydd shifted a tool box so he could perch a hip against the work bench. "Last month, I went to Arizona and spent a long weekend with Lew Whipple. Remember him? He was one of the officers I saw at Dong Phu. He told me that you sent him an email with a bunch of pictures of young grunts last spring, and he picked me out."

"Yeah. I did."

"He introduced me to four other former POWs from our era. I went down there with a cooler full of beef, and we grilled steaks and hamburgers and drank beer. His wife is a hell of a cook. In three days there," Dydd chuckled, "I gained five pounds!"

"You're getting fat, huh?" Blake joked.

"I've stabilized at a hundred-thirty, give or take. So when is this shindig at Andersonville?"

The smile in Blake Moffat's voice was audible. "They suggested Valentine's Day."

Dydd grinned. "Hey! That's the anniversary of my return to the States."

"They sorta planned it that way. So are you willing to speak to the group?"

"Sure. Like I said, I had a lot of time to perfect my public speaking skills in the box. And I've practiced a lot since I got home. In a typical month, I speak to

241

maybe four or five groups. And—" to allay Blake Moffat's concerns, he added, "I haven't had another panic attack. Not even when I read the articles about me in *Time* and *Newsweek* and saw the pictures of the box and the old man's house. I won't say I'm a hundred percent. I still have moments where I get a little wonky, but I'm good. I go to the American Legion meetings every month, and I've met some really cool guys there. It's good to talk to them."

"Outstanding," Blake relayed. He seemed about to say something else, but Dydd spoke first.

"Is it okay if I bring my girlfriend?"

"Girlfriend? Man, you don't waste time, do you?"

Dydd chuckled. "I wasted forty-six years, dammit."

"Tell me about your girlfriend," Blake prodded.

"She's a school teacher. Divorced. Three kids, one grandchild. Good cook. Good housekeeper. Really cute for an old lady."

"Old?"

"Yeah. She's fifty."

"Bring her along."

For the reader interested in learning more, the following books are available online at www.Amazon.com:

Bury Us Upside Down, The Misty Pilots and the Secret Battle for the Ho Chi Minh Trail, by Rick Newman and Don Shepperd. 2006

Baa Baa Black Sheep, by Col. Gregory "Pappy" Boyington, USMC, Ret. 1958

From the Holocaust to Hogan's Heroes: The Autobiography of Robert Clary, by Robert Clary. 2001

In the Company of Heroes: The Personal Story Behind Black Hawk Down, by Michael J. Durant. 2003

The Miracle of Father Kapaun: Priest, Soldier, and Korean War Hero, by Travis Heying and Roy Wentzl. 2013

A Shepherd in Combat Boots: Chaplain Emil Kapaun of the 1st Cavalry Division, by William L. Maher. 1997

Surviving Hell: A POW's Journey, by Leo Thorsness. 2008

Through the Valley: My Captivity in Vietnam, by William Reeder, Jr. 2016

Unbroken: A World War II Story of Survival, Resilience, and Redemption, by Laura Hillenbrand. 2010

Made in the USA
Middletown, DE
05 November 2022

14183652R00149